CASH MONEY

TIGGA

Cash Money Copyright 2021 by Tigga

ISBN: 978-0-9990847-1-7

Book Cover design and formatting by www.ebooklaunch.com

Book Edited by Dr. Jeff

This novel is a work of fiction. All characters, organizations, establishments, and events portrayed in this novel are either a product of the Author's imagination or is fiction.

Contact Information:
Lost and Found Publishing
PO Box 1032
Macon, GA 31201
(478) 308-5332
www.Lostandfoundpub.com
Email: varjr@lostandfoundpub.com

Follow us on social media:

Lost_andfoundpub@instagram.com

Lostandfoundpublishing@facebook.com

Lost & Found Publishing

CHAPTER 1

SKOOL DAYZ

Cash heard his mother calling him, but that was not the voice he was trying to hear at that moment. He was too busy beating his little brother on the PlayStation.

"Boy, if you don't get your ass in here and wash these damn dishes, your ass going to be sleeping in the van tonight!" his mother, Ms. Tina, yelled from the kitchen.

"Man, damn! Why she always callin me to do shit around here when your lazy ass don't do nothin'?" he complained to his brother, Money, while pausing the game to go see what she wanted.

"Nigga, you know you an ol' good dishwashin' ass nigga," Money laughed.

"Man, shut up!" Cash mumbled to himself, heading towards the kitchen.

Cashmere Lewis, aka Cash, was the oldest of his mother's three children, followed by his little brother Armani, aka Money. Then, right behind him was their baby sister, Mercedes. Being the oldest sibling at the age of fifteen with no father around pretty much made Cash the man of the house. He couldn't stand being in the position he was in as a child, so he found himself a part-time job at a local detail shop on Fletcher Street to keep him occupied and out of his drunk mother's way.

"Ma, why I always…"

Smack!

"Boy, don't question me in my goddamn house," she spat, after smacking him and bruising his pride. "Now get in there and clean that kitchen!" she instructed. She was on one tonight, so he did exactly what he was told in hopes she wouldn't hit him again.

While washing the dishes, he wondered why she was so abusive towards him and not his other two siblings. After all, he paid some of the bills and stayed out of her way most of the time, so why did she treat him so badly? He figured it was probably because of his punk ass daddy and his resemblance to him. He and his siblings never got a chance to meet their father because all he did was chase a crack-cocaine habit. His addiction led him towards the street life, where he neglected his children, leaving them to be raised by their mother.

After cleaning the kitchen, Cash took a shower and headed off to bed. It had been a rough day, and he was looking forward to going to school the next day.

***

"Hey, Cash!"

"What's up, boo?" he replied, greeting his sweetheart, Peaches, as they embraced.

"Where are you going? Class is this way," she said, reminding him as he broke away from their embrace, heading in the opposite direction.

"Hold on ma, I'll be right back," he told her, walking to the boys' bathroom to find his brother.

Cash was on a mission. He knew that dudes wanted to smoke before class, so he had to make sure Money was on deck in the bathroom, serving before the bell rang.

On his way in, he noticed JT was holding the door down to alert everyone on the inside if he saw Campus Police coming.

"J—tizzle, what it do?" said Cash, dapping him up.

"Man, you already know, Cash… same shit, different day," he replied, both reciting the second part together.

Cash knew JT like a book, and he already knew from being around him what his favorite line was. As he bent the corner, he called his brother, "Money, Money, Money, Moooooooooney!"

"Bruh, what I said about calling my name like that?" replied Money, looking up from counting the money he'd already made. He had been pushing nickel and dime bags of mid-grade weed all morning, and he knew his brother was coming by to see if he had sold out.

"Shit, nigga, you don't be complaining when the hoes be sayin' that shit," replied Cash, dapping up the rest of the students.

"That's cause they sang it while they're riding this dick, feel me." He grabbed his dick for emphasis and smiled.

"Boy, ain't nobody trying to ride that wee—wee."

Everybody in the bathroom erupted in laughter, leaving Money feeling played, so he hit his brother where he knew it would hurt to try and save face.

"Yeah, you right," said Money, lining him up for the joke. "But shit, I bet Peaches likes the taste of this here wee—wee."

"Ooooooooooooooooh!" was all you could hear from the instigators.

"Oh, you trying to be funny, huh?" Cash didn't like where this was going.

"Nah, I'm just fuckin' with you, bruh," he replied, still laughing at his own joke.

Money knew his brother was sensitive when it came to Peaches, because he had seen him smash plenty of dudes about disrespecting him, her, or their relationship.

"I'm about through with that ounce," Money said, counting out a hundred dollars to give Cash for re-up. "You got some more, bruh?"

"Yeah, but not right now. Holla at me after class and I'll hit the spot to see how much we got left, alright?"

"All right!"

Bell Rings

Everybody began exiting the smoke-filled bathroom and heading to their classes. As Cash walked out, he saw that Peaches was still standing there waiting on him. Approaching her, he thought to himself, my baby would wait for me until the end of time.

***

After school, he and Money walked Peaches and her two friends, Shay and Brittany, home, since it was on the way to their neighborhood.

"Aye, Cash!" yelled Shay, playfully slapping Money's hand away from her butt. "Come get your lil' horny-ass brother!"

She and Brittany were laughing at how Money kept trying to put his hand in their back pockets. Cash wasn't trying to hear it though, because he and Peaches were too busy doing their own thing.

"Man don't call me. That's y'all fault for telling him how cute he is," he replied, smiling at his brother's consistency. He and Peaches were too busy having their own little love connection to worry about what his brother was trying to do. It felt good having Peaches as his girl. She was the epitome of wifey material. He loved how her light brown caramel complexion complimented her beautiful hazel eyes. The box—braids she was rocking made her look even sexier, considering that was his favorite hairstyle for her. Just looking at her would remind you of the actress Sanaa Lathan, from the movie *Love and Basketball*, but with a body like a stripper. She was plump in all the right places, with curves that would send you flying over a cliff after her.

"Baby have you figured out what you're going to do when I go to Spelman next year?" asked Peaches, gazing into his eyes.

"What you mean what am I gone do?" he asked, puzzled, not understanding her question. "When you go to college, I'm gone stay down here and complete high school, then I am going to move to the A to be with you, isn't that what you wanted?"

"I mean yeah, you know that's what I want," she agreed, pecking him on the lips. She laid her head on his chest and took a whiff of his Curve cologne. "It's just that I'm going to miss you so much."

"I'm gone miss you too," he said in return.

"Well, just make sure you come and visit me at least once a month, cause I'm not trying to get snatched up by one of them ballers," she joked.

"Shit, that would be your loss."

"Is that right?" She playfully shoved him away.

Cash smiled after seeing how cute she looked mad. He knew she loved him.

Approaching her house, Peaches realized the time had come for her to make her move. She was so wet earlier thinking about him and how good it would feel to have him between her legs. She couldn't wait to get home and see if her parents were gone.

When she didn't see either one of their cars, she seductively bit down on her bottom lip once she realized she was about to get some dick.

"Babe, you want to come in and get some Kool-Aid?" she asked.

"What?" he replied, already knowing what she was up to. "Nah, I'm cool babe, and plus y'all shit don't never be sweet."

She rolled her eyes at him for playing hard to get. "Boy, whatever!" She knew he wanted her just as bad as she wanted him and she wasn't about to let him get away that easily. "Well…" She sensually wrapped her arms around his neck and in her sexiest voice said, "Are you at least gonna come in and taste some of this here Georgia peach?" She then quickly broke free from their embrace and sashayed away towards her house. She knew once he saw the sway in her hips as she walked, he would have no choice but to submit.

As he watched her strut towards the house, he knew he was going too. "Damn, this girl knows my weakness," he said to himself.

"Hold up girl!" he called after her, walking over towards his brother. "Hey Money!"

"Man, I already see the play a mile a way." When he saw her, he thought about fucking her too? "I'll holla at you later."

CHAPTER 2:

SINCE DAY ONE

"Damn baby," Cash groaned, "this shit feels soooo good, ma."

"Does it really, baby?" Peaches asked, seductively riding him like a horse in the Kentucky Derby.

They had been going at it for forty minutes straight, sexing each other up and down. As soon as they entered the house, she was all over him. Before they got a chance to make it to her room, she had stripped him down to his bare ass and kissed every part of his body. He didn't mind how aggressive and straight—forward she was when it came to the dick. In fact, he enjoyed seeing her like this, because it reassured him how much she loved him.

As she laid him down on her queen size bed, she took possession of his seven-inch manhood and placed it in her mouth. She took her time stroking his dick with her juicy lips, before she passionately licked the head.

That sent a sensational thrill through his body. As she continued taking care of business downtown, she eventually finished taking the rest of his clothes off. While he lay there, she did her best to prime him up so when it came time, she could jump straight on top of him and get what she had coming.

She positioned herself over him, putting his dick at the entrance of her pussy. He grabbed her athletic thighs and maneuvered under her to help facilitate the process. As she slowly slid down his shaft, her walls firmly enclosed around his dick, causing him to gasp for air.

"Mmmmmmm," she moaned, beginning to rock back and forth. "Boy, this dick feels good!"

"Does it, baby?" he moaned in response, grabbing ahold of one of her breasts and placing the nipple in his mouth.

"Yeah, it does," she cooed.

She looked into his eyes and saw her future husband and the love of her life. Cash was everything she wanted in a man, even though he was still a boy. As she slid up and down his pole, she hoped their lovemaking would last for an eternity.

"Mmmmmmm, baby I'm about..." she began bucking harder and harder.

"What?"

"I'm about to... to... cummm!" she screamed, continuing to rock back and forth, allowing him to go deeper and deeper inside her. "Oh my God, boy!" She bent down and passionately kissed him, letting him know that she was satisfied with his work.

The ecstasy he had taken earlier after school had him rock hard. So even though she was tired and worn out, he wanted to go at it for another round.

Feeling defeated, Peaches laid there with her head on his chest and listened to his heart beat while simultaneously rubbing his nipple.

"Cash!" She sat up so she could look into his eyes. "Baby, can I ask you a question?"

"Yeah, what's up?"

"Baby, why do you love me?"

He didn't understand why she was asking him that. What he wanted to do was go back to making love, but obviously she had something else on her mind.

"Shit, why do you love me?" he asked in response.

"Well, the reason I love you babe is because I know you truly love me. You're considerate of my feelings and I feel like I can trust you with my heart."

Damn, Cash thought to himself. He loved Peaches, but he didn't quite know how to express it in words like she did, so he did what any other man would do.

"Mmmmmmmmmm, baby, don't do that," she moaned.

Since he was still hard, instead of responding to her question verbally, he tried to communicate with her through body language. He started slowly pushing his dick in and out of her pussy.

"Baby, please stop and answer the question," she begged, enjoying how good his dick was feeling inside her. He knew she wanted an answer, so he stopped and said the first thing that came to his mind.

"Well, to be honest, babe," he started, "I don't love you."

"What?" she replied, shocked. She couldn't believe the nerve of him, after putting her true feelings out there on the table.

"Baby, let me finish," he said, realizing she was getting upset. She was even trying to get from off top of him. "I'm in love with you, boo, and it's been like that since I first laid eyes on you."

When she heard that, she gave him a breathtaking smile that genuinely warmed his heart.

"See boo, when I feel like I have no one to comfort me, I think of you and that's all I need to get by. You've always been a part of my support system and that's why I'm feeling you the way I am."

Her heart did backflips as she held back tears of happiness.

"Baby," he continued, "my heart has always and will always belong to Ms. Patricia Lanett Brown. Now, are you happy?"

She was more than happy. She leaned down and slowly began kissing him again, letting him know that it was time for round two.

***

"Okay, Money, you don't have to walk me all the way to my door," Shay told him, opening the screen door to her house.

"Girl, I got to make sure you're safe," he said, trying to convince her to let him in.

She already knew what he was up to and didn't want to lead him on. She did think he was cute, but to allow him into her home was too much of a step forward for her.

"Well, at least let me come and make sure nobody is gonna jump out of the closet on you?" he asked, standing behind her holding the screen door open so she could get her keys out.

She just laughed at how silly he was. The boyish grin he held on his young face let her know exactly what his horny ass was really up to. She knew if he was a little older, he would definitely have a chance at getting in her pants. He was too cute, and also too young, but that didn't stop her from wondering how good his thick, soft lips would feel on her pussy. She could see herself holding his wavy head down between her legs as he sucked on her clit and she nutted in his mouth. She would look into his eyes and see the lust and hunger he had for her.

Too bad for him though, that was all just in her mind.

"Boy please, ain't nobody that stupid around here," she replied while opening the door. When she got ready to close it on him, she looked across the street and noticed how some of the local gang members from her neighborhood were approaching her house. That's when she noticed the all-red 'Skool of the Hard Knocks' shirt Money was wearing.

"Matter of fact, why don't you come in and call Cash to meet you?"

"Why?" he asked, turning around to see what had caught her attention. "Man, them niggas ain't gone fuck with me, especially after I let 'em know I'm from Tha City.

Shay shook her head and smiled at how brave he was.

"Okay then, bye boy," she said, slowly closing the door.

"And it's not bye boy, it's I'LL see you later," he corrected her, putting emphasis on the *boy*.

Money turned around and began walking towards the Crips heading his way.

***

Cash was trying to call his brother on his cell phone to see where he was, but all he kept getting was his ring tone.

"Man, where the fuck is this nigga at?" he said to himself, growing impatient by the minute. He wanted to know where his bag of weed was and why his brother wasn't posted up on the block catching plays. He had already been to the crib, where their sister informed him that he hadn't made it there yet. So, he decided to scan the block to see where he was.

While walking up the street, he noticed his homeboy Trap getting out of a car, so he jogged over to where he was to ask if he had seen Money anywhere around.

"Aye Trap," Cash shouted, trying to get his attention. "Aye, slow up, my nigga."

"Yo, what up my nigga?" replied Trap, turning around to greet him.

He walked up to Trap and gave him some dap. "Aye yo, you seen my brother around here, cuzz?"

"Nah homie, I'm just now coming back from the store. Why, what's up, loc?"

Trap was his childhood friend from the projects they lived in. He was known for gangbangin' first and asking questions later. The neighborhood they lived in was called "Tha City" because all the streets throughout the projects were named after major U.S. cities.

Trap was a dark-skinned 18-year-old who stood six foot two. He had a big ass head that mostly sported Cornrolls. His mouth was full of open-faced gold teeth that spelled, "Since Day

One," which was their neighborhood response when fellow gang members asked them how long they'd been a Crip. It was pretty much a confirmation on whether you were a real Crip or not.

Cash admired Trap's outfit while they walked down Compton Street, heading towards Miami Ave. He had on a royal blue Dickies fit that was creased to perfection, with a blue bandana hanging out his left back pocket. On his feet he sported some royal blue Chuck Taylor's, and on all of his cuffs and shirt collar he had the pattern of the bandana stitched into the fabric. He was representing his gang to the fullest and Cash couldn't do nothing but smile at how Crip—crazy his best friend was.

See, Cash and Money got jumped into the Crip gang a while back, but never really truly picked up the flag. They didn't want to be known as Crips because they just wanted to be them. So, after many fights and them sticking with their position, the neighborhood eventually felt they had no choice but to respect their wishes. It was either respect them or kill 'em, and nobody in the neighborhood wanted to take it that far.

Cash's phone rings.

"Bruh!" Cash answered his phone. He knew it was Money from the ringtone, "Man, where the fuck you at?"

"Cash, this ain't Money."

It was a female's voice.

"Okay then, put his ass on the phone!"

"I can't!" she replied.

"What the fuck you mean you can't?" he asked, getting irritated. "And who the fuck is this answering his phone anyways?"

"It's Shay," she answered, sniffling, like she was crying.

He was caught off guard. Was Money over there fucking her? he thought to himself, a smile beginning to plaster across his face.

"Man, what's up Shay? What's wrong with you?"

"Money's in the hospital, Cash," she wept.

"What?" he asked, trying to make sure he heard her correctly.

"I said…"

"Man, tell that nigga to stop playing," he said, cutting her off. "Y'all probably over there hunchin' and shit." He laughed in hopes that she was just playing around. "Ha ha ha, real fuckin' funny, but I'm for real."

Realizing Shay was serious, he asked, "What happened?"

"He got jumped!" she cried, unable to hold her emotions any longer.

"He got jumped?" he shouted in disbelief.

CHAPTER 3

AGE AIN'T NOTHIN
BUT A NUMBER

"Lil' boy, you need to stop, because I am too old for you," said the nurse that was checking in on Money.

"Too old…too old," he replied in disbelief, looking at her as if what she was saying didn't make any sense.

After getting jumped and hospitalized, he was glad to see such a curvaceous woman. Shantell was his nurse for the shift and he liked everything about her. For a woman in her late thirties, Shantell had it going on. Every move she made in the room while the doctor tended to Money's wounds was very much observed by him.

She was short and cute, about 5'2" with shoulder-length, fiery red hair that looked nice next to her light-brown skin. She wore some cute designer frames that made her look sophisticated and intelligent, but her body is what caught his attention. He could tell even with her scrubs on she had a nice body, especially from how her shirt sat on top of her round ass.

"Woman, who you trying to confuse, me or yourself?" He was attempting to charm his way into heart until the food she placed in front of him caught his attention.

"Ma, you gotta be in college or something like that, right? Cause you lookin' fresh out of school you damn self," he said, digging into his tray.

She placed a hand on her hip and smiled at how adorable he was. She knew she had to be close to his mother's age, but the thought of his little 15-year-old ass wearing her pussy out had definitely crossed her mind. It's not like it wasn't a known fact that young guys have long stamina.

"I hear you, Mr. Lewis, she replied, smiling, signing his hourly check-in sheet and then leaving.

Thirty minutes after she left, Cash came rushing into his room with Shay, Peaches, and some of their homies from the neighborhood marching right behind.

"Bruh, what's up? You alright?" asked Cash, relieved to see his condition wasn't too bad.

"Yeah, he's good if you ask me."

Everyone turned around at the sound of Shantell's voice.

She was in the hallway when she saw them enter his room, deciding to go in and see who had come to visit her patient.

"Are you all his family?" she asked, while scanning the room.

"Yeah, we family," answered Cash, noticing how thick she was. "Why?"

"Bruh, don't mind my fiancée," Money grinned. "She's just a lil over—protective, that's all."

"Boy whateva!" she snapped, walking out to give them some privacy, allowing the boys a view of her behind.

"Man got damn she thick!"

"You got that right!"

"Straight up cuzz!"

Trap, Lil' C, Scrappy, and Fat Loc was dappin' each other up, all agreeing on how fine Shantell was.

Shay looked at them and rolled her eyes, "Men!"

"But ummmmm, yeah I'm straight, bruh. Them mark nig-gas from the Heights done violated though," he said, punching the inside of his palm to express his anger.

"Enough said though, homie," Trap interjected, letting him know to silence the situation around the girls.

"Yeah, you right Trap," he agreed. "Man y'all niggas come give a nigga some love, standin' there lookin' all crazy."

One by one, Trap and the rest of his homies walked up and gave him a hug. When Lil C walked up, he looked Money up and down for any sign of injuries, "Cuzz, what all they fuck up?"

"I just got a cracked rib and few bruises here and there, that's all."

"Well, be easy homie, alright?" "Alright bruh."

Lil C had seen enough and knew what time it was, so he joined Cash and the rest of the homies in the corner to discuss their plan for retaliation.

"Alright y'all," announced Cash after they finished talking in the corner. "Y'all let me holla at my brother for a minute." He wanted some privacy so he could find out from his brother what exactly happened.

Shay was busy rubbing on Money, trying to soothe him, when Cash asked everyone to leave.

"Come on, Shay, you too," he told her.

"Boy, here I come," she replied, rolling her eyes at him. She leaned over and kissed Money on the lips, "Get better, Money."

"Got damn girl," he said, caught off guard by her kiss. "That's what it takes to win you over... an ass whoopin'?"

"Boy shut up," she replied, smiling. "I'll see you later, alright!"

"I see you catch on quick too, girl. Keep on takin' them notes and next time I might just catch a few bullets instead."

That was the last thing she heard before walking out. "Damn my nigga, I feel bad as hell," Cash told him.

"Why?" asked Money, with a confused look on his face. "I'm the one in the hospital."

"I know, I'm just sayin'"

"Ah... SHIT!" Money shouted as the pain from trying to roll over hit him.

"Nigga you alright?" Cash asked.

"Nah man, this shit hurts even when I'm just lyin' here."

"Bruh, I thought your ass was somewhere bullshittin'," Cash said honestly. "I tried callin your phone lookin' for my weed and shit, and now look at you."

"Oh yeah, I almost forgot. Look over there. Your two ounces is in the bag."

Cash opened the bag up, and sure as shit stint, there was his marijuana."Nigga you didn't get robbed," he said in amazement.

"Hell nah, them fools from Match Blocc jumped me cause that 'Skool of the Hard Knocks' shirt I had on."

"What?" Cash couldn't believe it. "Them niggas didn't know you were from Tha City?"

"They weren't even tryin to hear it bruh," he replied, still thinking about the kiss from Shay.

"Well, them niggas definitely about to hear this!"

Cash removed his Glock 19 from his waist and pulled back on it, loading a round into the chamber.

Click Clack!

Looking at his brother, Money knew somebody was about to feel it. He just hoped that things didn't get out of hand because Shay lived right in their hood.

"Just don't bring no heat to Shay's crib, alright?"

Cash looked at his brother like he was stupid. He thought to himself, he gonna worry about a broad right now. He knew his brother when it came to women, so he told him what he needed to hear to keep him cool, calm, and collected.

"I got you bruh," he assured him, embracing him before leaving. "And Mama probably on her way down here too, so you better get ready to hear her cuss yo ass out."

Money laughed to himself, knowing how his mother was. "Alright then my nigga, be easy and stay safe fool."

"Always, fam," he said while heading out the door.

"Aye, say bruh," Money called after him to get his attention.

Cash turned around. "What up?"

"Tell my fiancée I'm ready to take my shower and I need her assistance."

Cash smiled and walked off, laughing to himself about how much of a clown his brother was.

CHAPTER 4

187

"Mmmmmmmmmm."

"Yeah, suck that dick, girl," said GC, looking down at Cat while she sucked him up good.

"Slurp slurp……mmmmmm."

"Oooooooooh shit!" GC wanted to punch her in the face for having such a good head on her shoulders. She had his legs shaking uncontrollably and his eyes rolling to the back of his head.

In the clean but worn-down project apartment, GC, a known Crip throughout the Heights, was getting his rocks off from a powder head named Cat.

Cat, who was ten years older than GC, got her name from her mother who said that when she was a baby her face resembled a cat. Her eyes were slanted and narrow but wide. She had a reputation of being a certified Brain Surgeon around the Heights, which she thought was a cute title for herself. In her mind, if that's all it took for her to get cocaine when she needed, then so be it.

She wasn't always like that, though. Just eight years ago, Cat had dreams of going to college. In high school, she was considered one of the popular kids. She was captain of the varsity cheerleading team, was nominated for class president twice, and was Prom Queen during her junior year. Now, her only dream was to keep the white girl a part of her life.

"Okay now GC, where my dubb at, because you're not gonna have me down here suckin' this thing all night," she complained looking up at him while still down on her knees and in—between his legs, with one had wrapped around his manhood while the other one fondled his balls.

"Man, goddamn Cat!" he shot back, frustrated. He hated when she stopped to ask him for her pay, especially since he hadn't even nutted.

"Just five more minutes and I'm gonna hook you up with the fattest dubb you've ever seen, alright!"

He slowly guided her head back down to his dick so she could continue doing what she did best, "brain surgery."

Cat wasted no time placing GC's seven inches back in her warm, wet mouth.

She took him in with ease, slowly bobbing her head up and down his shaft. She had a technique that was only used by the best, but she couldn't understand why it was taking him so long to nut.

GC was having the time of his life. The E—pill he'd taken earlier was paying off and he couldn't have been any prouder. Too bad for Cat; he had plans on making her work harder than she had expected.

"Mmmmmmmmm…. slurp slurp."

"Yah baby, just like

BOOM BOOM BOOM!

"Man damn!" he shouted, mad as hell at whoever it was banging on the door interrupting his moment of bliss. "Who the fuck is it?" he shouted loud enough to scare the person off.

"It's me, little dumb ass nigga!"

He pushed Cat off of him, pulled up his pants, and went to open the door. "Hold on cuzz!"

He slid the wooden two by four he had blocking the door and opened it for his big homie, T—Loc. "What up Loc?"

T—Loc walked right past him, glanced around, and after seeing that it was only Cat in the room said, "Cuzz, don't what up me. What the fuck happened around the corner earlier?"

T—Loc was a tall, dark-skinned dude with braids going down his head, decorated with blue and black beads. He was older than GC by 11 years and was recognized in the Heights as an OG.

Sensing his big homie's anger, GC thought it would cheer him up to know that they'd put work in on an opp.

Closing the door and waving his hand as if to dismiss his homies's animosity, he said, "Ah man, we ain't do nothin' cuzz but punish a slob for coming around here lit up like a Christmas Tree." He smiled at the thought of how it was only July and they got a chance to rearrange a Christmas Tree early. "Why?"

"Cause that wasn't a slob y'all jumped on."

GC looked confused as he walked back over towards Cat.

"That was somebody from Tha City you dummy!" T—Loc exclaimed angrily.

T—Loc looked Cat up and down, already having an idea why she was over there. Everybody in the hood had had her services at least once or twice. T—Loc had an expression on his face that said he was disgusted, mainly because she was his first love, so to see her over there like that only added more disappointment in knowing who she had become.

"Hi T-Loc," she barely whispered with her head down, too ashamed to look him in the eyes.

"What is she doing over here?" T—Loc asked him, not even acknowledging her.

GC snapped out of his daze and looked at her, "Come on Cat, time to go, ma." He got up to walk her out the door.

"But what about—"

"Cat, just come on," he said cutting her off before she said too much.

She was obviously upset as she grabbed her things and stormed out the apartment. Before she made it to the second step, GC called after her, "Cat." She was mad but turned around to see what he wanted.

"Here." GC tossed her a bag of cocaine, and before she could catch it and say thank you, he slammed the door.

"Now, are you sure this fool was from Tha City, cuzz, cause the nigga was flamed up, homie?"

T—Loc walked back into the room from grabbing a beer out of the kitchen. He looked at his little homie and laughed. It was funny to him how dumb the generation behind him was. He couldn't even blame GC, because he knew the streets had failed at raising him. See, T—Loc was more of a laid—back kind of guy, but quite deadly as well. He didn't believe in set tripping, just money tripping. He's the type of guy to give a dude a pass for making a bad wardrobe decision, but to play with his money was another story.

So, he sat down with GC and heard his side of the story, then said, "Cuzz, just stop bringin' heat to the block, because that is not what we need right now fam, alright?"

GC knew he was right, so he agreed, "Alright cuzz."

They chatted for a little while longer, smoking a blunt of purple haze, and then T—Loc made his way to the door. Before leaving, he shook GC's hand, locking the C's they vowed to forever represent.

Once GC secured the door, he decided to put the incident behind him and get back to hustlin'. He went to the back room in the apartment and opened the closet door. When he looked at the Brinks Security floor safe, it made him remember what the hustle game was really about.

He knelt down and entered the code to open it, and as he sat there and admired the contents, he realized how far he'd came in the dope game. There was a quarter brick of cocaine, three-and-a-half ounces of crack, two pounds of exotic weed, and three pounds of mid—grade weed. He looked in the corner of the closet for the scale and found it hiding behind his SKS Norinko Assault Rifle.

After grabbing the scale and the dope, he sat on the double-stacked mattresses in the middle of the room, placed his Ruger P90 beside him and began sacking up coke. He thought to himself, Man, I'm a young nigga out here gettin' the paper, and if anyone tries to get in the way of that, they better make plans for a funeral.

***

"You see that nigga right there?" Trap asked Cash, who was sitting behind the wheel of a 1987 green Chevy Caprice they'd rented from a crackhead.

"Yeah I see him, but who is he?"

"That's T—Loc, GC's big homie."

"Okay, but Shay said it was this nigga GC who started the shit, so that's who I want."

Cash was trying to keep an eye on the apartment door and load his Glock at the same time. The extended clip he had had enough room for 30, and he needed for all 30 to be ready for what he was about to do.

"Say cuzz," Lil Scrappy was sitting behind Cash who was sitting in the front passenger seat. "We need to bust a move, cause it's getting late and you know how my grandmother is."

Trap and Cash bust out laughing. Here they were about to commit one of the deadliest sins and Lil Scrappy was worried about missing curfew.

"Alright cuzz, we gone have you home before it gets too late, so just chill my nigga," Cash reassured him. He looked at his G—Shock watch and saw that it was 10:24, so he decided it was time for them to finally get their payback.

"Trap, pull up in front and keep the car runnin," Cash instructed while tying a blue bandanna around his neck. "Are you ready Scrappy?"

"Yeah cuzz, let's just hurry up."

"Remember," Cash turned around to see if he was really ready, "knock on the door and tell 'em you tryin to cop a quarter pound of weed, alright?"

"I got cha!" said Lil Scrappy. Then he got out of the car and approached the apartment steps.

***

"Yeah bitch, I got that and some good dick for you too."

GC was on the phone trying to line him up some pussy for later on when he heard someone knock on the door. "Listen, all you got to do is—"

BOOM! BOOM! BOOM!

"Man, hold on, baby." He got up from lying down and grabbed his Rueger, heading to the front door to see who it was.

BOOM! BOOM! BOOM!

BOOM! BOOM! BOOM!

"Who is it?" he asked, peeking through the front window blinds.

"It's Lil J cuzz," said Lil Scrappy, giving him a fake name. "T—Loc sent me over here to grab a QP from you, homie."

GC didn't understand why T—Loc wouldn't call him first and let him know he was sending someone by. He figured since Lil Scrappy said T—Loc sent him, it was all good. After all, it was his trap.

"Alright, hold on," he said, sliding the two—by—four from its resting place. He turned the bolt lock and cracked the door to see if he was alone. After peeking and seeing it was a young gangster in blue Chuck Taylors, he eased up.

Looking past Scrappy, he noticed a green Chevy sitting out front and asked, "Say, Loc, that Chevy with you?"

"Yeah, that's my ride, and they gone leave, cuzz, if you don't hurry up."

Realizing he was alone and everything seemed legit, GC opened the door, exposing the pistol he held in his hand. After letting Lil Scrappy in, he closed the door and placed the pistol back on his waist.

"Cuzz, I just saw T—Loc at the store and he sent me over here when I asked him about a QP." Lil Scrappy pulled some money out of his pocket to show GC he had come for business.

Convinced, GC said, "Hold on Loc, let me go weigh it up." He headed off toward the back of the apartment.

As soon as he was out of sight, Lil Scrappy crept back over towards the door and unlocked it to let Cash in.

"Where he at cuzz?" Cash whispered, walking through the door.

Scrappy pointed toward the back of the apartment, "He's grabbin' it now." He took the .38 revolver from Cash so he could secure the front door.

Cash proceeded towards the back, taking baby steps so he wouldn't alert GC. He silently made his way down the hallway. When he approached the last room, he saw that GC was sitting down weighing the weed up for Lil Scrappy.

Click Clack!

GC knew that sound too well not to recognize when someone was loading a round into a chamber. He stopped pressing buttons on the scale after realizing someone had gotten the drop on him and caught him slippin'.

When he looked up to see if it was the real deal, his heart skipped a beat at the sight of the pistol being pointed at him. He knew the person in front of him was not the little gangster he was supposed to be serving, because the person was too tall. The black Dickies suit and bandanna across the intruder's face let him know that the situation was definitely real.

"Cuzz, don't kill me!" he begged, throwing his hands up to surrender.

Cash didn't waste any time as he dashed across the room, smacking GC with his pistol. "Bitch, shut the fuck up!"

SMACK!

GC fell to the floor. The pistol made a gash across his face that sent blood spreading everywhere. Cash noticed the pistol in GC's waistband and removed it.

"Nigga, where the dope and money at?" he demanded, looking around the room and noticing the dope on the bed.

GC was trying to regain his composure from the painful impact of the pistol. "It's in the closet," he mumbled.

Cash's eyes shot over to the closet. "Alright then nigga, let's go get it."

Cash grabbed him around the collar and dragged him over to the closet. "Put everything in the bag and don't do nothin' stupid!" Cash pulled a black trash bag out of his pocket and handed it to GC, who was trying to find his way out of the situation.

As he put the contents of the safe into the bag, his eyes glanced at the choppa sitting in the corner.

Sensing by GC's slow movement that something was up, Cash stuck his head into the closet to see what else was in there.

"Nigga, I wish you would!" he dared him, digging the barrel of the gun into GC's neck.

"Cuzz, I'm not gone try anything, alright!" he replied, just trying to live to see another day. "Just don't shoot me, homie!"

"Nigga shut up!" yelled Cash, smacking him over the head with the pistol. "I ain't got time to play with you."

When GC finished emptying out the safe, Cash snatched the trash bag from him and kicked him in the ribs, making him roll over in pain.

GC looked at his tormentor, hoping he was satisfied but knew he wasn't when Cash removed his bandanna. He knew once a person revealed their identity during a 211, it could possibly turn into a 187.

"Man, come on cuzz, it ain't got to be like this," GC cried, begging for his life.

Looking into his eyes, Cash saw the soul of a person that would forever be his victim. He knew GC was not a killer, but a young gangsta that made a fatal mistake that would cost him his life. He raised his Glock to his head and whispered to him before pulling the trigger, "Make peace with God, Loc."

POW!

"Cuzz, everything okay?" Lil Scrappy asked, stepping into the bedroom doorway with his pistol raised, ready to bust. He was glad to see their mission was accomplished so they could go.

HONK! HONK!

"Shit!" Cash shouted. Trap was blowing the car horn to let them know that it was time to go. "Come on cuzz, let's bounce."

They ran out of the house and jumped into the car. They sped off, leaving Match Blocc in their rearview as they took Lil Scrappy home.

CHAPTER 5

ON

Two months after murdering GC, Cash decided it was time for them to get into the dope game. He wanted everything to cool down first before they pushed the dope in their neighborhood to avoid any questions being asked or suspicion being raised about where it had come from.

For a whole month, T—Loc was beating the block trying to find out who raided his trap, killed his little homie, and worst of all, got his dope.

Cash knew during that time, it wouldn't be wise to flood the block with dope, especially since the word was out about T—Loc's trap being hit. Nobody had a clue about who it was, but one thing people around the way knew for sure was that Match Blocc had a lot of enemies, so it could have been anyone of them who hit his spot.

Cash and his crew were ready to eat, so once they realized they'd gotten away, it was time to get on.

"Bruh, you feel like going to CripCo to get some blunts?" Cash asked Money. He, Money, Lil Scrappy, and Trap were all sitting in Lil Scrappy's grandma's basement. It was their hang—out spot.

Scrappy's grandma didn't stay directly in the projects like the rest of them did, but her house was right around the corner from Tha City, so it was still considered their neighborhood.

"Yeah, I'll go," he replied, getting up from the table they were seated at, bagging up nickel bags of weed.

"You'll stroll with me, Scrappy?"

"Yeah cuzz, come on." Lil Scrappy was ready for a break, because all the bagging up was starting to make his hands cramp.

"Man look, y'all niggas better not take all day either, cause y'all know we got shit to do!" Cash shouted as they walked up the steps of the basement. Truth be told, he was tired of bagging up weed too, but he knew it had to be done. Plus, considering all the weed they had to bag up, four sets of hands is always better than two. He and Trap were willing to put in the work, but not while his little brother and Scrappy ran the streets all day.

Overall, he was just thankful to be somewhere they could chill and get this stuff done.

Lil Scrappy's grandma was really cool and did not mind them lounging around at her house. She stayed gone most of the time, and on top of that, she loved her only grandson and spoiled him rotten.

Tramell Scott was Lil Scrappy's real name and he had it made. His grandma had turned her basement into his personal man cave. She even decked it out with a 52" plasma TV, which they mostly used to play the Playstation 5 on. He also had beanbag furniture, a mini—fridge, and a pool table. She figured if she gave him somewhere to hang out, she could keep him out of the streets.

Too bad it couldn't keep him out of the little girls around the neighborhood, because plenty of them had been given the opportunity to see the man cave. Not only did his grandma spoil his 14-year-old ass, she allowed him to have relations as well. Being light—skinned with green eyes and a head full of curly hair, this baby-faced teenager who always stayed fly in the latest gear couldn't stop enjoying the life he had been given.

"Aye Scrappy," said Money, grabbing his attention once they approached CripCo, a local convenience store, "did I tell you that Shay gave me her number?"

"Yeah fool, for the sixth got damn time," he replied, tired of hearing about how he did the so—called "unbelievable."

"I'm just sayin my nigga, she's gone give me some of that pussy sooner or later dawg, watch."

"Whatever, cuzz," he said, tuning Money out so he could focus on what was going on in front of the store.

"Cuzz, ain't that Peaches right there?" he asked Money, pointing to where a girl stood bent down in a car window.

When Money looked over at the gas pump where Scrappy was pointing, he saw that it was her. She was leaned over in the window of a candy painted, baby blue, round body Chevy Caprice sitting on some chrome 26" Asante rims. The driver, who she was talking to, was obviously trying to holler from the chemistry they had going on.

Before Money could get close enough to sneak up on her, their conversation had ended, and the dude was pulling off.

Peaches was waving goodbye until she looked up and noticed Money starring at the car. She took off in the opposite direction, hoping he didn't see her.

"Peaches!" he called after her.

She ignored him and picked up her pace.

"Peaches! Oh, you gone act like you don't hear me, huh?"

"Oh, what's up Money?" she replied, turning around to face him. "Where my baby at?"

Money smirked, "Shit, it look like he just pulled off," he said, letting her know he had seen her.

"Boy please. That nigga just saw something he liked and wanted to say hi."

"Yeah, I bet," he replied, not convinced.

"Boy, whatever," she shot back, waving him off as she walked away. "When you see Cash, tell him I am about to go home. Let him know that my parents will be gone for the weekend and I just made some Kool—Aid, alright?"

Money wasn't trying to hear what she had to say. He was already dialing his brother's number when he and Scrappy walked in the store.

***

"Man, where you tryin' to post up?" Trap asked Cash, "because I'm not tryin' to be steppin on each other's toes, cuzz."

"That's a good question, but we not gone be steppin on each other's toes, fam."

"How you figure that?"

"Cause…" Cash was trying to figure out the best way to say it, "we gone be eating off the same plate, ya feel me!"

"What you mean?" he asked. He was lost and didn't understand what Cash was saying.

"Cuzz, listen, once we dump this work, we gone need to re—up, right?" "Yeah," he agreed.

"Well, I got a connect."

Cash looked at his phone and saw that Money was calling him. "Bruh, where y'all at?"

"Say what?" he asked, making sure he heard him correctly. "Man, don't worry about her; she probably ain't on nothin', just hurry up and bring them cigars."

Money had just informed him about Peaches and how she was conducting herself outside of his presence. He took note of the description his brother gave him of the car she was leaning over in, but he was too busy focused on trying to get high.

"Kool—aid, huh?" he laughed to himself at the thought of her invitation. "Alright my nigga, I got you, now hurry the fuck up." He ended the call and informed Trap that they were on their way back.

The way Money described how everything went down, Cash assumed it was nothing serious. After all, he knew his girl was fine, so he expected dudes to try and holler. He just hoped for her sake, she knew not to holler back.

***

When Money got off the phone, he noticed he had a missed call, so he dialed the number back. After the first ring somebody picked up.

"Hey baby!"

"What's good Shantell?" he said pointing to his phone and smiling at Scrappy, letting him know there was a chick on the line.

"Nothin much, just sittin here thinking about you," she replied.

Nurse Shantell had crossed the line of ethics and succumbed to having a relationship with someone less than half her age. After being around Money for three days, she couldn't help but to give him her number. Every day she came to work, he'd tell her the things she needed to hear, which was the same things she wished she could hear from her husband.

"Ditto ma, but look, I'm tryin to see you soon, so when we gone make that happen?" he asked earnestly, wanting to see what Shantell was hiding inside of those scrubs.

Giggling from his response, she said, "Well, that's why I'm calling." He couldn't wait to hear more. "My husband goes out of town tomorrow for a week, so we could spend some time together then, the whole time if you want?"

"I'm down for it, what about you?" he asked, already knowing her answer.

"What you think?" she replied seriously. "I'm even gonna cook your favorite meal, so tell me what you like."

He didn't have a favorite meal, because he loved all foods, so he gave her the opportunity to guess.

"How bout you surprise me with something, cause I am pretty sure whatever you prepare will get eaten anyways."

"Mmmmmmmmmm, I bet it will," she thought to herself, imagining his head between her legs.

"Alright ma, tomorrow it is," he said as he and Scrappy turned onto the street where Scrappy's grandma lived.

"Bye, Money," she said in her sexiest voice.

"It's not bye ma, it's 'I'll see you later,'" he corrected her before hanging up.

When they made it to Scrappy's grandma's house, Money asked, "Nigga, do you know who that was?"

Oblivious to who the hell Shantell was, Scrappy asked, "Who?"

"The nurse from the hospital," he happily replied. "So you already know what she's talkin' bout, right?"

"Yeah," Lil Scrappy replied, smiling to himself, "your test results came back.

Money was lost.

"You got AIDS!" Lil Scrappy joked, laughing a little too hard. "Ha ha ha, real funny nigga."

CHAPTER 6

WORK

"I got 5 for 45 pimp, 5 for 45!"

Cash was standing on the block with a sock full of dime bags of cocaine. It was a sunny Saturday afternoon and the sweat from the intense heat had his white t—shirt sticking to his back.

He and his crew had been clocking some major hours, taking turns posting up to ensure that there was someone from their crew always out serving their product. Too bad for him, once he'd realized what time it was, his day would be cut shorter than he expected.

His boss, Mr. Mac, had been on his bumper about coming in to work late and missing so many days. Cash enjoyed his job at One Stop and wasn't trying to lose it just yet. After all, he was able to slang his product and work at the same time.

As he paced back and forth on the block watching for fiends, he decided to text Money and let him know he was going to be leaving for work soon and someone needed to come hold the block down.

***

"Ooooooooooooh baby, that shit feel good."

Money was laid back, getting his dick sucked when he heard his phone going off.

"Damn, hold on, baby!" he said, not wanting to stop Shantell as she skillfully sucked his manhood while simultaneously fondling his balls.

He pulled out his IPhone and read his brother's text.

Shantell used that time to get herself together. They were parked on the corner where he agreed to post and serve. She couldn't stand being away from him for even a day, so she decided to chill with him while he made his paper.

He couldn't believe how much of a nympho she was. She sucked and fucked him all week long once he showed her how strong his back was and how he could continuously bust nut after nut, keeping it hard.

She flipped the visor down to look at herself and apply some lip gloss. She couldn't believe how much she enjoyed having sex with this young jitterbug and how much her husband Roger was no match for Money. Comparing Roger's two minutes of sex to Money's hours of lovemaking was a no-brainer. Before she met Money, she was sexually depressed, but now, since she had a way to release her pent-up frustration, she literally worshipped the ground he stood on.

"Baby, who are you texting?" she inquired, applying some finishing touches to her make—up.

"Nobody, just hold up for a minute." He was busy trying to convince his brother in the text that he was standing on the block sweating to death, but in all actuality, he was sitting in Shantell's Lincoln TownCar, enjoying her AC.

After calling her an hour ago to bring him some Church's Chicken, he thought it would be okay if she stayed. Getting head and chicken wasn't part of the plan, but who could resist that kind of service?

"What do you mean nobody?" she asked, leaning over to see who he was texting.

"Man, damn ma!" he complained, irritated by her nosiness. "Here, since you lookin so damn hard." He tried handing her the phone; she declined.

"I don't want your phone, baby."

"Being nosy!" he cut her off.

"Baby, I'm sorry, please let me…" and she leaned over to suck on his neck.

"Chill, ma!" he said, moving away from her. "I got to go catch this play for my brother, but I'll catch you later, alright?" He opened the passenger side door and got out. Shantell was beginning to smother him, and he needed some space.

"Well, I'll take you," she offered, desperate to be around some hard dick.

"Nah, I'm cool boo. I'll call you later though," he stated, closing her door and walking off.

"Okay then, I love…" was all he heard before walking toward an apartment building.

"Man, this bitch is trippin'!" he thought to himself as he headed down the hill.

She was starting to work his last nerve, and he needed some time away from her to cool down. So, he headed to the neighborhood Candylady's house to get him a Huckle Buck, which was the nickname for frozen Kool—Aid in a cup.

***

Cash walked in the back door of their apartment and was instantly overwhelmed by the aroma of Southern-style cooking. He knew somebody was in the kitchen throwing down and he wanted to get him a piece of the action.

"Who is that?" shouted Mercedes.

He smiled at the sound of his little sister's voice.

"It's me, lil ugly," he answered, walking into the kitchen.

"Oh, hey, lil ugly," she greeted him. 'Lil Ugly' was the nickname they shared for each other.

"What you cooking?" he asked, looking around and noticing the carton of eggs on the counter. "And you better not use all of mama's eggs either, cause you know she gone trip."

"Nigga, I already asked her for some eggs, thank you very much," she replied, rolling her eyes.

Their little sister Mercedes was a good kid and an "A" Honor Roll student. They kept her away from the madness in the streets because they knew it wasn't for her. Instead, she ran track for the Middle School and played softball. She was the youngest of the three, trailing Money by one year. Weighing 106 pounds at five foot two inches, she was the spitting image of their mother when she was younger.

"Where's she at anyways?" he asked, grabbing a mango from the bottom of the refrigerator.

"Boy, you know mama gone raise hell about them mangos!"

"Do I look like I care?" he shot back, brushing past her as he walked out the kitchen.

"You need to learn how to say excuse me, lil ugly!" she shouted after him before resuming her cooking.

Once he got ready for work, he headed out the door and down the street, peddling his Mongoose bicycle non—stop the whole way.

***

As Cash rode down Fletcher Street, approaching the detail shop, he realized that today was going to be a very busy day. There were twice as many cars in the parking lot as usual, so he mentally prepared himself to do a lot of cleaning.

He parked his bike in the garage and noticed the 'For Sale' sign taped onto the window of a primed down 2010 Mercury Grand Marquis sitting on a chrome set of 24-inch rims.

It wasn't unusual for him to see cars for sale at One Stop, because people always brought their cars up there to advertise, but there was something different about this one. He saw something he liked. He knew he probably didn't have the money for it just yet, but it wouldn't be too long before he did.

"Is you gone clean the damn car boy, or just stare at it all day?" asked Mr. Mac coming from the back of the garage.

He snapped out of his trance. "Alright Mr. Mac, I got it."

"Don't got it, son, get it!" he ordered before walking to his office.

Man, this old nigga is something else, Cash thought to himself, pulling out his phone to enter the seller's contact information.

Cash liked Mr. Mac because he was a real man who came from the streets. Back in the day, Mr. Mac had got caught up in a big conspiracy and ended up serving ten years in prison. After coming home, he established himself as a successful and legitimate business owner. He was one of the few dudes who actually gave back to his community. He offered the youth jobs and helped single mothers financially raise their children, and that's how he earned Cash's respect.

Before getting to work, he walked around the shop admiring some of the vehicles that came in. He knew that one day it would be his turn to come by the shop and get his car detailed, and he couldn't wait for that day to come.

"What's up Tre?" Cash greeted his co—worker and Mr. Mac's son as he entered the shop. "Aye, whose Marquis is that over there?"

"One of my dad's friends brought it up here yesterday. Why?" Tre was getting ready to buff the paint on a Chrysler 300.

"Cause I'm about to cop that," he told him, smiling from ear to ear. "You know what he's asking for?"

"I think he told my dad $4,200, but how you gone get it, Cash? It'll take you damn near a whole year to make that kind of bread working here."

"Nah pimp, I'll have that in a few more weeks," he assured him, pulling out a wad of 5's, 10's, and 20's to show Tre he wasn't flexing.

Tre was shocked at how much money Cash had saved up.

"Damn bruh, you have been saving them tips, huh?" he asked, still amazed by all the money he'd just seen.

Cash put the money back in his pocket and said, "I guess you could say that," and then mumbled under his breath, "if only you knew." Then he grabbed the vacuum and proceeded to clean out his future car.

CHAPTER 7

RE UP

Boom! Boom!

Boom… Boom Boom… Boom!

Cash was on stunt mode as he bent corner after corner in his newly—purchased Grand Marquis. Two weeks hadn't even passed before he called the owner, offering to give him $3,500 cash for the vehicle. With his hustle money and Mr. Mac's help, Cash was able to get his very first car at the age of 16.

The two 15-inch Alpine speakers he had in the trunk had The Migos song "Jane" shaking the frame of his new toy. He had just left the local music store Beats For Us and was about to show off his whip to all his homies in projects. Nobody in Tha City, not even Money, knew what he was about to hit the block in.

He slowly made a right turn onto Miami Ave. and took his time driving down the street to the corner where saw his brother posted.

***

"Aye dawg, stop bringin' me these fuckin food stamp cards," said Money, serving a guy two bags of coke. He had already gotten two cards earlier and didn't see a need for any more. When the customer walked off, he pulled out his stash and started counting the money he'd made so far. A few seconds later, he noticed a greyish car coming down the street with its music blasting loudly, so he put his loot away to focus on who it was creeping down the block.

As the car got closer, he could hear Takeoff's voice booming through the stereo system. He tried looking to see who it was driving, but the glare from the sun was shining on the front windshield and blocking his view. So, just in case there was any trouble heading his way, he rested his hand on his waist, where he concealed a Larcon .380 handgun.

When the car finally pulled into view, he was surprised to see it was his brother behind the steering wheel.

"Nigga, I wish you would try and pull out that lil ass pistol!" Cash shouted over the music.

Money smiled.

"Boy, who the fuck car you in?" he asked, walking around to get in on the passenger side.

Before Money could utter another word, Cash tossed the Bill of Sale over onto his lap. When he looked at it and realized the car belonged to Cash, he shouted, "My motherfuckin nigga!"

They both smiled as Money bounced up and down in the car, excited, checking out the interior.

"Got damn, this bitch clean, bruh!"

"Ain't it though."

"Hell yeah nigga," Money agreed, looking in the glove compartment box. "Shit, you paid $3,500 for this?"

"Yeah, thirty—five hundred cash," Cash replied proudly.

"Oh yeah!"

"Yeah, bruh."

"Man, where the CD's at? Cause I'm not tryin to listen to no Migos," he said while looking through the console.

"Nah bruh, ain't no CD's." Cash picked up the IPod he had connected to the stereo. "Here, this is where the music is at."

As Money scrolled down the playlist, Cash turned down Atlanta Lane and saw the rest of his homies standing on the curb. He was about to pull and surprise them with his new ride.

***

"Hey, Peaches," Shay answered her cell phone. "What's up?"

"Nothin much, just callin to check up on your nappy-headed ass," replied Peaches.

"Weeelllll, if you must know, me and my naps are over here doing hair, thank you very much," she stated in her sassiest tone.

Shay was pretty good at doing hair, and the whole neighborhood made sure she knew it. She kept a long list of people on her waiting list.

"Bitch you need to stop movin then!" she spat at a customer who was busy trying to dodge her hot curling iron.

While Shay was occupied doing hair, Peaches was having problems of her own and desperately needed a friend to talk to. She had called Shay, hoping she could shed some light on her mood, but was beginning to second guess her decision.

"Peaches," Shay called her, breaking their brief silence.

"Girl, what's wrong with you? Why are you so quiet?" she asked, concerned about her friend. "Are you sick or something?"

"Something like that," she answered gloomily, feeling a little depressed.

"Well, what's wrong, you pregnant?" she asked, more as a joke than for real.

"Yeah," she whispered.

"Oh my God!" she shouted.

"Ouch!"

"My bad, girl," Shay apologized to her customer. "Is it Cash's?"

"Yeah bitch!" Peaches shot back, appalled at how she could think she was a hoe. "Who the hell else could it be?"

"Well excuse me for asking." She could tell she had touched a nerve, so she continued from a different angle.

"Are you gonna keep it?"

"I don't know, Shay, that's what I'm tryin to figure out now." Peaches began to cry.

After taking a home pregnancy test, Peaches cried on and off for hours trying to decide whether or not she wanted to keep Cash's baby. She knew the right thing to do was tell him, but first she wanted to make sure that she was going to keep it before she told him.

"Girl, don't cry," Shay sympathized, trying to comfort her friend. "You know Cash is a good nigga, and plus he loves him some Georgia Peach, so I'm sure he's gonna be happy to hear you're having his child."

"That's not why I'm crying, Shay."

"Then what's the problem?"

"I don't want to have a baby right now."

"Girl, why not? You're about to graduate."

"Because," she began, trying to regain her composure. "I'm tryin to go to Spelman next year and I'm not about to put my career on hold for nobody."

Shay couldn't believe how selfish her friend was but decided to keep her opinions to herself. She didn't want to seem like she was judging her, but deep down in her heart she knew an abortion was not the solution to her problems.

"So, what are you gonna do, Peaches? Cause I'm almost sure Cash is not gonna like the idea of you having an abortion."

Peaches knew her friend was right, but had already thought about how she was going to handle it if she chose to have an abortion.

"Who says he has to know?"

***

Trap and Money were enjoying the ride as Cash bent corner after corner through Tha City. He was letting it be known that him and his crew were on the rise.

"Say cuzz!" Trap yelled from the back seat.

Cash turned the music down so he could hear him. "What's up?" he asked, looking through the rearview mirror.

"Stop by Scrappy's crib for a minute, cause I got to re—up."

Cash nodded his head, then turned the music back up. After turning a few more corners, he pulled over to Scrappy's grandma's house. They could see Scrappy's grandma walking to her car as they pulled up behind her. They all got out and greeted Ms. Scott, and as always, she hugged and pinched every single one of them on the cheek.

"Cashmere, whose car are you driving with them shiny wheels?" Ms. Scott asked, checking his car out.

"Oh, that's mine, Ms. Scott," he answered proudly.

"Well, you drive careful in that thang baby, okay?" she replied while getting into her Dodge Caravan.

"I will Ms. Scott. Is Scr…I mean Tramell in the house?" Cash caught himself. He remembered she didn't like them using their aliases around her, so they made sure to use their government names instead when she was around.

"Yeah, he's in there. Y'all go on in there and play nice." When she pulled off, they all walked into the house.

***

"Cash, something gotta shake, cuzz," stated Trap, holding up a clear plastic Ziploc bag that contained their last few grams of coke.

They had been hustlin' so hard lately he had forgotten to check the stash to see how much dope they had left. They were down to 20 grams of coke, one ounce of purp, six ounces of mid—grade weed, and no crack.

Cash only had himself to blame, because it was his responsibility to collect and go re—up. But, never in the midst of hustlin' did he realize they were running out of dope. When the money came in and he saw an opportunity to get his very first car, he took it. Unfortunately though, he forgot about the obligations he had to his crew.

"I know dawg, this shit is crazy," he said, shaking his head. He tried thinking about how to get some more dope quick. "Aye yo, don't trip crip, I got it all under control," he said, pulling out his phone to give the one person he knew could help him a call.

He quickly scrolled down his contacts list until he came across the name he was looking for and pressed the call button. The phone rang three times before someone picked up.

"What it do, young Cash?" greeted Big Pete.

"I'm chillin, big homie, but what's good with you? How's the weather over there right now?" Cash was speaking in code to see if he had some weed on deck.

"Shit, you know how it is, windy as ever. These leaves blowin all over my fuckin lawn and I need someone to come by and rake this shit up. Why? You want the job?"

Cash understood that he had plenty of weed, which he always did, and he was looking forward to Cash coming by there to pick some up. Only thing different this time, Cash wasn't just trying to rake some leaves, he was trying to shovel some snow as well.

"Yeah, I can do that for you my nigga, but shit, I need to know if it's cold over that way?"

"Well… " Big Pete began contemplating his next choice of words, "matter of fact, I think the weatherman did say there was a light chance of snow."

CHAPTER 8

PLUGGED

Cash pulled into Bellvue Point, a gated community on the north side of Macon. He admired the six—figure homes that displayed the wealth and prestige of those who occupied them. Every house around every corner had a two-door car garage or better that housed elegant, expensive vehicles, each one representing its owner's taste.

After passing by a few more houses throughout the high dollar neighbor— hood, Cash pulled into a cul—de—sac that contained the cream-colored, modern-style house he was looking for. The house was separated from the one beside it by an 8—foot—tall wooden fence that hid any nosy onlooker's view of the backyard.

Pulling into the driveway, he saw Big Pete's pregnant baby mama walking towards her baby blue Beamer. He continued on up the driveway until his car was right behind Big Pete's Dodge Magnum, which sat on some chrome 24—inch Giovanni Floaters.

"Hey Leena," he greeted her as he got out of his car.

"Hey Cash!" she replied with her gorgeous smile that revealed beautiful white teeth with the two shiny golds on her bottom fangs.

"Pete told me to tell you to come to the back of the house if I saw you," she informed him, then she got in her car and pulled off.

Cash walked towards the backyard and thought to himself how much he liked Leena. She appeared to be a real down-to-earth woman. For seven—and— a—half months pregnant, she looked good, especially from how she was rocking her outfit. She was dressed down in a pair of Baby Phat Jean Capris that hugged her child-bearing hips, a gold tank top, and some open toe wedges that showed off her pedicured toes, with some newly styled braids she kept tied in a bun. She had plenty of ass too. Cash tried his best not to look at it out of respect for Big Pete.

When he approached the back gate, he opened it in search of his partner, but at the same time remained cautious of the two vicious pit bulls Pete kept in his yard. Therefore, he took baby steps in case he had to make a quick sprint back through the gate to avoid the wild beasts.

"Man, bring your scary ass over here, nigga!" shouted Big Pete, laughing at how Cash was creeping through his yard. "My dogs are put up in their cages in the back," he informed him, standing up to greet his guest.

"Alright then, nigga," he replied smiling, "I'm just making sure, cause them two lil bitches only got love for you and Leena."

"Yeah yeah, whatever, nigga," replied Big Pete, still smiling from how silly Cash looked tip—toeing through his yard.

After a quick dap and embrace, they sat down across from each other at the patio table. Cash enjoyed coming to see his connect, plus he liked the way he carried himself. For being such a big dude, Pete had swag and an aura about him that said, "I'm all about getting money." He was dressed in Giorgio Armani soft linen and wore a chain around his neck that held the letter P. His style of dress signified how wealthy of a man Big Pete really was. He stood at six feet four inches and weighed around 310 pounds. He had a bald head with a thick beard, resembling the rapper Rick Ross.

"So, you're tryin to venture off into new products, huh?" asked Big Pete, trying to read Cash.

Cash had been buying from him for the past six months and Pete wanted to know the reason for the change all of a sudden. It ain't that he didn't trust him, but he knew how the feds operated. Offering someone football numbers while threatening them with a Life Sentence always seemed to do the trick when it came to convincing someone to talk. So, Big Pete, knowing how Cash usually shopped, was just trying to understand what was up with the change in the forecast.

"Yeah, me and my homies been tryin to expand our hustle and take it to another level, and I figured since you were already plugged in, you should be the first one I talk to about doing that."

"Yeah, well that was a good look," Big Pete complimented his idea. He watched Cash's every move, observing him as he looked him in the eyes. Cash didn't flinch, and that was a good sign, meaning he was on real man time.

"So, what exactly are you tryin to cop, fam?" he asked, folding his arms across his chest and leaning back in his chair.

"What can you do for twelve racks?"

"Twelve?" he repeated him, making sure he heard him right. "Damn, I ain't know you was eating like that, lil bruh!"

"Well, to be honest with you big homie, we all chipped in together, feel me?"

Cash didn't think it was necessary to tell him that he had only a thousand to put in. Trap, Scrappy, and Money contributed the bulk of it, but he figured since he had the connect, his contribution was the most important. After buying his car and splurging at the mall, he was down bad and needed Big Pete to look out so he could bounce all the way back on his feet.

"Well, I'll tell you what," Big Pete started while getting out of his chair, "let me make a call right quick and see what I can do."

He slid the glass patio door open and walked into the house, pulling out his cell phone to conduct a little business of his own. He didn't sell cocaine, but he knew how to get it. So, for a small fee, he was willing to be a middleman in this transaction as long as he made him a few dollars out of the deal, especially since he was taking all the risk.

After about five minutes, he re—entered the patio and sat back down.

"Check it out, lil homie."

Cash was all ears.

"I can do 12 ounces for that twelve, and I guarantee that it's gonna be some top-notch quality, probably some Scale."

"Hold on dawg," Cash stopped him, trying to keep up, "What the fuck is Scale?"

Big Pete smiled at Cash's lack of knowledge when it came to cocaine. After breaking it down to him and getting a better understanding of what fish scale was, Cash couldn't wait to get his hands on the coke that, from Big Pete's description, resembled fish scales.

Big Pete schooled Cash on a few more things before asking him what he wanted to do.

"Well…" Cash was calculating in his head how much money they could make. He eventually came to the conclusion that it was a good deal, but he needed one more favor from Big Pete. "That sounds cool, homie, but I need you to front me some weed on top of that."

Seeing how he'd just made fifeteen-hundred off of Cash, he agreed to front him five pounds of mid—grade weed. It was going to be $150 more than the usual price for each pound, bringing it to a thousand a pound, but Cash wasn't tripping. It was known that any dope issued on consignment would have a little tax added on.

"Alright then, how we gone do this?" Cash asked anxiously.

"Look, I am gone give you the trees now, but come back tomorrow for the yayo."

"Alright then!" he replied, heading to his car to get Big Pete the twelve thousand for the deal.

***

"Hey mama!" Money greeted Ms. Tina as he walked in the house.

"Don't hey me, boy, hay is for horses!" she spat back in return.

"Okay then…" he began, walking past her. "How are you then, madam?" he asked in his best impersonation of a butler.

"Don't be comin in here tryin to be a smart—ass, Armani!" she shouted, cutting her eyes from the TV to look at him. "And where your brother at, cause I need some money?"

"I don't know ma," he snapped on his way to his room.

"What the hell you mean you don't know?" she shouted after him.

"That means I haven't seen him!" he yelled, before closing his door and laying down to take a nap.

***

"Oh shit!" Money jumped up out of his sleep, awakened by the loud sound of sirens blaring outside their home. He got up and ran out the door and down the street, chasing after the sound of an ambulance. He broke into a light jog until he reached the corner, which was blocked off by cop cars.

Walking up to the scene he noticed that a car accident had occurred, and from the look of it, Cash's Grand Marquis was involved. Looking around for his brother, he saw that the cops already had him on the ground, cuffed up.

"Man, what the fuck is y'all doing?" Money shouted, running over towards them.

Two cops in blue uniforms lifted Cash to his feet while another one stopped Money from getting any closer.

"You better stay out of this, boy, before we lock your little ass up too."

"Bitch, fuck you!" spat Money, grabbing his crotch. "Lock these nuts up, you faggot!"

One of the officers who was walking Cash to the cruiser heard Money's comment and decided he wanted to play a little dirty. He grabbed Cash's cuffs and slowly began twisting them, causing Cash to cry out in pain.

"Bruh, leave them alone!" he yelled, regaining the strength to continue walking to the cruiser.

Money felt helpless having to stand there and watch the cops mishandle his big brother.

"Hey, detective!" shouted one of the blue suits who was looking in the trunk of Cash's car, "you might want to come and take a look at this."

The detective he called was wearing a badge around his neck displaying his authority. He walked over to see what the officer was showing him. Money was surveilling the whole scene and wanted to know what was going on.

"It looks like a couple pounds of marijuana," the officer began, speaking loud enough for Money and the onlookers to hear. "And I found a .40 caliber handgun under the front seat.

"Is that right?" the detective asked sarcastically.

"That's not it either, sir. I also found what appears to be some kind of narcotics, maybe cocaine." He held up a big Ziploc bag with a white powdery substance in it. You could see the proud look on his face as he handed the detective the bag.

"Well, it looks like we got ourselves a federal case, boys!" he informed his partners before walking over towards the cruiser that Cash was in.

That was the last thing Money could hear before the police forced him to step away from the crime scene. He walked around the crowd to get closer to the cruiser that held his brother. When he made eye contact with Cash, he shook his head letting him know that it was all bad.

HONK! HONK!

HONK! HONK!

Money opened his eyes at the sound of the car horn. He woke up sweating and realized that it was only a dream. When he got up to see who was honking, he was relieved to see it was Cash waving for him to come outside.

***

"Man, what took you so long?" asked Money, getting into the passenger seat.

"Shit, I had to try and get the best deal, bruh!" answered Cash.

"Well… what's the 411?"

"I only got five pounds of some Mid right now, but he told me to come back tomorrow and pick up a tre-block of some fish scale."

"Fish scale?" Money looked at him, confused. "What the fuck is that?"

Cash laughed to himself as he thought back to how he reacted when Big Pete used the same terminology earlier. "Coke, bruh, just a better grade, my nigga."

While riding around Tha City, Cash really took time to reflect on where they were heading in the drug game. He didn't know about the rest of the crew, but he had plans on one day becoming the man on their side of town. He knew money was the number one problem solver, so he wanted as much of it as he could get his hands on. He wanted to make his mama happy and hopefully get her into a rehab center somewhere and be able to do something nice for his sister. He knew Peaches would be heading off to Spelman soon and he wanted to be able to do for her as he thought a real man should, because he truly loved her.

"Hey," Cash said, getting his brother's attention. "Where did Scrappy and Trap go?"

"Shit, I don't know, but let's go check the gym out, cause the swimming pool is open and they might be over there."

Money's mind wasn't on finding their homeboys, and Cash knew it, but he decided to stop by there anyways to find out. He didn't want to keep riding around with five pounds of weed in the trunk, but he figured it wouldn't hurt to stop by the gym, since it was on the way to Scrappy's grandma's house.

When the recreational gym came into view, they could see people all over the place in swimming trunks and bikinis. As Cash pulled into the parking lot he instantly saw how packed it was.

"Damn!" shouted Money, pointing towards the crowd, "look at the girl in the pink!"

Cash could see his brother was only concerned about the girls at the pool and not the weed in the trunk. So, he made a mental note to himself to only look for their homies, and if they didn't see them, then bounce and be on their way.

There was no need for them to go into the pool area, because first of all, they didn't come there to swim, and second, they didn't have on any trunks. They were only there to locate their friends, so instead they posted up on Cash's car and scanned the crowd.

"You see them niggas, bruh?" asked Cash, looking over by the pool's entrance.

"Nah, but I see Melissa and Jasmin," he replied with a smirk on his face.

"Look dawg, we gotta put this weed up first, cause I'm not going to be riding around all day with this shit in my car." Cash wasn't trying to fall into Money's pussy-chasing antics. They had more important things to do than to be around there chasing some cat.

"What's up Cash? What's up Money?"

They looked over by the pool and saw their friend Markus calling them, dripping wet from the pool. Markus was a teen from around the way who definitely wasn't into the street life. He was more of a bookworm who stayed in the house. His parents were very strict and expected for him to go to college one day and make something out of himself. Every once in a while, they would see him at the rec center and play basketball together, but that was pretty much it.

"We just chillin, Markus," replied Cash, looking past him as he walked around the gate surrounding the pool.

"Hey Markus!" shouted Money, calling him over, "Have you seen Trap or Scrappy around here?"

"Yeah, I think they're on the inside playin basketball," he answered.

Relieved, they both made their way over towards the front of the rec center. As they were about to walk in, Cash heard someone call his name, so he turned around to see who it was.

"Hey," Jasmin greeted him, "you were just not gonna acknowledge me?"

He smiled.

He liked the way she looked in her bikini, but lost his view when she wrapped a towel around her wet body. He thought Jasmin was a cute girl, but a little too petite for his liking. She was nice and he appreciated how consistent she was in making her presence known whenever he was around, but he liked thick chicks and she was far from being that.

"Oh, what's up Jasmin?" he asked, returning her greeting. Then he waved Money off to go look for their homies. "I ain't even see you, girl."

"I don't see how you could have missed me; I was standing right in front of you," she said, sounding disappointed.

"Nah, I just been looking for Scrappy and Trap, that's all."

"Oh well, I was just wondering who car you were driving, because that ride is hot."

"Oh yeah, you think so?" he said, enjoying her compliment. "Well, that's mine if you must know, lil mama."

Her eyes lit up as she glanced at the car again. It was music to her ears to hear that he had his own car, because she wanted to be the one in his passenger seat. Jasmin couldn't control herself around Cash. Every time she got around him, the juices between her legs began to stir. She had had a major crush on him since the first day she laid eyes on him. His swagger and confident attitude made him look even sexier, and she enjoyed being in his presence.

She was only 14 years old and a freshman in high school, but she carried herself like someone older. She knew in order to one day be Cashmere Lewis's girl she needed to step her game up. She was well aware of the fact that he was already involved with a pretty senior at their school, but she didn't care.

"That's a nice car, Cash," she complimented him again. "So when are you gonna take me for a ride?" she asked flirtatiously.

He smiled.

"Whenever you want, lil mama," he replied, realizing he was really making her day. "But we gotta get you a baby seat first."

He burst out laughing after seeing her facial expression change from a smile to a scowl. She playfully punched him in the arm to let him know she wasn't feeling his sense of humor. Jasmin's towel started to unravel because she kept shifting her body around, so when she tried to fix it before it fell, Cash took another peek at her body. She was completely unaware that he was staring at her until she looked up and their eyes met.

They shared a moment of silence before she spoke.

"Damn Cash, you must see something you like." She was obviously flirting but glad to see that he was finally checking her out.

"Nah, I just couldn't tell if you were wearing that bikini or if the bikini was wearing you, because y'all look good together."

She smiled at his compliment, thinking to herself, Nah nigga, we look good together.

"Well… " she said, still blushing, "there goes your homeboys, so I'll catch you later, alright?" She quickly grabbed ahold of his hand and wrote her number on it, then walked off towards the pool area.

"Man, what did Jasmin want, bruh?" asked Money, being nosy.

"Nothing," he replied, eyeing his brother, "she just wanted to know whose car I was driving."

"Yeah cuzz, that motherfucka a straight pussy magnet my nigga!" stated Trap as they all walked over towards the car.

***

"Girl you won't believe who I saw earlier all up in your man's face," said Kissy, ready to spill some tea.

"Who?" asked Peaches, putting her ear closer to the phone so she could hear clearly.

"Jasmin's hot little ass," she answered.

"Jasmin… Jasmin…" Peaches kept repeating the name to see if it registered. "Who the fuck is that?"

"Oh, just some little cute thang that's 14 and ready."

Kissy was one of Peaches' closest friends, but also a full—time gossiper. Peaches didn't know how credible this information she was listening to was, but being that Kissy said she saw it with her own two eyes, she considered it.

"Kissy, what do you mean ready?" asked Peaches, trying not to get upset.

"I mean ready to fuck, bitch, what the hell you think?" she spat back, not liking the fact that her friend was acting slow.

"Well, if Cash wants him some little girl pussy, then that's on him. I don't have the time or energy to be chasing behind his ass like some sick puppy."

Peaches felt herself getting upset and Kissy could hear it in her tone, but it wasn't her intention to throw shade on Cash. She was just hoping that Peaches would get mad at Jasmin and beat her up.

Kissy didn't like Jasmin because the boy she liked at school liked Jasmin, and every time she came around he would pop up to either walk her to class or carry her books. Kissy didn't like that one bit and she despised the fact that he never offered to walk her to class or carry her books. So, after seeing how she was all up in her friend's man's face at the rec center, she thought this would be the best way to get revenge on her for stealing her man. It was just too bad her plan wasn't going as well as she thought it would.

"No, I'm not sayin that Cash was on her like that, I'm just sayin—" was all she could say before Peaches cut her off.

"Well bitch you're sayin too much!" she snapped in return, getting irritated by where the conversation was going.

"Well excuse me for tryin to inform my homegirl about what was going on with her man," replied Kissy. Her feelings were clearly hurt.

There was a brief silence between them.

"Look Kissy, I'm sorry, girl. I'm just not up for the gossip today." Peaches apologized for hurting Kissy's feelings.

"I hear you, girl, and sorry too. Did you at least get to drive his new car yet?" she asked, thinking that Peaches already knew about Cash's new car.

"What new car?" she replied, surprised by what she'd just heard.

"Ummmm…" for the first time in years, Kissy had put her foot in her mouth and didn't know what to say, so she just said, "Never mind."

CHAPTER 9

WHIP GAME PROPER

Only a few days had passed since Cash and his crew re-upped. Big Pete came through just like he said he would with the 12 ounces of cocaine. Thanks to his deep connections in the drug game, he was able to negotiate a pretty good price, allowing him to make a healthy transaction fee. Cash didn't see a problem with Big Pete making some money out of the deal, because he was the one putting his name on the line. In his line of business, being plugged-in meant those who weren't plugged-in had to pay to play, especially when there were risks involved. Cash and his crew had not been exposed to the risk-taking just yet, but when you sold dope, risks were inevitable.

Cash and his crew were working the block, slanging coke left and right, but it seemed like their clientele had slowed down a bit.

"Hey Cash," said Trap while they were standing on the corner, "what are we gonna do about these rock heads who keep coming up? Because I'm getting tired of telling them we don't have no hard."

"I don't know yet cuzz, but I'm out of coke for tonight," he replied while firing up a blunt.

They were posted up on Trap's side of the projects, which was close to the Swamp, a neighborhood up the street from Tha City.

The Swamp got its name from the heavy traffic of crack smokers it once held. Trap had no problem getting rid of the coke he had on his corner, but Cash did.

The clientele coming from the Swamp had a heavy demand for the rock substance and Trap wanted to supply all of the fiends coming his way.

"Man, you don't know how to cook do you?" Trap inquired, holding his hand out to receive the blunt Cash was passing him.

"Nah my nigga. This my first time even dealing with coke like this, but I see why niggas be rockin their shit up though," he replied, realizing how much more money could have been made if he turned their powder into crack.

"Well look, I got a nigga who can cook it up for us, so I'm gone hit him up and see what he talkin about." Trap pulled out his cell and prepared to call his homie when Cash told him to hold up.

"Hold on cuzz, if we gone do that, we need to get him to teach us how to cook, so we don't have to come back."

Trap thought that was a great idea. "Yeah, that sounds even better, but we probably gone have to pay a lot more for the lesson."

"So?" Cash began pulling out a wad of cash, "I don't see us having no problems with that.

***

Beep!

Gangsta opened the white microwave to remove the bowl that contained a white, jelled substance. As he sat the bowl on the counter, he reached over to another bowl that held some ice water and dipped the teaspoon he had in it. He then took the teaspoon of water and splashed it in the bowl containing the jelled substance. After repeating this process two more times, he picked up a fork and began whipping the water into the substance, holding the bowl at an angle.

They were caught up watching every wrist movement and every motion. To them, learning how to cook crack was like learning how to paint, do hair, or draw. It was an art that required practice in order for one to become skillful. Lucky for them, they were being taught by one of the best.

"You payin attention?" Gangsta asked Cash and Trap, whose eyes were glued to Gangsta while he cooked. "After you whip the water back in it, put it back into the microwave for fifteen to thirty seconds so it could blow up. Got it?"

"Got it!" they answered in unison.

After two more hours of showing them the game on how to cook crack, Cash and Trap started putting their own wrists to work.

Gangsta, who was old enough to be both of their fathers, was a well-known Crip from their projects, and he repped it from the C to the Y. He was considered a Big Homie to Trap but played the backfield in running the streets. He didn't mind helping his little partners get to the money the dopeboy way, especially since they were paying him. He was really kind of flattered they would come to him for his expertise, but it was already known throughout the Mac that Gangsta's whip game was proper.

"Make sure when y'all get through, y'all clean them dishes with that bleach up under the sink," he instructed them before walking off to watch the movie *Paid in Full*.

"Aye yo, Trap," said Cash, placing big round pieces of crack on a newspaper so it could dry.

"What's up?" he asked turning to face him. "You know what this means, right?"

"What?"

Cash smiled.

"Time to get paid, my nigga."

***

Once Cash and Trap left Gangsta's house, they met up with Money and Lil Scrappy to discuss their future in the dope game. By Trap and Cash being the oldest out of their crew, they pretty much directed traffic for the other two. They knew Money and Scrappy would follow suit on any decision they made, so they decided to just fill them in on what was up.

They were all sitting in Scrappy's grandma's basement going over the plan that would ultimately change their lives.

"Listen y'all," whispered Cash, as if what he was about to say would determine whether someone was going to live or die, "here's what we are gonna do…" He ran the plan down to the crew and they were all in agreement about how it should be executed. It was understood that they would re—up once a week unless they ran out early. Whatever amount each individual produced for re—up, he would be provided with that much work.

Cash had easy access to the weed and he liked the clientele, but as the others began to see the quick turnover in dealing crack, they slowly bridged off into selling nothing but the cooked-up cocaine. That allowed Cash to get all of the weed customers in his pocket, so he didn't mind.

At the moment, crack was the preferred drug in Tha City and it had the smokers going wild. It brought a desire into some of the purest souls to do some of the most humiliating things.

"Can I suck your dick?" "I'll let you fuck!"

"You tryin to holla at my daughter?" "I'll let you rent my car."

"Who do you want me to kill?"

Those were just a few of the proposals that desperate smokers offered to Cash in exchange for a crack—fiend high. It was just that bad. The thing about Cash and his crew was that they only wanted paper. That's what it took for them to pay their connect and keep their operation rolling, so the paper is what they were after.

***

"Hey Money baby."

A female smoker approached him, wildly scratching the exposed titty that was spilling out of her tank top.

"What's up Cat? You tryin' to cop, girl?" he asked, eyeing her up and down.

Money thought to himself how just a few months ago he would've loved to fuck the hell out of Cat, but from looking at her now and seeing what she'd become, he wouldn't dare. Cat had gone from smoking weed, to snorting powder, to all-out smoking crack. She was still in pretty good shape, but the dingy, overworn clothes she wore over it made her look unattractive.

"Baby, I don't have no money right now, but you know I'm good for it," she begged, stepping closer to him while wiping snot from her nose.

"Cat, keep it moving ma." He waved her off. "I ain't got nothing else for you."

"Ah, come on Money," she whined, stomping her feet as if throwing a desperate tantrum. "Nigga, I know you been wanting some of this here cooty Cat," she said, rubbing her hands over her pussy. "So do me this one little favor and I'll give you some."

She stuck her hand out as if the deal was sealed.

"Bitch, get your stank ass away from me!" he shouted, flinching like he was about to slap the taste out of her mouth.

She didn't stick around to see if he really would; instead she took off like a bat out of hell. Money checked the time on his phone and decided it was time to go home. The fiends were beginning to act up and he didn't want to stay around to see who had enough balls to rob him. He was going to take it in for the night.

CHAPTER 10

PMS

Cash was beginning to get fed up with Peaches and her stank attitude. She had been calling his phone constantly complaining about anything and everything her drama—ridden mind could think of. He didn't have time for it, plus he and his crew were slowly on the rise to becoming the biggest thing to hit their projects.

He thought allowing her to drive his car a few times to school would give her some security in their relationship, because he knew once people saw her driving his car they would know that she was his main chick. Too bad for him though, it didn't work out that way, especially after she got around to hearing about this chick and that chick being seen in the passenger seat. He did keep a few chicks on the side, but they were only temps because everybody knew Peaches was his one and only full—time lady.

"I'm just sayin, Cash," pleaded Peaches while lying next to him, "why I gotta keep hearing about you and all these hoes?"

"Baby listen," he began, lifting her face so he could look her directly in the eyes. "Bitches lyin on me and they tryin to fuck up what we got going on, don't you see that?"

They were trying to rest after their long session of lovemaking. Their naked bodies were entwined together under her plum-colored sheets.

She had asked him to strap on a condom earlier, but he didn't know why. He didn't see a need to, because they had been having unprotected sex for months now and it was never a problem before. He figured it had something to do with all the rumors she probably heard about him sleeping around with other women.

Besides that and the drama, he had noticed how strange she was acting lately. For the past three weeks she'd been dodging him and avoiding his attempts to make love to her. The first week it was PMS. The second she was too sick and now, out of the blue, she wanted him to use a condom while they had sex. He couldn't figure out what was going on between them, but he knew whatever it was wasn't going to get in the way of him getting paper.

"Babe," he whispered, kissing her on the lips, "are you nervous about going to Spelman?"

Peaches thought about the question and knew that that was far from how she felt about going off to college. She rolled over and positioned herself over him, straddling him so she could look him in the eyes. She truly loved him with all of her heart, but she was not ready to have his baby. After having an abortion without his permission, the doctor told her not to have any sex for a month, but after hearing her man plead for some of that Georgia Peach, she decided to go against the doctor's orders.

She sat up and entwined her fingers with his.

"Nah baby, why you ask me that?" she curiously asked, to see what he was thinking.

"Because you've been acting strange lately and I want to know what's the deal. I'm worried about you girl," he said sliding his hands across her thick thighs until he reached her firm, soft ass.

"Hmmmmmm, don't worry about me, boo," she moaned, reaching over to her nightstand to grab a condom. She made sure to have plenty on standby, because she was not trying to get pregnant again and have to go through the process of having another abortion. Honestly, she didn't even think she could do it again, especially after the many nights of crying and emotional stress she had to endure.

Her only concern as of right now was to please her man, so she moved from straddling him to going down on him. She grabbed ahold of his semi—hard dick and placed it in her warm wet mouth, instantly bringing it to life. She took her time easing it down her throat and taking him in completely. She pushed his dick to the back of her throat so she could choke a little bit and build up enough saliva to lubricate his manhood. With one hand fondling his balls and her mouth covering his dick, she went to work.

"Mhmmmmmmm, yeah baby just like that," he moaned while his eyes continued to roll around in his head.

After minutes of deep throat action, Peaches began to feel the head of his dick swell, so she knew he was on the verge of nutting. She took her mouth off and slid a Trojan condom over it before he even had a chance to protest. She then climbed on top and positioned herself right in the path of his rock-hard dick. Easing her way down, enclosing his shaft with her tight pink walls, she bit down on her bottom lip, reacting to the mind-blowing sensation of their perfect fit.

"Ooooh shit, that feels so damn good baby," she cooed, her body quivering from stroke after stroke of sliding up and down his manhood.

"Mhmmmmmm, yeah baby," he groaned in response before closing his eyes.

Her juices flowed as she rode him like a horse, galloping into ecstasy as she slowed her rhythm. She brought her head down to his mouth and slid her tongue between his lips. They passionately kissed, taking turns sucking on each other's tongue.

After fifteen more minutes of her riding, Cash wanted to take control. He rolled her over onto her stomach and grabbed a pillow to place under her for support. She arched her back and raised her ass up in the air. He probed around between her legs until he found what he was looking for.

Parting her lips, he entered her from behind. "Sssssshhh, that's my spooot!" she cried out.

"Whose pussy this is, girl?" Smack!

"It's yours!" she shouted.

"Whose?" he asked again, pumping harder and harder.

"It's yours, Cash."

Smack!

"Whose is it?" he repeated, watching the moisture of sweat build up on her back.

"Oh baby, just like that, daddy," she urged him on.

Smack!

"Ohhhh Cash!" she winced from the pain of him smacking her ass.

He could feel her pussy muscles tighten with every slap, making the sex more intense.

"Baby, I'm about to cummmm!" Peaches was breathing heavy now.

"Yeah, cum for daddy then," he said while picking up pace.

"Oh my god, I'm cum… I'm cum…" Peaches couldn't even spit out what she was trying to say.

Instantly, they both released their cream of passion at the same time then collapsed on each other, satisfied and out of energy.

"Damn ma, your pussy is off the chain," he said exhaustedly. They both laughed.

CHAPTER 11

STACKS

Money prepared for this day a whole month in advance. He knew when the time came, he was going to be stepping out fresh to death, letting everybody know how it is; you only turn sixteen once. Today was his birthday, and the brand-new Akoo outfit he wore with the J's to match said he was ready for it. After weeks of saving his money from hustling on the block, he was ready to celebrate.

He had bought himself a car two weeks ago, but because of its old age and wear, it needed some work done to it. After having all the needed parts ordered, he put his '73 hard top Chevy Caprice in the mechanic shop to bring it back to life. The car would have everything it needed to be showroom ready. He planned on doing the interior all white with blue trim and put some chrome 26-inch DUB's in Pirelli tires. Right now, though, it was far off from being completed, but he wasn't even tripping. He was on his way to pick up a Dodge Charger from Enterprise.

Cash had made some improvements to his car as well. The Grand Marquis was looking real good with the windows tinted, two six—by—four-inch LCD monitors in both headrests and new 26-inch Asante rims sitting on its feet. He was definitely stuntin' on them in the neighborhood.

Money was on his way out of the apartment when he noticed his sister sitting on the couch, staring at him.

"Dang lil ugly, you done got clean for your birthday, huh," said Mercedes, getting off the couch to brush his shoulders off.

"Shut up, lil ugly," he smiled. "You're just glad to have a brother like me on your team."

She rolled her eyes at him and went back over to the couch to watch the rest of *Cheaters*.

Money walked out the front door and snatched his phone off his belt clip to call Cash.

***

As Cash was turning the corner in his Grand Marquis, he felt his phone vibrate on his lap.

"Money, Money, Money, Moooooney!" he sang.

Money shook his head, "Man where you at?" he asked while walking into the street.

"Turn around, fool," Cash told him.

He was pulling up to the curb when Money looked behind him. He hopped out without turning the car off and gave his brother a hug. "Happy Birthday nigga!" he shouted.

"Appreciate that my nigga, but let's go get this whip."

Money walked to the passenger side of the car to get in, but just as he was about to close the door, Cash grabbed the corner of it.

"What are you doing?" asked Money. "Get out," he demanded.

"For what?" Money was confused.

"Cause this your car for the next 24 hours, bruh," he stated, smiling from ear to ear.

Money hopped out of the car and ran over to the driver's side. He was happy as hell as he pictured himself pulling up to the club in his brother's ride. He told himself that he was going to definitely pull something bad tonight.

"Oh shit, I'm 'bout to be stuntin' hard tonight!" he shouted.

Cash knew it would make his brother happy to be able to drive his car for his birthday. Money had taken the test for his driver's license last weekend, so Cash figured since he passed, he might as well let him use his car for his birthday. He was proud of Money for hustling so hard lately. After all, it wasn't like he didn't have a car in the shop just in case he wrecked his.

"Listen, bruh," said Cash, preparing to lay down some car rules, "this is a luxury car, not a race car, so slow down."

Money was flying through the projects doing about 45 in a 25 mile per hour area.

"Only put Plus gas in my tank, and watch how you bend corners in my Asantes too, dawg, cause if I see one scratch—"

"Bruh, I got it," he said, cutting him off.

Money knew how much Cash cherished his ride, so he knew not to go crazy in it. He drove the car over to the rental place so Cash could pick him up a car for tonight. This was going to be Money's first night in club Stacks and he couldn't wait to see what was in store for him.

***

The vibe in Stacks was off the chain. The DJ was playing the hottest tracks and had the crowd going HAM. Women had the dance floor packed as they twerked, popped, and rocked their hips all over the place.

Cash and his crew pulled up looking and smelling like straight money. Cash, Trap, and Money were all driving their own vehicles, with Scrappy riding shotgun with Money. They wanted to make a statement pulling up to the club in Cash's car; they were two of the youngest boys out there getting to the check.

After parking in their reserved VIP parking spots, they headed straight for the VIP express line, taking in the whispers from the onlookers who were waiting in the regular line.

Cash was the first to get patted down for weapons and pass through, but not before he slipped the bouncer $200 for the rest of his crew. He knew that in order to get Money and Scrappy in, he was going to have to break the bouncer off with a pretty penny. He didn't mind at all because it was for his brother's birthday.

"Damn, my nigga, look at the hoes in this bitch!" shouted Money, looking around in amazement.

"Shit, it's still early though," stated Cash while checking the time on his phone.

The club usually didn't get packed until around midnight, so after seeing it was only 11:15, he decided not to get any drinks just yet. He and Trap were no strangers to the club scene, so it was nothing to them, but Money and Scrappy's eyes were glued to the new atmosphere before them. The women were dressed in everything from jersey dresses to scanty garments.

There were curves all over the place.

Cash and Trap expected them to look thirsty, so they chilled in the cut and watched them from a distance.

"You see shorty right there, Scrappy?" Money pointed.

Scrappy was too busy looking around the club to focus in on the girl with the fat ass. He never saw so many grown women with so much sass and sex appeal in one room before. He needed a few minutes to wrap his young mind around what was transpiring right in front of him. For a minute, the music, the women, and the weed smoke didn't seem real to him. He'd only seen stuff like this on TV, but once he realized it was reality, he was wide open.

"I can't believe what we've been missing, cuzz," he said, staring at a thick, dark-skinned Amazon who was walking past them in a leopard skin—tight outfit. As he watched her stride towards the bar, he thought about meeting her over there.

"Aye, we gone get some drinks or what?" he shouted to Cash and Trap. He knew him and Money didn't stand a chance at getting anything from the bartender with their baby faces.

Cash and Trap looked at each other and smiled.

"Be easy dawg. I'm gone get y'all something to drink in a minute," he shouted back. "Here!"

He placed two Ecstasy pills in each of their hands.

"Pop one now and then pop one in three hours," he instructed them.

He knew the E—pill would keep them from getting drunk. Cash wanted to have a good time but watching over two young drunks wasn't his idea of having fun.

Once the E kicked in, Cash and Trap walked over to the bar to get them something to drink. After receiving their drinks, they headed back over to where Money and Scrappy were.

"Here," said Cash, handing his brother a cup filled with Grey Goose and cranberry juice. "Y'all listen up for a second."

Lil' Boosie Bad Azz was bussing through the club's massive speakers so Cash damn near had to yell over the music.

"I'm about to walk around and see who's in here, is y'all gone be straight?" he asked the two youngest, looking them both in their glassy eyes.

They both nodded in agreement.

"Okay then, just remember what I told y'all," he said, reminding them about the unofficial club rules. He could look into their eyes and tell they were geeked. Their pupils were as big as dimes and he knew exactly what that meant.

"Don't pick up your drink once you set it down, stay low if you see the police make a round, and most importantly…no means no, got it?" He gave both of them some dap and walked off. Trap was already off doing his own thing and enjoying himself. He was on the dance floor receiving a dance from a chick who looked pretty drunk. Her breasts were moving all over and moments away from popping out of her too small shirt.

While Cash was making his way around the club he spotted someone he knew from school. He asked her to dance and she happily obliged, turning around so he could grab ahold of her hips. While she did her thing, swaying her hips from side to side, he kept an eye out for his brother. Although he came there to party, he knew today was his brother's birthday, so he didn't mind playing security for the night.

"Hey, birthday boy." Money turned around to see who was speaking to him.

Once he saw that it was Shay, a big smile broke across his face.

She was standing there posed like a model. She stepped back to give Money a full view of her curvaceous body. She was looking edible in her tightly fit 'Kiss Me' jeans, which had Money thinking about all types of things he could do to her.

"Boy, are you just gonna' stand there smiling or ask me to dance?" she said with a bright smile revealing her pretty teeth.

"Shit, lookin' the way you look, I'd rather ask for your hand in marriage," he joked, grabbing ahold of her hand and bending down on one knee.

Shay felt embarrassed as everyone in the crowd backed up and gave them some space. Everybody thought Money was really proposing, so Shay began blushing. She pulled him back to his feet, closing the space between them. She said in his ear, "Boy, you are crazy." Then she guided him over to the dance floor.

The DJ was playing one of Usher's hottest hits, "Love in the Club." It seemed like perfect timing, because all she wanted to do was whine and grind on him. She took away his Goose—filled cup when they found a spot to dance and took a sip. Then she turned around so he could grab a hold of her waist as she danced on him.

Money was in the zone, enjoying the view and the feel of her ass rocking back and forth on him. It felt amazing to have her this close to his manhood and not tease him like she'd done before.

***

"Cuzz, look at your brother over there," said Trap.

"Yeah, I see him," replied Cash.

They were both staring at how Money was trying to hang on to Shay's wide hips.

"He's in love with that girl, my nigga, and he ain't even got the pussy yet," joked Cash, shaking his head.

"Yeah, the boy is definitely in love, but shit, to me it looks like she feelin' him too."

They looked at each other and bust out laughing.

"Say cuzz, where's Lil' Scrap at?" asked Trap.

They quickly scanned the club to see if they could find him.

"I don't know, but check the bathroom, cause he might be taking a leak," replied Cash.

***

As they danced together, Shay noticed Money go in his pocket and retrieve a pill. When she saw he was about to pop it in his mouth, she asked, "What's that? Give me half," she commanded, sticking her hand out.

Money couldn't believe what she was asking him. He wondered if she'd ever popped pills before. He didn't mind giving her a piece, but to hear her ask for it shocked him. So, seeing how this was the perfect opportunity for him to place his lips next to hers, he quickly put the pill between his teeth and leaned forward so she could bite off half from his mouth. She leaned in and bit half, taking her portion in and then drinking from his cup to wash the taste down.

She then passed him the cup and leaned forward to whisper something in his ear.

"So, you think you grown now, huh, poppin' pills and shit," she stated, grabbing his hands and placing them on her butt. "You think you're grown enough for some of this?" she asked seductively.

Money was in a trance and didn't know if it was the Ecstasy talking to him or if Shay was really offering to give some pussy.

"Hell yeah I'm ready, girl," he answered, looking down to where her hand was gripping his dick. "And as you can see…I'm growing by the second." She smiled at his quip.

"Yeah, I see you," she replied, leaning closer to his ear. "But what are you gonna do with it?"

He was on the verge of busting a nut right there, but he wasn't about to let her embarrass him like that. So, he just aggressively squeezed her ass and smacked it.

"I'm tryin' to put this thang to sleep," he said, looking into her eyes.

"Hmmmmm, now that sounds real good," she said, impressed. "Well, I guess this pussy is all yours tonight then."

They leaned into each other and passionately kissed. Both of them had forgotten they were still in the club, but once Shay felt the spot between her legs get wet, she knew what time it was.

She broke from their embrace and turned to walk away still holding his hand. "Come on baby, we bout to go!" she said, leading him towards the entrance.

***

"Aye say, cuzz," said Trap, urgently approaching Cash. "We gotta go."

"Why?" he asked, looking around to see if there was any beef.

"This nigga Scrappy in there huggin' the toilet, throwing up and shit," he replied, shaking his head.

"Damn, off one drink?" asked Cash, not believing his little homie went out like that.

Cash had been sure the two of them could hold their liquor after popping the ecstasy, but it looked like his assumptions turned out to be wrong, at least in Scrappy's case.

"Alright then," he began, realizing that the night had just ended for them. "Let me holla at my brother to see what he gone do and then we out, alright!

"Alright fam."

"Go get Scrappy and we'll meet y'all outside." They dapped each other and headed in opposite directions.

Cash walked over to where he last saw Money and noticed Shay leading him towards the entrance. He could see that his brother's eyes were wide open, so he knew he wasn't drunk, but he did want to know where she was taking him. He sped up to catch them before they reached the front door.

"Bruh, where you going?"

"I'm going with her," he stated, pointing at Shay's voluptuous behind.

"Don't worry about Money for the rest of the night, Cash. He's in good hands," she said, winking at him before continuing out the door.

Cash couldn't do nothing but smile because he already knew what time it was.

"Nigga, just make sure you take care of my ride!" he yelled after them.

He was glad to see that his brother was about to get some pussy for his birthday. He thought Shay was a bad chick and had even contemplated on hollering at her before he fell in love with Peaches. Now, he knew it was out of the question because they were too close of friends for him to try his hand.

***

Money couldn't believe he was about to make love to Shay. The ecstasy had him so geeked up that he had to pinch himself to make sure he wasn't dreaming.

Once it eventually settled in that he was at the Holiday Inn Express with Shay, a great big Kool—Aid smile broke across his face. He was laying across the soft, queen-sized bed while he waited on her to come out of the bathroom. She was getting herself ready to make his birthday a night to remember.

He wanted for this day to come so badly, but in his mind he thought it was only a fantasy. The thought of them having hot, passionate sex made him a little nervous because he wanted to make sure he satisfied her just right. However, what he didn't know was the power behind the E—pill to knock her socks out of the park. He was definitely about to tear her ass up, so now it was just a matter of when the action was going to take place.

He rolled over, sat up, and kicked off his shoes. He snatched one of the Swisher Sweet cigars he'd bought earlier off the nightstand and rolled up some weed. After firing it up and taking a long pull, he sat back and relaxed. As he continued taking hit after hit of the blunt, he heard the water from the jacuzzi stop and that's when he knew it was about to be showtime.

When Shay cracked open the bathroom door, he could see the steam from the jacuzzi roll out. She slowly stepped out into his view wearing a big white towel that only covered her plump breasts and very little of her round ass. There was nothing that could hide the tractor trailer she had back there, and it wasn't her intention to hide it.

As their eyes met, she could see how much lust and desire he had for her. She enjoyed his admiration because it made her feel even more beautiful. The E—pill they shared earlier had them both feeling horny as hell. She strutted across the room towards the bed but stopped along the way to turn the TV off. She then proceeded to walk over towards the nightstand and turn the radio on to a local Slow Jams station. Never losing eye contact with him, she unwrapped the towel and dropped it to the floor, revealing her naked body.

He held his breath.

Shay then slowly sashayed to the end of the bed to allow him a minute to take in what was headed his way. Satisfied with his look, she began to slowly crawl onto the bed while seductively singing to him.

"Happy Birthday to you…" she sang while simultaneously using her tongue to slide his shirt up to his chest.

"Happy Birthday to you…"

She continued singing to him as she crawled up his body, kissing every part of him.

"Happy Birthday…"

Kiss Kiss

"Dear Money…

Kiss

"Happy Birthday to you." She ended the song by sucking on his neck. Then, he exhaled.

***

Cash was super geeked as he sat at the red light trying to figure out where he wanted to go. He knew the party wasn't quite over for him yet. The pills he popped in the club had him rolling to the third power. He was grinding his teeth non—stop, which made him feel like his jaws were about to lock up. The cool air hit him when he walked out of the club, intensifying the high he was already feeling, so now he was looking for a way to smooth it out.

He looked up the street and saw a Waffle House ahead. He knew everybody that left the club hungry was probably there, so he figured he'd stop by to see what was popping.

Trap had agreed to drop Scrappy off home because he was planning on taking it in too. Cash appreciated him, especially after the surge of alertness he received from the Ex.

When the light turned green, he pulled off heading towards the Waffle House. From what he could see, the parking lot was packed with cars and broads. He was very much aware of the Waffle House's atmosphere, which consisted of dopeboys, drunks, gangsters, and plenty of women.

When he hit his turn signal to turn into the parking lot, he noticed a Macon—Bibb County Police car pull up behind him and hit their lights.

"Fuck!" he shouted, already knowing this wasn't going to end well. "This is the last thing I need right now," he told himself, reaching down under the seat to grab his semi—automatic handgun and place it in on his lap. The fully loaded Glock was not registered to him and the drugs in his possession were not legal.

He had to think quickly as he coasted the Charger down the street, past the Waffle House. He knew everybody was probably thankful he didn't pull in because there was no telling what kind of illegal activity was going on over there. Just leaving the club, he was sure the parking lot was filled with all types of government violations. Plus, he felt like leading the police into a den of criminals was the equivalent of snitching, and he didn't get down like that.

Whoop! Whoop!

"Pull your vehicle over to the side of the road NOW!" demanded the cop over the loudspeaker.

That's when he realized what was about to take place.

"Yeah, alright bitch, let's see what this baby is made of." He pressed down on the accelerator making it touch the floorboard, and quickly started seeing the cop car get smaller and smaller in the rearview.

***

Shay slowly slid her tongue in and out of Money's mouth as he sucked on her tongue. She was sitting on top of him giving him the ride of his life. She sucked on his ear, licked on his chest, and kissed all over his face. She was no stranger to lovemaking and Money was thankful for that.

About a year ago, she had been in a relationship with a guy she met from a nearby college, and he showed her every trick there was when it came to pleasing a man. He would pick her up at night and take her to various places to have sex; the park was their favorite. He taught her how to properly ride a man's dick and coached her on how to give toe—curling head. It didn't take long for her to catch on and when she did, college boy was on to the next one.

Now, she was showing Money everything she learned. She slid off top of his manhood, leaving it glossy and wet before bending down to put it in her mouth. Some would consider that nasty, but after doing the 69 with college boy, she felt comfortable tasting her own juices.

She took his whole dick in her mouth with ease and slowly began to bob her head up and down. Money's eyes were closed as he took in the moment. His body trembled from her warm mouth stroking him. It felt unbelievably good and he didn't know how much longer he could hold on before busting a nut.

"Mhmmmmmmmmmm," she moaned, allowing his dick to go deeper and deeper down her throat. With every stroke, he expanded her esophagus and she handled it very well. She knew exactly what she was doing to him. He was falling in love and didn't even know it.

Slurp!

Slurp!

Slurp!

Shay stopped when she knew he was on the verge of nutting. She could feel the head of his dick begin to swell and from hearing how loud his groaning got, she could tell he was about to blow.

"You ready for mama, baby?" she cooed, climbing back on top and sliding him right back in between her juicy walls.

He groaned out loud from the sensation. Her pussy was hotter and wetter than her mouth and he felt himself beginning to lose control. He was moaning and spitting out words that he didn't even understand.

"Damn Shay!" he gasped, trying to catch his breath. "Girl what... are you... doing tooooo me?"

She continued rocking back and forth on him until she saw his eyes start to roll towards the back of his head. She knew right then; it was the perfect time to cast her spell.

She leaned down and whispered into his ear, "Now that you got this pussy, daddy, do you promise to keep it wet?"

"Yeeeah!" he groaned, not really aware of what he just agreed to.

As she continued rocking she said, "Are you gonna love this pussy like it needs to be loved?"

"Yeah baby, yeah!"

"Are you gonna take care of this pussy, baby?"

"Oh shit!" he shouted, on the brink of exploding. "Yeah baby, I swear!"

"You swear daddy?" she moaned, making him repeat his commitment to her.

"I swear ma, I swear to God," he said, mistakenly committing himself all the way.

That was all she needed to hear. She placed her hands on his stomach and spread her legs as if she was about to do a split. She leaned forward so she could arch her back and slowly began to bounce up and down on his dick.

She knew that from this day forward, Armani Lewis belonged to her.

***

The police had Cash surrounded. Every corner he turned and every street he sped down, it seemed like there was a different police car already there waiting on him. He decided the time had come for him to jump out of the vehicle and take his chance on foot. The only problem was he didn't know where he was. By the looks of the middle-class area he was in, there wouldn't be too many places for him to run.

The sirens continued in the background. He knew his time was running out, so he quickly unfastened his seatbelt and looked for a possible escape route.

"Fuck it, it's now or never," he said, bringing the Charger to an abrupt halt.

Scurrrrt!

Hitting a garbage can, he bailed out of the vehicle and took off behind an old brick house. The police were late exiting their vehicles, which gave him a ten-second head start.

Once he was out of their view, he pulled the handgun out his waistband, preparing to toss it. As he dashed through different yards looking for a place to get rid of it, he saw a pool with the cover over it. He quickly ran over, raised the tarp and tossed the gun inside. Now, he needed to put some distance between himself and the illegal firearm.

Bark!

Bark! Bark! Bark!

Bark! Bark!

When he heard the K—9's, he knew he was pressed for time. He hopped over a wooden fence in an attempt to lose the dogs. Instead, he ran into a pitbull that chased him into another yard, but not before he could toss the drugs down for the hungry animal to devour.

As he started running again, he noticed he had a bulge in his other pocket and remembered that he still had weed on him too. He reached into his pocket and pulled it out, preparing to toss it. That's when an officer's flashlight shined on him.

"Don't move, motherfucker, or I'll shoot you in the face!"

He stopped immediately, scared to death. He started screaming loudly so the cop wouldn't shoot.

"Alright, alright, alright, don't shoot!" he yelled, throwing his hands up to surrender.

"Get down!"

"Get on the fucking ground!"

Don't you move, maggot!"

All of the approaching officers were yelling different demands making Cash confused. He didn't know whether to get down on the ground or stand still, so he remained standing until an officer forced him to the ground. They twisted his arm around his back and cuffed him.

He wasn't even concerned about the excessive roughness he was enduring from the cops who had him pinned to the ground. His only concern was that they didn't find that gun.

CHAPTER 12

JUVENILE

"Now presiding in Juvenile Court, the State of Georgia calls the case of Cashmere Lewis to the attention of the Court!" announced the burly, white bailiff.

"Good morning your honor, how are you doing today sir?" asked Cash's attorney.

"I'm just fine, Mr. Pendelton, but I can't say that I am too pleased to see this young man back in my courtroom," replied the judge, tilting his head forward to peer over his glasses.

This was Cash's third time coming in front of Judge Banks, and he didn't like being there just as much as the judge didn't like seeing him. Cash couldn't stand Juvenile Court. It seemed like everybody there was against him. The judge, the prosecutor, his attorney, and hell, even the court reporter all seemed to be giving him dirty looks. Yeah, from the look of it, he was pretty sure they all wanted him locked up. He maintained his composure and sat patiently in his seat while court took its course.

Sitting next to his Case Manager, Mr. Daniels, Cash slowly glanced around the courtroom for any familiar faces. In the small courtroom, mothers of all ages and races sat quietly as they waited to support their delinquent child.

He didn't see his mother anywhere in the courtroom and he wasn't surprised about it either. It was a common thing for him not to expect her to show up. All she wanted was her drink. She was willing to let the state raise her son, even if it meant his going to a Juvenile Detention Center. Point blank, Cash had to fend for himself, and no matter how bad he wanted Ms. Tina to be there, he was basically alone.

"We understand your position, Your Honor. Myself and Mr. Daniels have discussed Mr. Lewis's conduct and feel that maybe a little youth detention time will correct his behavior," stated his attorney, clearly selling him out.

"What you mean discussed!" shouted Cash, jumping up from his seat.

"Order in the Court!" The judge announced, banging his gable to make his point. "Young man, if you disrupt my courtroom like that again I will hold you in contempt and reschedule your court date for a much later time, do you understand me?"

"But my lawyer—" he tried to plead but was cut short.

"Do you understand me?" said the judge, raising his voice louder.

"Yes, sir," he whispered, lowering his head from defeat.

"As I was saying, Your Honor," his lawyer continued, "maybe my client does deserve another chance, but it's totally up to you."

Cash wanted to smack the hell out of his lawyer. He just continued to stand there with a stupid grin on his face. This is not what they talked about earlier, so Cash was wondering what type of game he was playing.

"What do you have to say about your client, Mr. Daniels?" Judge Banks asked the Case Manager.

Mr. Daniels rose to his feet. "Your Honor, my client has done a good job since the last time he entered your courtroom."

Cash exhaled in relief.

Mr. Daniels continued. "Mr. Lewis has maintained a job, completed his tenth-grade year in high school, and completed the probation time you ordered for him to serve. So, to be honest your honor, I do not believe that time served at a detention center best fits this situation."

"But he took officers on a high-speed chase at three o'clock in the morning, Your Honor, and might I add, he was in possession of illegal drugs."

"Your honor, it was marijuana," stated Mr. Daniels, down—playing the drugs. "True, my client was a little under the influence and probably not fully aware of the damage he caused, but keep in mind he does have to finish school, Judge. I propose you commit him to the state and reinstate his Supervised Release until his twenty—first birthday."

Got damn, Cash thought to himself, this motherfucker is trippin', but if that's what it'll take to get me out of jail, then so be it'.

"Well…" began the Judge, contemplating his suggestion, "is his mother in the courtroom today?"

Everybody began looking around, as if expecting someone to come forward and claim him.

"I don't believe so." The lawyer started to speak, only to be interrupted by a woman bursting her way through the two double doors at the front of the courtroom.

It was his mother, Ms. Tina.

"Where's my baby?" she shouted, clearly drunk as she stumbled down the walkway. "Where's my got damn child?"

"Ma'am, who are you here for?" asked the judge, disgusted by her appearance.

Ms. Tina's long hair was in a tangly mess, and her clothes were obviously completely mismatched. She looked a hot mess. Cash began to feel embarrassed and slouched down in his chair hoping she couldn't see him and leave.

After realizing she was standing in front of a judge, she quickly tried gathering her composure. "Yes, how do you do, Judge, I'm here for Cashmere Lewis. I am his mother," she stated proudly.

Cash slid further down into his seat.

"Well ma'am," he began, readjusting his glasses, "we are in the middle of his hearing right now. Do you have anything to say on behalf of your son?"

"Yes I do, Your Honor," she said, combing her fingers through her hair. "My son is a good child, Judge. I blame his father and them crackers at his school for this shit! Plus, I need my damn rent money."

The Judge banged his gavel.

"Ms. Lewis, if you use anymore racial slurs in my courtroom, I will hold you in contempt, do you understand me?" He was clearly upset by her statement.

"I hold you in contempt, Judge!" she spat back. "Matter of fact, I hold all you bitches in contempt, tryin' to railroad my child!"

She spun around dramatically, pointing to everyone in the courtroom.

"Bailiff, remove this woman from my courtroom now!" He had enough of the mockery she was making of his authority. Once the deputy removed Ms. Tina the court resumed.

Judge Banks felt a little sympathy for the young man after seeing the display his mother just gave in his court. He had seen his share of unfit mothers, but nothing like this. Out of remorse, he decided to give Cash one more chance.

"Okay," he began, "here's what I am going to do. Cashmere Lewis, you are now committed to the State of Georgia until your twenty—first birthday. This means, young man, you will be under the supervision of the probation office until you are a legal adult. Do you understand?" Cash rose to his feet.

"Yes, sir!"

"Okay, good." The judge shuffled some papers around on his desk. "I'll also order for you to pay in restitution $250 for the damage done to the property of 1279 Hillridge Circle. This includes one mailbox and one trash can. Do you understand? Any questions?"

"No, sir!"

"All right then, court is adjourned."

***

"Man, I can't believe mama," said Money, disappointed by his mother's behavior in court.

"Yeah, bruh. After that lil' display, I just knew I was about to get juvenile life," laughed Cash. He was referring to how juveniles get sentenced to prison until their twenty—first birthday.

They were riding around in Money's old school Chevy Caprice. He had gotten it out the shop a month after Cash got locked up. They laughed and joked about their mother's ridiculous behavior while smoking and drinking.

Cash had just been released from the Regional Youth Detention Center earlier that day and Money was right there to pick him up. Three months had passed since they celebrated his birthday. Throughout it all, Money was right there by his brother's side. He went to go see him every weekend while he was locked down. Every now and then, he would bring Jasmin, too. Whenever she saw Money in the neighborhood, she would always ask about Cash and how he was doing. So, when he relayed to Cash how bad she was sweating him about coming to visit, he told Money to bring her along.

Because of Cash's incarceration, the crew couldn't re—up, and that left opportunity for someone else to steal their customers. Money informed him that there were some dudes up the street from the projects who opened up a dope house and was serving their old clientele. Cash wasn't trying to hear it though. Now that he was out, it was time for them to get back to work.

"You see bruh," said Money, driving by their trap house, "them niggas always deep, and they slangin' the same thang we be slangin'."

"Yeah, I see them niggas," replied Cash, surveilling the house.

The Chevy's tinted windows hid their identity as they crept by, but at this point, Cash didn't really care. He knew what needed to be done in order for them to get their customers back. Going to war with these cats wasn't a good idea. For one, they weren't violating, and two, it wouldn't be very long before the police raided their trap house anyways. Cash knew when they passed the house, whoever those guys were, they weren't that smart. Standing out front of your trap with that many people, doing hand to hand transactions, was the easiest way to catch a case.

Money drove around a little while longer while him and Cash devised a new plan on how they were going to sell their dope.

"So, how much bread you got on the table?" Cash asked his brother, firing up a blunt.

"Like $1,300."

"That's it?" Cash replied.

"Yeah, but shit." Money grabbed the blunt from Cash and took a couple of hits before he continued. "We can pump that shit right back up in no time."

"Yeah, I guess you're right, but don't trip though. I still got most of my bread anyways, so I got you my nigga," he said, giving his brother some dap.

He knew Money wasn't the kind of person who was serious about saving money. Plus, he heard how he was in a relationship now, so he pretty much knew from there where it went.

He noticed that Money passed by the street to their crib, "Bruh, you know you passed the crib, right?"

"Yeah, I know," he replied, looking at Cash like he was crazy. "Well, where are you going?"

Money knew his brother was high because he had already forgotten what they had to go do.

"Man, don't we have to pick mama up from the County?" he asked.

"Oh yeah, I forgot," he replied, feeling stupid.

The weed had him gone.

CHAPTER 13

THE TRAP

"Listen," said Cash, getting everyone's attention, "here's what we are gonna do…"

Cash, Money, Trap, and Scappy were all sitting around Scrappy's grandma's basement.

The lights were down low and it was quieter than usual. You could tell they were engaged in a serious conversation. They were all sitting around the table with the money they had left in front of them. From the look of it, Cash had the biggest amount, but that was only because he didn't have a chance to spend it while he was incarcerated.

"I'm gonna holla at my man and see if we can cop two bricks and ten pounds with what we got here. And also, we're no longer gonna hustle on the corner," he told them.

They all looked at each other, confused.

"I'm gonna take $1,500 out of this and get us a trap."

No one opposed his idea. Not only was he the one with the connect, but he was the one with over $20,000 to put up. Everybody else had either splurged all their money away or had some bills to pay. Trap had a total of ten stacks in front of him, Lil Scrappy was down to five, and Money was depending on Cash.

Trap already knew what Cash's focus was going to be on when he got out, so he made it his business to save as much as he could. Scrappy, on the other hand got tired of riding shotgun, and brought himself a motorcycle, along with some clothes, jewelry, and a big ass ego. Money had his Chevy fixed up really nice and even bought Shay a Honda Accord so she wouldn't ask to drive his car as much. Cash didn't approve of Money's choices, but he knew how his brother was when it came to Shay. All he wanted to focus on now was them getting back on track and getting their hands on more dope.

"You really think your man is just gonna serve you like that, after being MIA for three months?" asked Trap, leaning forward and crossing his fingers.

"Nah bruh, that nigga cool, plus I've already talked to him," replied Cash. He stood up and started filling a Louis Vuitton bag with the money on the table.

"Say bruh, how in the hell are you gonna get a trap when you're not even 18 yet?" asked Money.

He already had it mapped out in his head. Cash looked over to his brother and said, "Don't worry about that, my nigga, I got it under control."

***

"Hold on, what the fuck you mean you don't know about that?"

"Just like I said, I don't know about that!"

Cash and Peaches were going through it over the phone. The whole time he was locked up, Peaches hadn't written or visited him. Now she had the nerve to say she wasn't going to help him get an apartment. He wasn't trying to hear it, though. He understood while he was away she went off to Spelman, and congratulated her for accomplishing her goal, but to not keep in touch with the person you supposedly love was unacceptable.

As much as he tried overlooking it and moving on, he just couldn't. He was always there for her when she needed him, so he felt like she owed him a little support as well.

Here they were, arguing about what she was or wasn't going to do. All he knew was that if she didn't get this apartment for him, their relationship was going to need some serious help. He figured it was the least she could do for abandoning him when he needed her most.

"Listen, Patricia," he said, calling her by her government name. "I don't ask you for shit, now do I?" he said, fed up with her bullshit.

She was heated. She didn't understand why he was so upset. He was acting as if she was the one responsible for him almost being sent to YDC. Plus, she didn't feel comfortable getting an apartment in her name, especially one she wasn't going to be living in. As far she knew, he could be trying to shack up with another chick.

"Do I?" he yelled repeating himself.

"No!" she screamed back, on the verge of tears.

"So why can't you do this fuckin' favor for me then?"

"Because…" she hesitated, trying to think of an excuse, "what if you miss the rent or something and it messes up my credit?"

He couldn't believe her. With all the lame excuses she could've came up with, she chose that one. Cash was sick and tired of her excuses and told her that this one wasn't going to work.

won't ever have to worry about that, alright!"

"Man, check it out, I'm gonna give you three months in advance, so you…"

"Whatever, Cash," she agreed, giving into his request, "When I do this for you, don't ask me for nothin' else!"

It took every bone and fiber in his body not to say, 'even your hand in marriage,' but he was already treading on thin ice. It took 45 minutes of them arguing back and forth to get her to do it, but he got what he wanted, so it was time to move on.

"Alright then cool, I'll holla at you later," he said, attempting to end their call.

"Oh, so you too mad now to tell me you love me?" she replied, sounding hurt.

He didn't want to make her cry, because he still loved her. He was looking forward to one day spending the rest of his life with her, but only if they could get on the same page in their relationship.

"I'm sorry baby," he apologized, "I love you Peaches."

"I love you too, Cash.

Then they both hung up.

***

After Cash visited his connect, Big Pete, they were back in business. Big Pete blessed him with two bricks of cocaine and ten pounds of weed. He even threw in two pounds of an exotic bud called AK—47. He didn't have a problem with fronting Cash anything because after he took his cut off the top, he was going to make a profitable commission from the transaction.

Money and Lil Scrappy decided against Cash's advice not to drop out of school. They felt like they could make more money trappin' than from reading a book.

Cash, on the other hand, didn't have much of a choice, so he continued to go. His Probation Officer was on his bumper, so he needed to continue driving straight or not be able to drive at all. He didn't mind, though, because he knew how important an education was. In the morning he went to school, and afterwards he was in the trap. Education and getting money created the perfect balance in his life.

After he left school, he went straight to the trap house. When he pulled up he noticed a customer approaching their front door. As he got out, attempting to serve the person, he saw some girls walking down the street towards him. Squinting to get a better look, he noticed that one of them was Jasmin.

He knew there was already someone in the trap to serve the customer, so he directed his attention to the crowd of girls. Jasmin had earned a special place in his heart when she rode the three months out with him. She wrote him twice a week and sent plenty of pictures, so he felt obligated to return the favor.

"Hey Cash," all the girls greeted him.

"Hello ladies," he returned their greeting. "Say Jay, come holla at me for a minute." He reached out and grabbed her hand.

"Cash, where is your brother?" asked one of the girls.

"He in there," he replied, pointing at the house.

"Alright." All the girls, except Jasmin, followed suit as she walked up the steps and knocked on the door.

Turning his attention back to Jasmin, Cash said, "What's up, sexy? Where are y'all going?"

"Nowhere in particular, probably to the store," she replied, blushing.

"Oh yeah," he pulled her closer to him.

"Yeah," was all she could say before their lips touched and their tongues began to dance.

As they passionately kissed, he explored her body with his hands. He caressed her ass, rubbing around her thighs and between her legs. He took in her scent and quickly became aroused. He was really feeling Jasmin. Her determination to stay in touch with him while he was away gave her some major brownie points in his book.

"So, you want to spend the rest of the day with me or what?" he asked, breaking their embrace.

She nodded in response, still a little shocked from their kiss.

"Come on, he said, walking around the car to get in the passenger seat.

She stood there for a minute lost, trying to figure out why he walked to the other side of the car. He could see she wasn't catching the hint so he asked, "Are you gonna drive or what?"

A big smile spread across her face. He knew what kind of impact he was making on her. When a man allowed a woman to get behind the wheel of his most precious toy, it really meant something. Only a girl of importance could drive a man's car and Cash wanted her to know how much she meant to him.

"I don't even have a license," she said, getting in the car.

"Well then…" he began putting on his seatbelt and laying the seat back, "just don't get pulled over.

She just sat there and stared at him confused. She was beginning to think this was a bad idea, but quickly dismissed her thoughts. She didn't want to act like a little girl in front of him in case this was a test. He was clearly trying to tell her he trusted her, so she wanted him to continue feeling that way.

She adjusted her seat to her short legs, moved the rearview mirror around to straighten her view, and turned the keys in the ignition. The loud music flooded her eardrums, making her cringe.

"Hold on," he exclaimed, reaching over to turn it down. "Let your friends know you gone be with me before we leave."

She honked the horn and waited for someone to come to the door.

When Money opened it and peeked out, Cash said, "Say, bruh, tell them girls that Jasmin is with me for the rest of the day, alright!"

"Alright!" he replied, then closed the door.

CHAPTER 14

BOTTOM BITCH

After weeks of showing Jasmin how much he really appreciated her loyalty and support, Cash started to notice how she always seemed to try and turn their making out sessions into a full sexual encounter. He knew she wanted to make love to him and he wanted the same in return, but there was something special about Jasmin that made him want to wait. He didn't want to treat her like the rest of the girls he met in the past. When he looked into her eyes, he saw a beautiful young lady with an honest heart. He wanted her to be more than just a friend; he wanted her to be his ride or die chick, or for lack of better words, his bottom bitch.

Peaches, on the other hand, had her mind made up that school was her number one priority. Cash had no other choice but to respect her decision. he just couldn't understand how she was easily willing to jeopardize their relationship in the process. After all, school didn't buy her clothes, support her financially, or make love to her; he did!

To him, school wasn't worth losing the love of your life. He wanted her to realize that, but he still loved her despite their disagreements. He truly wanted Peaches to be his woman for the rest of his life at some point, but after realizing he couldn't have her like he needed her, his perception of their relationship changed.

He needed someone to be there and give him something that only a woman could provide. If she couldn't give it to him, he was more than willing to go and get it from somewhere else.

"Baby, why do you only have a bed and a TV in here?" asked Jasmin, looking around his bedroom.

They laid down on his king—sized bed to watch *Love and Basketball* and spend quality time together. Lately, Jasmin had been spending a lot of time with Cash in the trap. Whenever she came over, she'd intentionally pay no attention to the oval-shaped table in the living room that always contained a digital scale, some small colorful baggies, and razors. He tried his best not to expose his drug dealing lifestyle to her, but it was becoming harder, because of her tendency to frequently stop by. When she came over, he would whisk her away to the confinement of his room until it was time for her to go.

"First off, babe," he started, adjusting her head on his shoulder, "I rarely be here, so there's no reason to keep anything other than a TV and bed here."

The real reason he didn't want to keep a lot of stuff in the trap was because he knew that at any moment the doors could be kicked in. It would be a lot easier for him to just get up and leave without missing anything. They already had it planned to flush the dope; therefore they only kept a small portion of it in there. The rest of it was being held at Scrappy's crib.

"Well look, I'm about to start working, so if you need me to buy you some stuff just let me know, alright?"

He smiled at the thought of Jasmin spending her money on him.

"Babe," he said, gazing into her pretty brown eyes, "I got enough money to do whatever I want to do in here." He pulled out a thick wad of cash from his pocket, letting her know that he was financially capable of taking care of himself. "But thanks anyways, boo!"

He pulled her to his lips and they began kissing.

Suddenly, two loud knocks were heard at the bedroom's door.

Money walked in. "Bruh," he exclaimed, rushing in and peeking out the window.

"Man, what!" shouted Cash, not liking his brother's rudeness.

"You might want to come and see who just pulled up, nigga."

Cash moved Jasmin from off top of him and hopped off the bed.

"Peaches," Money whispered.

"Oh shit!" He rushed towards the front of the house. By the time he got there, she'd already put the key in the door and was turning the knob but not before he could grab the drug instruments and paraphernalia off the table. He tossed them over to Scrappy to hide in the kitchen. It was hard enough persuading her to rent the house in her name; so if she was to see any sign of illegal activity going on, she'd probably flip out.

"Heeey baby!" he said, catching the door halfway open.

Peaches was caught off guard.

"Damn boy, you liked to scare the shit out of me!" she said, pushing away from him and placing her hand over her chest.

"Well, since you ain't shitted yet," he said, trying to bring some humor to the situation, "what are you doing here?"

"What do you mean, what am I doing here?" she questioned. From seeing how nervous he was acting, she immediately started to feel like something was going on. She began looking around the living room for signs that he had a chick in the house.

"What's wrong with you?" she said, noticing how funny he was acting.

Then it dawned on her.

"Who's in here?" she asked with an attitude. She tried walking past him to go towards the back, but he kept cutting her off. "Move out my way, Cash!" she shouted. "Why the fuck are you blocking me from going back there?"

"Girl, what the fuck are you talkin' about? I'm tryin' to talk to you for a minute," he stated, loosening his grip on her arm.

She snatched away from him and said sternly, "Cashmere, move!" He moved to the side to let her pass.

She took off flying straight down the hallway, running into Money and Jasmin. Money had his arm draped around her shoulder as if she was his girl.

He was whispering in her ear what to say in case Peaches tried to stop them. He knew he was putting himself at risk because Peaches and Shay were best friends, but he had no choice but to help his brother out.

"Hey Peaches," he greeted her, attempting to walk right pass.

Peaches looked at both of them. "Don't 'hey' me boy, who is that?" she asked, determined to find out what was going on.

Cash didn't know what to do, so he just stood there dumbfounded. At first he didn't catch on, wanting to know why Money's arm was around Jasmin, but then he realized what his brother was doing. He was saving him from what would've been their biggest argument ever.

"Ummmm, first of all, my name is Jasmin, and why are you asking about me?"

Peaches couldn't believe the nerve of this girl. She wanted to punch her in the face for getting fly at the mouth but decided against it. She'll just let her friend have this fight. After witnessing Money's blatant infidelity, she knew Shay was going to go crazy when she heard about how her man was hugged up with some thot.

"Well, little girl, I was just trying to make sure you weren't here with him," she said, pointing her finger at Cash.

Jasmin smiled as she contemplated on telling Peaches that she was there for her man. She knew that would crush her and probably destroy their relationship, but she didn't want to get Cash that way. She knew in due time he would be hers, so she played her part and kept her mouth closed.

"Peaches, bring your ass on and leave that girl alone!" Cash grabbed Peaches by the hand and began leading her towards his room.

Jasmin rolled her eyes as she continued to let Money walk her out the door. As soon as Peaches turned her back, Jasmin blew Cash a good—bye kiss.

Scrappy was sitting on the couch, in the midst of it all, watching it play out. He laughed to himself when everybody parted ways.

"I can't wait to tell Trap about this shit," he joked, reaching down to pick up the controller to the Playstation.

***

Cash and Peaches spent the rest of their evening together. Even though they were enjoying each other's' company, Cash couldn't seem to get Jasmin off his mind. Throughout the night, his thoughts always came back to her, worrying about where she was or what she was doing. Earlier, she kept it real cool and didn't blow up his spot, and he loved her even more for that. She could've spoken up about their relationship and turned the situation into an all-out war, but she didn't. He also enjoyed the fact that he was able to keep both women on his team, at least for now.

"Bye boo," said Peaches, making her departure as she got into her car.

"See you later, babe," he said in response, bending down to kiss her before she headed off back to Atlanta. "You need some money?" he asked.

Her eyes lit up when she saw him reach into his pocket and pull out a wad of cash. "I thought you'd never ask."

He quickly counted out five-hundred dollars and placed it into her hands. He knew she needed money to live comfortably in the A, especially since her parents had to struggle to get her there. They were putting themselves in debt so she could go to college, so he didn't mind helping out.

They embraced for one more long kiss before she took off. When he began walking back towards the trap, he noticed a Lincoln TownCar pulling up. The driver flickered the lights to get his attention. He assumed it was a customer, so he turned around to see what they wanted.

"What's good ma, what you lookin' for?" he asked the women.

"Is Money here?" she asked, licking her lips as she eyed him up and down.

"Nah, he ain't here, but ummm… what are you tryin' to get?" He pulled out a few sacks of weed, because she didn't look like the type to smoke crack.

"Oh, I'm good on that sweetie," she said, declining his offer, "I just came by looking for him, that's all."

"Well, he should be back any minute. Do you want me to tell him to call you when he gets here?"

"Yeah, could you do that for me?" she asked.

"Yeah, I got you, Miss…"

"Oh I'm sorry, how rude of me. My name is Shantell."

"Alright then, I'll let 'em know you dropped by," he assured her, stepping away from the car.

When she pulled off, a junkie walked up to cop some dope. While making the transaction, he repeated her name over and over so he wouldn't forget. There was something familiar about Shantell, but he couldn't quite put a finger on it.

All he knew was that Money left the house hours ago and hadn't even called. He assumed that wherever he was, he and Jasmin were still together and that didn't sit too well in his mind.

He called his brother's number again, but it continuously went straight to voicemail. Cash was starting to get upset and couldn't wait to get in touch with him.

***

After the episode at the trap, Money took Jasmin home. She was in love with Cash and since she was already aware that he had a woman, she wasn't going to put him on blast about what had really been going on between them. Even though she envied Peaches, she was willing to wait her turn for Cash to open his heart to her. She knew they were meant for each other; she just had to give him enough time to figure it out too. In the meantime, she had other matters to deal with.

When they pulled up to her house, she noticed all of her neighbors standing out on their front porch. They were listening to the commotion that was going on in her house. She quickly got out of the car and ran inside, already knowing that her mother needed her help.

Her mother's boyfriend, Corey, was always coming home drunk and taking his frustrations out on her mom. For the past two hours, they'd been going at it and the whole neighborhood was there to witness.

Now, here they were engaged in a standoff. On her way in, Jasmin stopped by the kitchen to grab the biggest butcher knife she could find, just in case he tried to put his hands on her. When she finally made it to their bedroom, her mother was balled up in a corner crying. Corey was pacing back and forth across the room, holding a belt. Jasmin ran over to her mother, looking for any cuts or bruises. Still clutching the knife, she stood up to confront her mother's abuser.

"What kind of man does this to a woman, you piece of shit!" she screamed.

"Shuuuuuut up, yoooou litttle bitch!" Corey spat back, pushing himself off the wall he was leaning on.

"Nigga, if you come near my mama again, I'm gonna chop that little-ass dick of yours off!" she threatened, raising the knife to let him know she was serious.

She hated Corey with a passion and honestly thought he was a pervert. Whenever she'd leave the bathroom, she'd notice him always somewhere nearby, as if he was trying to catch her coming out the shower or something. He wore some goofy-looking glasses that covered his beady little eyes. He reminded her of Marvin from the movie *Players Club*.

He knew she meant business, so he backed away from the sight of the blade. He was in no condition to fight someone with a knife, so he decided to just leave. He was still drunk from his long night of partying and didn't want it to end with him dead.

"Fuck you, stupid ass hoes, I'm outta here, and don't even think to call me for rent money either," he said, walking towards the bedroom door.

As he was trying to leave, someone stepped through the door blocking his exit.

"Who the fuck is you?" asked Corey, wondering who the hell was interfering with his business.

Jasmin couldn't see who was blocking him from leaving, but she wished they would move. As she peeked around Corey, she saw that it was Money.

"Nevermind who the fuck I am dawg, wasn't you just leaving?" stated Money, moving out of his way.

Corey was taken aback and didn't like how someone half his age was trying to handle him.

"Man, who the fuck is this boy, y'all super—save—a—hoe?" he laughed, looking back at the women. He didn't like Money's tone of voice, and the fact that he was intruding in on their business angered him even more. Corey took two steps towards Money, but stopped when he lifted his shirt, revealing a chrome handgun.

"My nigga, this ain't what you want, so I suggest you bounce up out of here before the police get here, cause I'm gone body you," stated Money, resting his hand on his Glocc. It was a dangerous situation to get involved in, but he knew Cash wouldn't have wanted him to turn his head the other way. He had brought his pistol with him to ensure that the odds were in his favor.

Sirens were heard in the distance.

Once he heard the sirens approaching, Corey snapped out his daze and walked right past Money, out of the bedroom.

"Y'all alright?" he asked the girls, looking at the two as they consoled each other.

"We good," Jasmin answered while hugging her mom, "and thank you Money."

He nodded his head and decided it was time for him to go. The sirens were getting closer by the minute and he wasn't trying to stick around to explain anything to the cops, or get caught with an illegal firearm, so he left.

***

After Money left Jasmin's house, he rode around town for a while to clear his head. He had witnessed more than enough drama for one day and needed some peace and quiet for a change. He knew that once Peaches had a chance to speak with Shay, he was going to have to do some major explaining about why he was hugged up with Jasmin.

Shay had his nose wide open and he couldn't even deny it. After his birthday he got to know her better and realized that she was everything he could ever want in a woman. She was classy, jazzy, and sassy. He was truly happy and as long as she was happy, then they'd be happy together. He just needed to cut a few strings loose before their happiness got rudely interrupted.

Shantell had been blowing up his phone all week long and he was getting tired of it. She just couldn't catch the hint that he was through being her sex toy. There was no type of future for them because she was a married woman. Although she wasn't happily married, she was still in a relationship with another man. Money didn't want to have to deal with any more problems than the ones he already had. He appreciated the long nights of hot, passionate sex when she would suck his dick for what seemed like hours and share that warm spot between her legs with him, but it was time for them to bring this thing they had to a close.

He checked his caller ID and saw that for the 30th time she called his phone. He also saw that his brother called him too, so he made a mental note to call him back after speaking with Shantell. It was time for him to end this chapter in their lives. They both had to move on, whether she liked it or not.

He pressed the call button on his phone and waited for her to pick up.

"Hello," he said, after hearing her answer.

"Oh my God, baby, Money where have you been?" she asked.

"What you mean, 'where have I been?' I been doing me, why?"

"Listen baby, whatever I did let's talk about it and work this out. Just tell me where you are so I can come pick you up."

"Shantell, listen." He pulled over to the side of the road so he could concentrate on how he was going to break it down to her that it was over between them. "We can't keep doing this, babe," he finally said.

"Wha— wha—— what?" she stuttered, trying to make sense of what was going on.

"Hold on, let me finish," he said, cutting her off. "You're married, shawty, and I don't want to be the reason for your divorce. Try and work things out with your husband and continue doing you. What we had was special, but ma, it's time to put this relationship behind us, okay!"

There was a brief moment of silence before he heard her utter something into the phone.

"What?" he said, barely hearing her.

"I said, I love you," she whispered, "so this is not over AND IT NEVER WILL BE!"

Just like that she hung up the phone, leaving him puzzled by what had just transpired. He wasn't expecting for her to confess her love for him. He felt sorry for her and how the situation turned out, but it needed to be done.

Now that it was over, he was just hoping in time she would see that it was for the best.

Pulling off from the side of the road, he wondered to himself what she meant by 'it will never be over?'

CHAPTER 15

DRAMA

It was a bright and colorful Saturday morning when Cash decided to take his car out for a drive. He was enjoying some purple haze as he listened to music, thinking about how far he and his crew had come in the dope game.

Two weeks ago, he had quit his job at the detail shop, committing himself full—time to selling dope after school. Mr. Mac didn't want him to leave, but he knew Cash's time working for him was limited, especially after hearing about his rise in the drug business. He hated to see him fall victim to the same game that cost him years of his life, but he knew he had to let him make his own mistakes in order for him to learn. Hopefully for Cash, his mistake wouldn't cost him his life.

"You be careful, young man," was the last thing Cash remembered Mr. Mac telling him before leaving. He knew Mr. Mac cared for him like a son and he appreciated all the love and support he gave him, but it was time for him to start making some real money and he couldn't get that working at no detail shop.

Today felt special, but he didn't know quite yet why. What he did know was that they were starting to bring in some real paper, and if they kept it up, they'd be running the Mac—Town in no time.

Thanks to Big Pete, they no longer had to go pick up their work. Big Pete didn't like the heavy traffic that came with serving weight, so he made the offer to deliver their package to the trap instead. He had one of his loyal family members pick up and drop off his packages for him because he wasn't going to do it himself. He admired how Cash and his crew had stepped their game up, from copping a few ounces to a few bricks. He was impressed and decided to throw them some Ecstasy pills their way for hustlin' so hard.

As for their competition around the corner, they were no longer a factor in Cash's eyes. They seemed to always run out of dope, and he heard that the quality wasn't all that good either. That allowed him and his crew to grab all of their clientele back. His crew kept good dope, so it started not to even matter if anyone else sold dope in their neighborhood, because everybody knew they had the best product around.

As he bent another corner in his Grand Marquis, he decided it was time to go put in some work at the trap. He had done enough driving for one morning, so he headed off towards their money—making domain.

***

"Baby, I'm pregnant!"

"Hold on, Shay, what you mean you're pregnant?"

Money couldn't believe his ears. Was he really about to become a Da Da, a Pa Pa, or even an Old Man? These were words he wasn't expecting to hear at such an early age, but once he realized he was about to start his own family, a smile broke across his face.

After going through it with Shay about the situation with him at the trap, they were hardly on speaking terms. He tried on numerous occasions to explain to her that it wasn't what it sounded like, but she clearly, at the time, wasn't trying to hear him out. Now, after weeks of barely communicating, she was calling to tell him that she was pregnant.

"I said I'm pregnant, Money," she repeated herself. She couldn't believe he was acting like he hadn't heard her the first time. She knew they were having a rough time right now, but she didn't know how else to break the news to him. She knew for sure the baby was his, so she had no problem telling him, but now after hearing his response, she wished she'd told him in person.

He was sitting down in the living room of the trap when she informed him that he was about to become a father. He jumped off the couch and began pumping his fist in the air, as if he'd just won a million bucks.

Trap and Scrappy were both playing the game when he got the news. They both looked at him with confusion, wanting to know what made him so happy.

Cash was walking through the front door when all this took place. He also wanted to know why his brother was so happy. He looked over at his homies for an explanation, but they just shrugged their shoulders.

He walked over to where his brother was celebrating and mouthed, "What's up?"

Money put the phone to his shoulder so she couldn't hear him.

"Shay about to have my child, nigga. She pregnant! I'm 'bout to have a little Money Jr. on the way."

Cash smiled and dapped him up, congratulating his brother on becoming a father. He was happy for him but shocked at the same time. He knew Money loved himself more than anything or anybody in the world, so to see him happy about having to share that love with a child was unexpected.

While Money was informing everybody in the house about his latest news, he forgot Shay was still on the line.

"Money…Money, are you still there or what?" She was shouting through the phone trying to get his attention.

"Get dressed boo, cause we going out to celebrate."

He hung up without saying another word. He was getting too excited so he sat down, allowing it all to sink in. While sitting there, he noticed that everyone in the room was staring at him.

"What?" he asked, embarrassed about how he was just acting.

All his homies broke out laughing.

"Man, fuck y'all," he said, smiling.

They just continued to laugh. "I'm da pappy!"

"I'm dat dere kid's pa, boss!"

They were all laughing and cracking jokes on how he was acting when he heard he was about to become a father.

"Damn dawg, what you think I should name him, Scrappy?" he asked, already assuming that it's going to be a boy.

"I don't know cuzz, but Tramell sound like a good name to me."

Money looked at him like he was crazy. Cash and Trap broke out laughing again.

"Nigga, I wouldn't name my dog after you," Money joked, making them all burst out laughing.

***

An hour later, Money was on his way out the door to pick up Shay. He called his sister and gave her the news. He told her to relay the message to their mother because he wasn't in the mood to deal with her yet.

On his way out, he passed Cash, who was weighing 63 grams of crack for a customer. When he stepped out on the front porch, he yelled at the top of his lungs, "Got damn!"

Everybody in the trap froze once they heard him. Cash, not knowing what for, pulled out his Glock and pointed it at the customer. If he was being set up, he was going to make sure this dude never had the chance to set up another soul.

"Nigga, who the fuck you got out there with you?" he asked, demanding an answer.

"Dawg, you trippin'," replied the customer, throwing his hands up to surrender. He was pleading with Cash not to shoot because he was just as confused.

Trap grabbed the AK—47 that was leaning against the wall and ran to the front window. When he peeked out and saw Money bent down by his car, he turned around and smiled, letting Cash know that everything was straight.

Cash returned his pistol to his waist and apologized to his customer. It was better to be safe than sorry when it came to his life, plus he didn't like surprises. The customer took it well and they continued doing business. The fact that Cash pulled out his pistol though had him ready to go, but not before he grabbed what he'd came there for.

After serving the customer, Cash and Trap walked him out the door so they could see what was going on. They began laughing once they saw the damage done to Money's car.

"Man, this shit ain't funny, y'all," he said, clearly upset.

In pink chalk, someone had engraved the words, 'IT'S NEVER OVER' in big letters across his $2,400 paint job. He couldn't believe how someone so grown could be so childish. He knew he couldn't pick up Shay with his car like this. Too many questions would be asked.

"Damn, bruh," said Cash, still laughing, "one of your other hoes must know you got a baby on the way too."

More laughter erupted.

Money looked like he wanted to cry. His car was his most prized possession and he took pride in keeping it in good condition. To see someone damage its body cut him deep. He knew there were going to be consequences, but first, he had to go out and celebrate with his new baby's mother.

"Say, bruh," he stood up, calling Cash.

Cash tossed him his keys. "Just make sure you fill it up with Plus."

"Man, whatever," he shot back, still upset about his car.

He walked over to his brother's car and turned around, "Here, just in case you need to go somewhere," he said, tossing Cash the keys to his car.

Cash and Trap walked back into the trap and closed the door. Money sat in the car for a minute, going through his selection of music to find a song that matched how he was feeling at the moment. After finding one, he cranked up the car and pulled off, bumping Jay Z's "99 Problems."

***

Money pulled up to Shay's house and honked the horn. He didn't see a need to walk to the door and get her because she had more than enough time to get ready.

When she stepped out onto the porch, his mouth dropped wide open. She was wearing an all-white, skintight dress that barely covered her perfect, round ass. The dress had an open back that showed off her sexy smooth skin and he was loving it.

Strutting her way towards the car, he got out to meet her along the walkway.

"Hey baby," she said, raising her arms to give him a hug. "Why you...ouch! Boy stop!"

He reached around and pinched her on the ass.

"Money, why you do that?" she whined, rubbing the spot where it hurt.

He stood back and looked at her, "Girl, I had to make sure you were real, because the way you stepped out that house had me thinking I was in some kind of dream."

She smiled at how charming he was.

"Mhmmmmm hmmmm," she mumbled. "Why are you driving your brother's car?" He opened the passenger door for her to get in.

Once he got in he said, "Because, I'm about to get mine painted. Somebody scratched my shit up when I was at Wal—Mart earlier, so I'm gonna put it in the shop."

"That's so crazy, babe, how people can't even go to the store anymore without someone running into them," she said, looking herself over in the visor as she applied some lip gloss.

He was watching her thinking to himself how he couldn't wait to have those juicy lips wrapped around his dick. She was looking gorgeous, giving him second thoughts about whether they should be going out to dinner or not. He was ready to skip dinner and start on dessert, but he knew his stomach wouldn't agree, since he hadn't eaten all day.

He was thankful she bought his story about the car. He didn't feel like arguing with her, especially since this was their time to celebrate.

"Don't trip about that though, boo, cause I was plannin' on changin' the color anyways."

"Oh yeah," she said, not taking her eyes away from her reflection, "to what?"

"Candy hot pink," he replied smiling.

***

"Cash," said Jasmin, calling his name once she heard him answer the phone, "will you come pick me up from work?"

He was at the trap playing video games when she called. He and Scrappy had been battling over who could last the longest on Grand Theft Auto, and it wasn't looking too good for him since he was already at five stars.

"Yeah, I think I can do that," he said, tossing Scrappy the controller.

"What time you get off?"

"Ummmm," she looked at the clock on the wall, "in about an hour."

Cash looked at his watch and saw that it was 8:45. "Alright then, I'll be there at 9:30."

"Okay babe, I love you."

"Say what?" Cash thought he was tripping.

"I said," she emphasized, to make sure he was listening, "I love you. Why, is there something wrong?"

Jasmin didn't have a problem confessing her love to him, even though it really just slipped out. She already knew she loved him; she was just waiting to see when he would finally confess his love for her.

"Nah, ain't nothin' wrong with that, ma. I'll be there to pick you up in a few, alright?"

"Okay."

After they hung up, he began feeling awkward. Hearing her say she loved him made his heart do backflips. He didn't want to tell her he loved her back, because, at the time, he wasn't sure. Peaches was the only girl he'd ever confessed his love for, so to hear it come from someone other than her felt strange.

He didn't see how Jasmin could truly love him when they had never even had sex. Could that even be possible? he thought to himself. He sat back on the couch to gather his thoughts. He was at a loss for words, replaying what she said over and over again in his head.

I love you.

I love you.

I love you.

A smile began to spread across his face as he let those words sink in. Before today, Peaches had been the only woman to make him feel the way she did, but after this he wasn't so sure. Jasmin held a special place in his heart, but he wasn't quite certain yet if it was love or not. He needed to clear his head some, so he got up and went to his room to have some time to himself. He wanted to get his mind back in order and on what really needed to be done.

Big Pete had just sent them some more weed and he needed to bag it up for distribution. Ever since they started copping 50 pounds, it seemed like they had to bag-up weed every day. At first, they weren't keeping more than a pound at the trap at a time, but once they started selling weight, they had to keep at least ten on deck to keep up with the demand.

When he walked in the room, he went over to the closet where he kept a four-foot-tall security safe. He turned the knob until it opened, then removed two pounds of compressed mid, busting them open into a large trash bag. He grabbed a box of sandwich bags off the top shelf and started bagging up quarters, halves, and ounces.

After 30 minutes, he looked at his watch and saw that it was time to pick Jasmin up from work. So he told Scrappy to do what he could until he got back, and then headed out the door.

***

Cash pulled up to Straight Stuntin' at 9:38 and remained in the car until Jasmin got off. She could see him through the front glass window, so he didn't call to let her know he was already outside.

As he sat there staring at the neon Straight Stuntin' sign hanging above the building, he realized how lucky he was to have Jasmin in his life. There was nothing in the world she wouldn't do for him and he knew it. She even risked losing her job one day by giving him a 25% employee discount when it was only meant to be used for workers. If her boss found out, she would be fired, but she didn't care. Providing for her man was more important to her than some clothing store job.

He smiled as he watched her sashay through the front door 10 minutes later. He loved her sexiness and sense of style. Even with work clothes on, she knew how to rock an outfit. He saw that she was carrying some bags, so he reached under the dash to pop the trunk.

Once she loaded her stuff, she got in the passenger side of the car.

"Hey baby," she greeted him, leaning over to give him a kiss on the lips. After they shared a long, intimate kiss, he returned her greeting.

"What's up babe? You must've had a good day at work?" he asked, noticing how cheerful she was.

"I guess you could say that," she replied, opening the bag she still had in her hands. "Look what I got for you, babe."

She pulled out a two-piece lingerie set that looked sexy and inviting. He imagined how good she would look wearing it. He looked at the bottom part and saw that a piece of it was missing: the part that was supposed to cover her private area was completely gone.

"Where's the rest of it?" he asked, pointing at the missing section.

She laughed while wearing a devilish grin.

"I thought I would place you right there instead. What you think?"

He smiled and said, "Mmmmmmm hmmmmm, we'll see."

While making his way out of the shopping center, Cash thought to himself, maybe it's time to finally make love to Jasmin. After all, she earned it and after seeing the lingerie she had, he couldn't resist the temptation any longer.

***

Shantell was walking out of the nail salon when she noticed Money's car parked six spaces down from hers. She saw a girl walk towards the car, place her things in the trunk, and get in on the passenger side. From where she was standing, she couldn't tell who was in the driver's seat, but she knew it had to be her lover.

Stepping closer to the vehicle to get a better peek, she witnessed the two occupants share an intimate kiss. Nearly yelling from frustration, she hurried and got into her car. She decided after seeing Money with another woman, today was going to be his last day disrespecting her. She thought she'd made it clear earlier that their relationship would never be over. She started crying after cranking her car, saddened by the memories of their lovemaking. She spent countless hours training him on how to make love to a woman and make her feel good, and she'd be damned if her hard work was wasted on some little, young thing.

When she saw his car pull off and head towards the exit, she pulled off heading in the same direction.

***

"Cash, what happened to the side of Money's car?" asked Jasmin. She noticed the big pink letters on the side when she put her bags in the trunk.

Cash laughed to himself as he replayed Money's reaction in his head.

"What's so funny?" she asked, not catching the joke.

"Nothing," he replied, "he's just having a little fatal attraction going on right now."

"Oh yeah," she said, beginning to laugh herself, "well, it looks like he got a real heartbroken bitch on his bumper."

When Cash approached the exit to the shopping center, he put on his turn signal, preparing to pull out the parking lot. While slowing down to see if any cars were coming, somebody rear—ended them, sending their car flying across the median into the opposite lane and hitting another car before coming to a halt.

Cash was knocked unconscious when his head hit the front windshield. He had made a huge mistake not buckling his seatbelt before pulling off. Jasmin, however, did, and she was okay, but she was still a little shaken up. When she came to and realized what had just happened, she looked over at Cash to see if he was okay too, but he was out cold with blood gushing from his head. She nearly panicked when she saw it. She quickly unfastened her seatbelt and leaned over to check on him, and that's when his door flew open.

"I told you this wasn't over…look what you made…" Shantell was screaming at the top of her lungs when she opened the car door.

"Oh my God," she gasped, realizing Money wasn't the driver of the vehicle.

"Bitch, are you crazy?" shouted Jasmin, still trying to wake Cash up.

"Oh my God, I'm so sorry," Shantell covered her face from the shock of what she'd just done.

"You non—driving ass bitch! You better hope he's okay!" Jasmin was steadily trying to wake him up. "Come on baby, get up! Get up Cash, please baby wake up!" Tears streamed down her face as she began to cry for help. "Somebody help me, PLEASE!"

Other drivers had stopped and got out to help. Police sirens could be heard approaching from afar and Shantell didn't want to stick around to explain why she did what she did. She hopped in her Lincoln and sped off.

She didn't expect for somebody else to be driving Money's car and felt bad for what she'd done. All she wanted to do was mess up his car and show him how bad he'd hurt her, but it wasn't turning out as she had hoped. It was turning into a bad situation for her. She wouldn't know how to explain this to her husband, so the best thing to do was leave the scene, but not before someone was able to take down her plate number.

CHAPTER 16

CONVICTED FELON

When Cash awoke, he noticed he was lying in a hospital bed. He had been unconscious for the past 16 hours and was waking up out of a slight coma. His eyes quickly scanned the room in hopes of seeing a familiar face. He began to feel lost when he realized nobody was there by his bedside. He tried to replay the events before he slipped into a coma to get an understanding of why he was in the hospital, but his mind was completely blank. He needed some answers, and lying in bed wasn't going to get them. He slowly tried to get up but realized he couldn't. His arm was cuffed to the bed.

"What the fuck is this?" he said out loud, reaching over to untangle the cuffs from his wrist.

As he laid back down, he felt something wrapped around his head.

"What the fuck?" he said to himself, using his free hand to see what was on his head.

Was I in some kind of accident? Is someone playing a sick joke on me? Who am I? What am I doing here? These were some of the questions that ran through his mind as he searched for some kind of explanation.

The fact that he was cuffed to a bed made him worry about his future. He didn't like how this was turning out, because he was confused and didn't even know what the hell was going on.

"Who am I?" he whispered to himself, realizing he didn't even know who he was.

Frustrated by his lack of knowledge, he tried to snatch his arm away from the bedrail again, making a loud clinking sound.

"That's some fancy new jewelry you got there, Mr. Lewis." Cash looked over towards the door where he heard the mysterious voice but couldn't make out who it was. The lights in the room were too dim for him to see, so he tried squinting his eyes in an attempt to get a better look.

"Who is that?" he asked, hoping this person could give him the answers he was looking for to calm his nerves.

The detective stepped closer. He was a black man in a tan suit. He looked to be around the age of 40 and was carrying a folder in his hands.

"Mr. Lewis, I am Detective Fairbanks from the Macon Police Department, and you sir, are under arrest," said the detective, looking at him and then closing the folder.

"Man, I don't even know who Mr. Lewis is, but somebody better come take these fuckin' cuffs off me right now!" demanded Cash, trying to snatch his arm loose from the bedrail.

"Sir, I suggest you calm down before I assume you are trying to escape." Fairbanks opened his coat, revealing his service weapon.

He wasn't trying to give him an opportunity to shoot, so he laid back down and waited to hear what else he had to say.

"Mr. Lewis, are you aware that you were involved in a car accident yesterday at 4 o'clock on Pio No No Avenue?"

Cash didn't have a clue as to what he was talking about. He tried really hard to remember the accident, but he couldn't. From what he was hearing, his name was Lewis and he was involved in some kind of accident, but the fact that he was under arrest wasn't making any sense to him, and that's when it hit him.

"Oh my God, did I run someone over?" He was praying that wasn't the reason for him being cuffed to the bed.

"Well, no Mr. Lewis, you were the only person hospitalized, from what I can see," replied Fairbanks, flipping the folder back open to see if his statement was accurate.

Cash was convinced the folder contained information pertaining to him and the matter at hand, so he waited to hear more.

"You and a young lady by the name of Jasmin Myers were victims of a hit-and-run incident, don't you remember?" He looked at Cash to see if it was starting to register.

Cash didn't know anything. He didn't know who he was, and he didn't know who Jasmin Myers was, but he did want to know how he could be a victim in a hit and run incident but was cuffed to a bed.

"No, I don't remember," he answered truthfully, "but if I'm the victim, why am I being treated like a criminal?" He pointed at the cuffs around his wrist.

Fairbanks nodded as if he understood the question clearly. "Mr. Lewis, I can see that you're having a hard time remembering, so I'm going to inform you about what's going on."

Cash braced himself.

"When MPD arrived on the scene, you were unconscious with head injuries."

Cash touched the bandage again that was wrapped around his head, now knowing why it was there.

"After removing you from the vehicle sir, we searched the car for any signs of drugs and weapons. Upon searching the vehicle, a fully loaded handgun, one Glocc 17 .40 Caliber, was retrieved from under the driver seat in the car. The serial number was filed off, and by you already being a convicted felon, it made this incident a very serious offense."

He was in a daze. The only thing he heard was loaded gun and convicted felon and knew he was in deep trouble. He didn't know how he got put in this situation, but until he found out, he wasn't going to say another word.

"I want a lawyer," he stated, looking away from the detective.

"Alright, as you wish, Mr. Lewis, but I'm almost certain that no attorney in the state of Georgia is going to be able to get you out of this jam." He turned around and approached the door.

Cash just laid there thinking about how his whole life was coming to an end. He couldn't believe what had transpired. He needed to find out who this Jasmin Myers girl was, because right now she was the only one that could help him connect the dots.

***

"Excuse me, nurse," Money said, leaning over the counter in the lobby trying to get one of the nurses' attention. "Excuse me nurse, which room is Cashmere Lewis in?"

He patiently waited as the nurse who responded to his call keyed in his brother's information. He and Shay were at the house making love when he received the messages about the accident. He had his phone off the whole time, so when he finally turned it back on, he instantly knew that something was wrong. He had 11 missed calls and six text messages from the same number.

He told Shay to hold on while he checked his phone. She remained laid out on the bed with her legs sprawled open. Just a few minutes earlier, he had been eating her pussy like it was the last supper until he realized he left his phone off. For 40 minutes straight, he experimented with all kinds of edible treats to bring a new taste to her juices. She was enjoying every minute of him savoring his dessert.

While Money looked through his phone, reading every message, Shay rubbed her pussy to keep it wet. The whipped cream and chocolate he was using wasn't quite gone from between her legs, so she took two of her fingers and wiped the remains off to feed it to her man. She rolled over and placed the two fingers in his mouth. As he sucked on them, he read through his text messages to see what was going on.

"Money, your brother is in the hospital. We got into a car accident and he's fucked up pretty bad. The police found a gun in the car and they're talking about he's in police custody. Call me back PLEASE, because I don't know what to do. Jasmin."

He spit Shay's fingers out his mouth and quickly got dressed.

"What's wrong baby?" Shay said, sitting up on the bed.

"My brother's in the hospital. I gotta go see if he's okay," he answered, wrapping his G—Shock watch around his wrist.

"Oh my God, is he okay?" she asked, rolling off the bed to get dressed.

"I don't know, but we about to find out." They were out the door two minutes later.

Now, as they stood in the lobby of the hospital waiting for his brother's room number, Money looked around the lobby for Jasmin but didn't see her. When the nurse gave him the room number, she warned him that there was a police hold and he couldn't receive any visitors.

Money wasn't trying to hear that, so he stormed off through the lobby in search of Jasmin. Shay stayed close on his heels as she informed Peaches about what was going on. She had called her the minute they left the house and had been on the phone with her ever since. When she told her that Cash had been in-volved in an accident, Peaches got upset and started crying.

Money found Jasmin sitting in the corner room of the lobby with her head between her legs. When he called her and she looked up, he could see the worry written all over her face. She had been crying nonstop since the moment they told her she wasn't allowed to visit him.

"What's good, lil' mama, you alright?" He walked up to her and gave her a hug.

"No," she whined, "they won't let me see him."

She wasn't taking it too well, and he already knew it was because she loved his brother.

"Don't worry about that shit, 'cause we about to go up there now," he told her, leading the way towards the elevator.

When they got in the elevator, Shay whispered into Money's ear, "Who is that?"

He mumbled back, "She's a friend of the family," and then introduced them. He knew better than to tell her the truth about Jasmin because not only would he be telling her; he would be telling Peaches as well.

When the elevator stopped on the fifth floor, they got off and went looking for Cash's room. Money saw at the end of the hallway there were two uniformed officers and what looked to be a detective standing around. He assumed, considering what the nurse had told him, that's where his brother's room was.

They walked cautiously down the hallway until Money saw the number on his door. It was definitely his brother's room. Even though the officers were standing right in front of the door Money decided to take his chances.

He proceeded to walk in the room as if he didn't even see them standing there.

"Hold on, buddy, where do you think you're going?" asked one of the officer's, placing his hand against Money's chest to stop him.

He looked down at the officer's hand and said, "Man, get your motherfuckin' hands off me, cuzz!" He knocked the officer's hand down and braced himself.

The two blue coats both tightened their stance, placing their hands on their weapon.

Sensing the tension in the air, the detective decided to intervene.

"Hold on for second, y'all," he said, ordering the officers to stand down. "Sir, do you know the patient in that room?"

Money was still a little tense from the standoff and upset about the cop touching him, but he steered his attention towards the detective.

"Yeah, the nurse downstairs told me my brother was in this room and I want to see if he's okay."

"Alright," replied the detective, pulling a notepad from his pocket,

"and your name is…"

"Armani Lewis."

"And who are these two young ladies?" he asked, pointing towards Shay and Jasmin who were standing behind him. "Oh, you're the young lady who was in the car with Mr. Lewis, right?" Jasmin nodded her head. "Well I'm sorry to have to tell y'all this, but Mr. Lewis is now in police custody."

"Why?" Money snapped, not liking where this was going.

"We found a loaded handgun under the seat of the vehicle he was driving. By him being on probation and a convicted felon, we have no choice but to detain him."

Money couldn't believe it. It was all his fault. He was so pissed off about Shantell messing up his car that he forgot to tell Cash about the pistol under the seat. Cash was in some real trouble now and Money didn't know how to get him out of it.

"Man, that shit ain't his!" he protested.

"It's not?" the detective's eyebrows shot up. "Then whose is it?"

Money knew right then he'd said too much without a lawyer, so he decided to change the topic of their conversation.

"Can we at least see him, got damn, he was in a car accident for goodness sake," Money pleaded with the detective, hoping he would be sympathetic to the situation. "Come on detective, we all his family," Money complained.

The detective considered his request and figured it shouldn't be too much of a problem.

"Yeah, pleeeeeeease," begged Jasmin.

The detective shook his head. "No can do, only immediate family, and you got ten minutes, sir."

"Don't worry y'all, we gone go see him when he hits the county alright, so just be easy."

The detective ordered the officers to pat search Money and allow him into the room.

***

Cash's eyes shot towards the door when he heard someone entering his room. The young teenager that came in looked familiar, but he couldn't quite place where he knew him from.

"Aye dawg, who is you?" Cash eyed his brother suspiciously.

"What you mean 'who am I?' Nigga stop playin'. Is you alright?" asked Money, walking over to his bedside.

Cash looked at him, trying to see if he could recognize him, but there was no hope.

Money saw the deranged look on his face and wanted to know why he was looking at him like that.

"Bruh, is you okay, nigga?" he asked, concerned.

"Bruh?" said Cash, trying to figure out why he referred to him as his brother. "Are we family or something, dawg?"

Money stood back and looked at him.

"What you mean? I'm your brother. Nigga, have you lost your mind?"

He believed so, but he wanted Money to confirm it for sure. By the way Money was speaking to him, they had to be close, so since they were relatives, he could expect to receive some kind of explanation as to why he was in this situation.

"Aye dawg, I don't know shit right now, so please tell me something, cause I'm lost, homie." He was getting upset and irritated because his visitor was unaware of his current amnesia. He was getting tired of everyone assuming he knew what was going on. All he wanted was for somebody to give him a reasonable explanation to why he was cuffed to a bed.

Money stood there for a minute thinking to himself, is this nigga for real? Did he bump his head that got damn hard? Man, I hope this nigga ain't retarded. Damn, he don't even remember his own brother.

"Aye, listen dawg, cause obviously you done bumped your head a little too hard. I'm your brother, your blood brother at that, so you should remember me. But since you don't, I'm gone put you on game right quick, alright!" Cash paid close attention while he spoke.

"You were involved in car accident, my nigga, and I guess you hit your head pretty hard, knocking something loose up there," he pointed towards Cash's bandaged head before continuing, "but just chill though. The police found a gun in the car after you wrecked, so you gotta go to jail, but I'm gone bond you out when you get there, okay?"

Money looked at his brother to see if anything he said was registering. "We gone get you a lawyer and everything, so don't worry about shit. We got money, so you good." He pulled two big wads of cash out of his pocket to emphasize his statement. "Just try and remember who the fuck you is in the meantime, my nigga."

He grabbed Cash's hand and gave him a pound. Money headed towards the door, remembering the detective's timeframe.

"I'm gone be down there to visit you asap, so make sure you put me on your visitation list, alright?" Money told him, approaching the door.

"Yeah, I hear you, but what is your name, bruh?" he asked, not having the slightest clue.

Money couldn't believe he was this lost. It made him angry to see his brother like this. Even though he didn't cause the wreck, he felt somewhat responsible for his brother's condition.

"My name is Armani Lewis and yours is Cashmere Lewis. We got a sister named Mercedes, so put her on your list too. Oh yeah, one more thing, our street names are Cash and Money, so just call me Money, alright?" Cash nodded in response. "Anyways, I'm gone my nigga, go ahead and get you some rest," Money told him, getting ready to walk out the door.

"Alright, but hold on, who is Jasmin Mmmm…"

"Myers," Money finished his question.

"Yeah, Jasmin Myers." Cash was glad to know he knew her name. "Where is she at? Because the detective said she was involved in the accident too."

Money laughed to himself and said, "Just put her on your list too and then you'll find out if we have to visit you." Then he stepped out of the room.

Cash laid there and replayed the conversation over and over in his head. There were a couple of things he knew for sure as he went back over the memory he'd just accumulated. One, he had definitely been involved in a car accident. Two, he was with a girl by the name of Jasmin Myers. Three, although he didn't like the sound of this one, he was definitely going to jail. And last but not least, his name was Cashmere Lewis.

Cash and Money. Cash and Money. Cash Money. It had a nice little ring to it and he could live with that for now. So he didn't forget it. He pressed the nurse's request button the side of his bed to get some assistance. He needed a pen and some paper so he could write those names down. After all, he wasn't trying to forget them all over again.

CHAPTER 17

THE FEDS

Over the next few weeks, Cash slowly regained his memory. After staying in the hospital for three days, they transferred him over to the county jail. Due to his injuries, they kept him in the infirmary until he got better. Over time, he gradually regained his strength and returned to tip—top shape.

In the meantime, Money, Jasmin, and his sister Mercedes visited him every week. They were there to support him 100% and he needed it.

The judge denied him bail at his first appearance hearing, pending the outcome of his probation hearing, so Cash had to sit and wait. Money told him he was going to claim the firearm at his probation hearing, but Cash wasn't so sure that was going to work. If it did, they had already planned-on Money bonding him out.

Cash's probation officer, Mrs. Atkins, was a real headache. She enjoyed making his life hard and kept her foot on his neck. Every time he reported to her office, it was the same routine: "Piss in this cup, let me see your school attendance record, and make sure you keep a job." He was surprised she didn't make him bend over, squat, and cough like they made you do in the county.

What it was was that she couldn't stand Cash. She knew he was doing something he had no business doing, so she made it her personal business to find out what it was. Watching him pull up to her office every month in his fancy car with fancy rims irked her nerves. Her intuition told her he was selling drugs, but she couldn't prove it, so she did what most probation officers did, hate.

"Cashmere Lewis!" yelled the female officer that was standing in front of the pod.

"Yeah?!?" he shouted, walking out of his cell.

"You got a professional visit!"

"A professional visit," he repeated to himself, confused. He'd never heard of one of those before.

After washing his face and brushing his teeth, he walked towards the front of the pod to let the officer know he was ready. They opened the door for him to enter the sally port where another female officer was standing to transport him to the visiting area.

"What's up, Miss Black?" he greeted her, stepping into the sally port.

"Hey Mr. Lewis," she said, returning his greeting with a smile.

Miss Black was a senior officer at the jail, so it was no problem for her to transport him by herself. Although she was thick, short, and cute, Miss Black was far from an easy pushover. She knew how to handle herself around the inmates and everyone respected her.

Cash liked her attitude and personality because she didn't act like her shit didn't stink. He considered her cool people who just came in everyday to get her check. She treated him with the same respect he gave her and he enjoyed how they could converse on a man to woman level. Every time they saw each other, they would smile and acknowledge one another. So, now since they were alone, he was ready to feel her out.

"Hay is for horses Miss Black, so I'm guessing you see the thoroughbred in a nigga, huh?"

"Boy whateva," she said, rolling her eyes at his statement.

As they continued on down the hallway, he continued flirting with her.

"Say," he said, getting her attention. "Why you always coming to work smelling like Bath and Body Works?"

She smiled, knowing it was her perfume he was smelling.

"Boy, this is an everyday thang with me. It just comes natural."

"So, you tellin' me that's your natural juices smelling like that?"

"Juices?" she asked, wondering what he meant by that.

He locked his eyes between her thick thighs and tilted his head forward to let her know what juices he was talking about. "Boy, you is crazy," she replied, blushing.

"Yeah, you right. Crazy about them juices." They both laughed as they bent around a corner.

"I see right now you're probably a handful when you're free."

"Nah, not really. I'm more a of mouthful," he said, licking his lips seductively to entice her.

She could feel the moisture between her legs build up while she stared at his lips, picturing them sucking on her fat pussy.

"Ugh ummmmm," she grunted, trying to regain her composure, "go through that door over there and I'll be back to get you when you're done," she said, pointing towards the gate to the visitation area.

"I can't wait," he replied, walking through the gated door.

As he walked down the hallway, there were three rooms to his left. In the first one he passed, he saw a black dude with dreads sitting down at the table across from what appeared to be an Arab in a suit. He looked like he was having a bad day while the Arab waved some papers back and forth in front of him. Cash figured the Arab was probably his lawyer and was trying to get him to take a plea.

When he approached the second room, he saw his probation officer, Mrs. Atkins, engaged in a conversation with a white man dressed in a short-sleeved collared shirt and blue denim jeans. When he entered the room, they both stood from their seats to greet him. He noticed the guy was wearing a badge on his belt but couldn't place the symbol.

"Hello, Mr. Lewis," Mrs. Atkins greeted him.

He knew whatever they had to say couldn't be too good because she actually looked happy to see him. She waved for him to take a seat across from them.

"What's up?" he asked, refusing to sit down.

"You can sit, Mr. Lewis. We have some important information to discuss with you."

"I'm cool. I'd rather stand," he replied, rejecting her offer. "What's up, though? My hearing is still next week, right?" he said, referring to the probation hearing that would determine if he should receive a bond or not.

"Well, not quite, she said, opening the folder in front of her. "This gentleman here is with the FBI and he would like to ask you a few questions."

Cash couldn't believe what he was hearing. Was the FBI on to them? Did they know about his trap? Just hearing those three letters made him cringe.

"Questions about what?" he asked defensively.

"About a Mr. Pete McDaniels, also known as Big Pete," the agent interjected.

"Nah, that name don't ring no bells, dawg, and I'd rather not speak to y'all without my attorney." He turned around to walk out.

"Well, what about being a convicted felon in possession of an illegal firearm?"

Cash stopped and turned around. Both of them held smirks on their faces, so he knew what type of games they were trying to play. He couldn't believe they were asking him about his connect. Had they been watching Big Pete all this time? Was he under investigation? Those were questions he wanted to ask, but not to these two clowns. He stood there while the agent spilled more venom from his lips.

"Mr. Lewis, I would recommend that you cooperate with us. We are considering picking up this case, but it's totally up to you if we do or don't." He crossed his arms and waited for Cash's response.

Cash wasn't about to cooperate with anybody and he definitely wasn't going to stand there and listen to any more of their bullshit.

"How about this…" he began, a smile spreading across his face. "Don't bring your old funky ass back down here with this shit, Mrs. Atkins, alright! And you…" he steered his attention over towards the agent. "As for picking something up, pick these nuts up, you faggot ass bitch!" He grabbed his crotch in a blasphemous way and then walked out.

Mrs. Atkins was shocked and appalled. The smile she had in the beginning of their meeting had turned into a big hole, with her jaw damn near touching the desk. The federal agent just shook his head, shouting after Cash, "We'll see who's the bitch when your ass is sitting in a federal penitentiary!"

Cash wasn't trying to hear another word. He banged on the gate and waited on someone to release him from the visiting area. A few seconds later, Miss Black sashayed her fine self around the corner to transport him back to his pod.

"Done already?" she asked, signaling the booth to let him out.

"Yeah, I'm done, but ummm…. let's get back to you and them juices."

It was like he hadn't received any bad news at all, because he was back to flirting like it was nothing. "What are you wearing anyways?" he leaned over to and took a sniff. "Let me guess…Edible by Black." They both smiled and continued where they left off.

***

"Aye, we gotta close the shop down for a little while," said Money, walking through the front door of the trap. He quickly started gathering his things.

"Why?" Trap and Scrappy asked in unison. They were in the living room playing the PlayStation.

"My brother just told me that the feds is watching the connect, so they could be watchin' us too." He was packing and talking at the same time. His main goal at this point was to get everything he owned out of the trap.

He didn't have the time to explain in detail what was going on, but he knew they needed to get out of there fast, just in case they raided the place. He thought it would probably be best if he took everything with his name and DNA on it out first, then later, come back for the drugs.

Trap and Scrappy saw the seriousness of the situation in his eyes and decided to do the same. They collected all of their clothes and games, loading their cars one by one. Everyone had their own vehicle, so it wouldn't be hard for them to part ways once everything got packed.

"What about the dope and the heat?" asked Scrappy, grabbing the AK—47 out of the corner.

"Listen, I'll take the guns with me and put 'em up, but y'all are gonna have to walk the dope over to your grandma's."

They both nodded in agreement as they continued to pack. Once they were all ready, they headed off in different directions. Scrappy and Trap agreed they would come back for the six keys of cocaine, 30 pounds of weed, and 500 ecstasy pills later on that night.

Money didn't really have a place to stash the guns, so he brainstormed while he rode around. He knew his mom's house was out of the question. He pulled out his cell phone and began scrolling down his contact list for any potential prospects.

While scanning, the name Jasmin popped up on his screen, alerting he had an incoming call. That's when the light bulb in his head came on.

"What's up J? Where you at?" he asked.

"Ummmmm, I'm on my way home, why?" She was caught off guard by his urgency to know where she was.

"I need to holla at you about something important."

"Well, I'll be there in about ten minutes."

"Good, I'll be there waiting on you," he said before hanging up.

He knew Jasmin would be willing to keep the guns at her house. She was willing to do anything for his brother, so he figured she wouldn't mind helping out the team. Plus, ever since he walked in on the domestic dispute between her mother's boyfriend and them, she'd been trying to show him her appreciation.

Every time he came over to pick her up for visitation, her mother would always come outside to say hey. It was her way of telling him how grateful she was for his help that day. He figured the more they saw him, the safer they would feel, and he didn't mind being super—save—a—hoe for a change.

When Jasmin made it home, she saw his car already parked outside her house. When she walked up to the passenger's side door, she saw him laid back in his seat, smoking a blunt and listening to music. She also noticed all the clothes he had in the backseat and wondered what was going on. She knocked on the window to get his attention.

Money unlocked the door to let her in. "What's up J? Where you coming from?"

When she got in, she could tell he was high as a kite. His eyes were bloodshot red and his movements were slow.

"I'm coming from my homegirl's house. What up with all them clothes in the back?" she asked, looking over her shoulder at the pile.

"That's kind of why I'm over here. I need to ask you for a small favor, babe."

"Okay, what is it?"

"Look, I got some guns in the trunk and I need to put 'em somewhere safe for awhile, because it's getting kind of hot."

She eyed him suspiciously, wondering why he was asking her, out of all people. She thought to herself, don't they have stash spots for stuff like this? In her heart, she'd already decided to help him, but she wanted something in return.

"I don't have a problem with that, but what's in it for me?" she said, crossing her arms.

Money was high, but he was enjoying how she was trying to negotiate a deal.

"How about this," he began, sitting up in his seat to address her, "when bruh gets out, I'll drive him over here personally so you can get the dick first," he giggled, knowing that was what she really wanted.

"Well, that would be nice, but what else?" she replied smiling.

He was lost. He didn't know what else to offer. He could give her some money, but he knew she wouldn't take it. He needed more time to think. The weed had him on cloud nine and he wasn't about to make a commitment under the influence.

"Give me a few days to come up with something, or do you already have something in mind?"

"Nah, I'll just wait for you to get creative, but ummm…I need a ride to work in the meantime. That's why I called you in the first place."

"When?" he asked, checking the time on his phone.

"Right now, but let me go and get ready first." She got out the car and went inside the house.

He waited in the car while she got dressed. He saw why his brother liked her so much. She was cool and down for the cause. He made a mental note to tell Cash the next time he went to see him, how she was keeping it real and when he comes home, she gets the dick first.

***

"All presiding in the case of the State of Georgia versus Cashmere Lewis," announced the bailiff. Cash and his lawyer stepped forward.

A few minutes earlier, he had been in a holding cell until an officer came to retrieve him. The other inmates who were in there with him were having regular jail conversations and he couldn't wait to get a chance to get away from them.

When they brought him in the courtroom, he saw his lawyer, Ms. Debra Cox, heading towards the front to meet him. The middle-aged, petite black woman was one of the best attorneys in the city and he needed her to produce a good outcome today for the $2,500 his brother gave her for his bond.

"Mr. Lewis, how are you doing this morning?" she asked, greeting him as they approached the podium.

"I'll be a lot better if you can get me out of these cuffs," he replied.

"I'll do my best," she reassured him.

The judge was taking his time starting the hearing as he sat in his chair, flipping through a stack of papers. Cash wondered if they were about him. When he turned around to see if anyone was there to support him, he saw Money and his mom sitting in the back row. It made him smile to see his mother there sober. Even though she was an alcoholic, she made time to come support him in court and that's what counted. He knew Jasmin and Mercedes wouldn't show because they had tests to take at school, but where was Peaches?

He had called her cell numerous times to let her know about his court date, but she never picked up. He even had Money call her in hopes she would show. He didn't understand. The more she turned her back on him, the farther they grew apart. The more he thought about Jasmin, the less he thought about Peaches. He didn't know how much longer Peaches could hold a spot in his heart, but as for right now, love was the last thing on his mind.

"Ms. Cox," spoke the judge, letting the courtroom know he was ready to proceed, "you are representing the defendant Mr. Lewis today, is that right?"

"Yes I am, Your Honor," she answered, rubbing Cash's shoulder.

"Okay, and what does the prosecutor have in regard to the defendant?"

The district attorney who was presiding over his case jumped up out of his seat when he realized the judge was talking to him.

"Your Honor, this case involves a felon in possession of a firearm where the serial number was completely obliterated. It is to my knowledge that the U.S. Attorney's Office plans to pick up this case, Your Honor, and being that Mr. Lewis is on probation..." he paused to look over at Cash, "I'm asking that bail be denied for now, at least until we know what they're going to do."

"Your Honor," Ms. Cox interjected, "my client has no history of escapes or absconding. He has been a resident of Macon, Georgia most of his life and I see him posing no threat to the community if bail is imposed." The judge listened attentively while she spoke.

"To be quite honest, Your Honor, my client has reported to his probation officer faithfully ever since probation was imposed in juvenile court last year. He attends school on the regular and would like to continue his education from outside of jail. Furthermore, we simply ask that you grant him a reasonable bond and lift his probation hold."

Cash couldn't believe it. He wanted to lean over and kiss Ms. Cox right there in the courtroom. She knew exactly what to say, as if it had been previously recorded in her brain.

"And what says the probation officer about this young man?" Cash held his breath.

Mrs. Atkins stood up to address the judge. "I am Mr. Lewis's probation officer, and I agree, he has maintained a good report with my office."

He exhaled.

"But these are very serious charges, where, might I add, a fully loaded semi—automatic handgun was involved."

Cash went back to holding his breath.

"And let's not forget about the obliterated serial number. I feel like this type of charge doesn't warrant the lifting of his hold. I have spoken with the U.S. Attorney's Office as well, and they are highly considering taking this case to the federal level."

"Your Honor," Ms. Cox interjected, "my client was unaware that a firearm was even in this vehicle. The car legally belongs to my client's brother, Armani Lewis. Also," she shuffled through some paperwork until she pulled out the document she was looking for. She held it up high enough for the judge to see it. "I have a sworn statement from Armani Lewis stating the weapon belongs to him. In it, he states that my client had no knowledge that the firearm was in the vehicle."

Cash exhaled.

"May I see that statement, Ms. Cox?"

"Yeah, sure, Your Honor." She walked around the podium and handed the affidavit to the bailiff, who then handed it to the judge.

After moments of reading over it, the judge looked up at Cash and his attorney.

"Is Armani Lewis in the courtroom today?" he asked, looking at them.

Ms. Cox leaned over towards Cash to ask if Money was there or not. Once he confirmed it, she addressed the court. "Yes, Your Honor."

"Your Honor," the District Attorney interjected, "if I may have some input on this, I think we should at least wait for the fingerprint analysis to come back before we decide on this matter. The defendant's brother is a pretty close relative and he may be lying to help his sibling."

"I ain't got to lie for him. That shit ain't his!" shouted Money, jumping up from his seat to defend his brother.

"Order in the court! Order in the court!" the judge exclaimed while banging his gavel. He didn't like Money's outburst and he was not willing to let him continue to disrupt his courtroom. "Young man, do not shout like that again in my courtroom or I will have you removed, do you understand?" said the judge, pointing his gavel in Money's direction.

Money nodded his head and sat back down. The judge removed his glasses from his face and massaged the bridge of his nose, obviously indecisive about what to do.

"How long will it take for the fingerprint analysis to come back?" he asked the prosecutor.

"Probably a week or two, Your Honor."

"Okay then," he said, putting his glasses back on, "we will adjourn until the fingerprint analysis is completed. Mr. Lewis, you will remain in custody until then. I will make my ruling two weeks from today. Court is adjourned."

"Don't worry about it, I'll be down there to talk to you later." Ms. Cox lightly pinched his hand to let him know that everything was going to be alright.

Cash was shocked. He didn't know how to respond to what just took place. He didn't like the fact that fingerprints were the only thing keeping him in jail. The worst part of it was that he believed his prints were on the weapon. After all, he sold the gun to Money in the first place.

***

Two weeks later, after his second probation hearing, Cash was still in jail. The fingerprint analysis had returned a week prior and the evidence was conclusive. Three of the prints on the weapon were a match for Cash, making his chances of getting out slim to none. The U.S. Attorney's Office immediately decided to indict him on the charge. At his arraignment hearing, the prosecutor over his case requested he be detained until trial. The judge accepted the request and made it the order of the court.

Cash was sick. It had never dawned on him that he could be facing some serious prison time. Time and time again, he could hear the agent's voice in his head, the word penitentiary repeating itself over and over again.

Penitentiary

Penitentiary

Penitentiary

He was not ready to deal with the feds. He knew a jury trial was a potential option, but considering the feds' high conviction rate, he was unlikely to succeed. Plus, the evidence they had against him wasn't so helpful either. His only focus now was to try and get the best deal possible.

As he walked down the hallway to see his lawyer, it crossed his mind that he wasn't being escorted on this trip. It seemed kind of odd as he looked around and didn't see anybody.

They housed him in a more secure part of the jail once he healed up from his injuries. Being that he was an official federal inmate, they placed him in the maximum-security part of the county jail, which housed some of the city's most violent criminals, along with a few federal inmates. He knew a lot of the dudes from the streets, so it wasn't hard for him to fit in. However, the red wrist band he sported around his wrist brought him a lot of unwanted attention.

Everyone in the county jail wore a colored band to represent what type of charge they were locked up for. Orange bands were for felony charges while blue was for misdemeanors, but when it came to the red bands, also called the Rolex because of its high-profile status, everybody knew you were federal. Whenever someone would inquire about his Rolex band, Cash would be quick to tell them to mind their business because he was never in the mood to explain why he was in federal custody.

He continued making his way down the hallway towards the visitors' gate when he noticed it was already open. He thought to himself as he walked in, they must think a nigga won't escape around here. He peeped in the officer's station through the window to see where the officer was, but he didn't see anybody.

While making his way down the narrow hallway, he began to hear a woman moaning from one of the rooms.

"Oooooooh oooooooh…awwwh." He slowly started tiptoeing, attempting to sneak a peek of someone getting their rocks off.

A grin spread across his face as he listened to the rhythm of the desk squeak back and forth. The woman's cries intensified, which had his dick growing by the second.

When he made it to the room, he leaned on the side of the wall so he could brace himself to take a peek. He didn't want to disturb as he watched from the doorway.

When he peeked around the corner to see who it was getting-it-in, his eyes nearly popped out of his head. The sight of Peaches buck-naked, bent over a desk with a white dude ramming his dick in her, enraged him. He quickly noticed the white dude was wearing a badge around his neck. As they locked eyes, he immediately recognized him.

"Now who's the bitch, Mr. Lewis," said the FBI agent who came to see him with Mrs. Atkins.

Click… click…click…click…BOOM!

Hearing the loud bang of his cell door woke Cash from his dream, his dick rock hard. Adjusting himself, he took a deep breath after realizing it was only a dream.

He got out of bed and began washing his face. That's when he remembered today was Saturday, visitation day.

***

When Cash walked into the visitation room, he noticed that it was as busy and crowded as usual. Baby mamas, family members, and friends were all up there to support their loved ones as they sat on the opposite side of the half—inch thick Plexiglass.

He walked around the room until he saw a familiar face. It surprised him when that familiar face turned out to be Peaches. His heart did backflips when he saw her wave from behind the glass, looking as good as ever. All the anger he felt towards her for not being supportive had temporarily disappeared and for once, he was glad to see her.

As he stepped in the booth, they both looked into each other's eyes and shared a smile.

"Hey baby," she spoke cheerfully.

"What's good, ma? Where have you been?" He was glad to see her but wanted to still hear some kind of explanation as to why she was just now showing up. "I've been calling your phone for the past couple of weeks, but it always goes to your voicemail. Why you ain't been picking up?" he said, searching for an answer.

Peaches sighed. She was expecting to get the 411 treatment. Cash had been locked up for four months now and she knew he would be looking to hear from her. She was just so busy with school and she didn't quite know how to be there for him. Now that she was here to explain herself in person, Peaches knew she needed to be up—front with him.

"I'm sorry, babe, I've just been so busy with school, that's all. The phone calls probably show up private on my cell so that's why I haven't answered them."

"Yeah, I forgot about that," he replied, remembering how she didn't answer unknown callers. "But what about my letters? Are you at least getting them?"

"Yeah, I got' em and I promise I'm gone write you back."

Cash wasn't feeling her lame excuses, and the fact that she got his letters didn't help the situation at all. By her not responding to any of his letters only added to the flames between them.

"So, what are they talkin' about doing, babe?" she asked, trying to change the subject.

"I don't know yet, but it looks like I might have to do some fed time." He looked up at her expecting to see some kind of reaction but didn't get one. "They found my fingerprints on Money's gun, so I'm pretty much hit."

She nodded her head as if she understood everything he was telling her.

"But ummm, don't worry about that right now, just focus on school and keeping in contact with me, alright! I need you right now, babe, so please make me a priority."

"Okay babe. How much time are you lookin' at?"

He looked at her, trying to figure out her angle. He wasn't trying to waste his hour discussing how much time he was looking at because to him, that didn't even matter.

"Peaches, I'm not gonna be gone long; it's only a gun charge. You make me feel like you not even tryin' to wait on a nigga or something." He was starting to get upset because it sounded like she was trying to abandon him.

"Nah, I'm just sayin' that, I'm just..." she paused when she felt someone tap her on the shoulder. When she turned around to see who it was, she saw Money, their sister, and another girl standing there.

Cash looked up to see who was interrupting their visit. He braced himself as he saw Peaches and Mercedes greet each other with a hug, while Jasmin stood off to the side trying to get his attention. He winked at her to let her know he saw her and to be cool. At the moment, he was just hoping Peaches wouldn't pay her no mind.

After Mercedes waved and briefly spoke to him, she pulled Peaches off to the side for a little one on one girl talk. She looked up to Peaches as a sister, admiring her. She was planning on attending Spelman as well, so she wanted to holler at Peaches to get the full scoop on college in the A.

"What's up, my nigga? You good?" smiled Money, noticing Cash breaking a sweat.

"As good as it gets. What up though?" he replied, looking over Money's shoulder hoping Mercedes could keep Peaches busy.

"I see your girl finally made it," Money said, looking over at Peaches.

"Yeah, she finally showed up. I've been waiting on her to pop up, I just can't believe she didn't write me and let me know first."

"Yeah, I know, right!"

"Anyways, did you do that?"

"Yeah, I did it and boy does she love you for that."

Cash told Money to take $2,500 out of his stash and buy Jasmin a car. He bought the typical girl car, a Honda Accord, but he also told him to dress it up real nice for her and that's exactly what he did. So, after putting some beat in it, tinting the windows, and placing some 22—inch rims on it, Cash spent a hefty $8,500 instead. He wasn't really tripping though because he knew it was going towards a good investment.

For the past few months, Jasmin had been keeping it real, so he felt like she deserved an award for her loyalty. She wrote him three times a week, sent him pictures on the regular, and even put $100 on her phone every paycheck just so he could call. She was doing all the right things to keep him happy and he truly appreciated her.

"Say bruh, what's good on the block though?" asked Cash. He was concerned his homies wasn't making any money right now with the feds around.

"They good," he replied, nodding his head. "They told me to tell you what's up too. They both gave me $250 to put on your books, so you should see that on there today."

"That's what's up and tell them niggas I said that's love too. Let Trap know that I got them pictures too bruh."

"Alright my nigga, you want to holla at Jasmin or what?"

He didn't know what to do. He at least wanted to say hi, because after all, she was his ride or die chick.

"Yeah, let me holla at her for a minute, but keep Peaches busy for me bruh, alright?"

"I got you player," he laughed standing up from the booth, signaling for Jasmin to come take his place.

Jasmin walked over and sat down, smiling from the excitement of seeing her boo. "Hey baby," she greeted him.

"What's going on sweetheart?"

"I see your number one finally came to see you." She didn't like how Peaches just all of sudden decided to show and take the spotlight off her. She wanted him to cut her loose and make her the love of his life, but she knew that wouldn't come right now. If she continued playing her part and hold him down, her patience would one day pay off.

"Look lil mama, don't trip bout her. You're getting your ten minutes of fame, right?"

"Mhmmmmm hmmmm," she mumbled.

"So, how have you been, road—runner?"

All of a sudden the expression on her face changed as she thought about her new car.

"Thank you so much, baby. I love my new car. I've been driving everywhere in it. I just wish you could see me drive babe, cause I drive real good," she said excitedly.

"Trust me ma, I can't wait to see how good you can drive," he replied, licking his lips.

She smiled after realizing he was flirting with her.

"In due time boo, in due time," she replied, leaning closer to the glass. "Anyways, I miss you, do you miss me?" She was gazing into his eyes.

"Ummmm, excuse me!"

Cash looked up and saw that Peaches was standing right behind Jasmin with her arms folded across her chest. He could tell by the expression written all over her face that she did not like how Jasmin was in the booth talking to her man.

Jasmin turned around to face her. "Ooooooh, I'm sorry boo boo, you're excused," she stated with heavy sarcasm as she rolled her eyes.

"Bitch, who the fuck are you getting smart with?" replied Peaches, not liking her attitude.

"Bitch?" Jasmin shot back, "who the fuck are you calling a bitch?"

"I'm talkin' to you!"

BANG! BANG! BANG!

Cash couldn't just stand there and watch his visit get out of control. So, he banged on the window to get both of their attention. When they looked his way, he directed Peaches to step in the booth.

Peaches rolled her eyes at Jasmin and sat down.

"Man, leave that girl alone," he told her.

"What the fuck is you sticking up for her for, huh?" She was mad and could tell something was up between them. "And I remember that girl from the apartment too, Cash, so tell me, is you fucking her or what?" She shouted loud enough for everyone in the visitation area to hear.

"Man, nah, and stop yelling in my motherfucking ear!" he shouted back, getting mad too.

"Nigga, I ain't got time for games either, playing with these stupid ass hoes."

The next thing he heard was Jasmin's blow to Peaches' head. After hearing Peaches continuously refer to her as a hoe, she couldn't take no more and stole off on her right there in the booth.

Cash couldn't believe it. Everyone in visitation had stopped their conversation to watch the Jerry Springer brawl. Jasmin had Peaches' hair in one hand and was swinging on her with the other, and from what he could tell, Jasmin was winning. He couldn't do anything but stand there and watch, but it didn't take long for the deputies to rush in and break it up. While Money grabbed Jasmin, some of the deputies grabbed Peaches, ushering them both out of the room. They sent all the inmates back to their pods and announced that visitation was officially over.

CHAPTER 18

PAYBACK

"Yeah man, you should 've see that shit bruh. Shawty got a little spunk in her for real."

Money and Trap were sitting on Trap's porch smoking a blunt while Money replayed the events from his brother's visit. Trap was enjoying every minute of the story as they sat around getting high.

"Man, that's crazy. She really took off on shawty in the booth?" he asked in amazement.

"Yeah nigga, right there!"

"So what happened when y'all broke it up?" He passed the blunt to Money, urging him to continue.

Money phone rings.

"Yeah, who dis?" Money answered his phone.

"Yes, I'm calling to speak to an Armani Lewis." He sat up in his seat at the sound of a female's voice.

"Speaking," he replied.

"Hello, how are you doing? This is Ms. Cox, the attorney you hired to represent your brother, Cashmere Lewis."

He tried to sober himself up a little. He knew this wasn't the time for him to be high and not pay attention. This woman was trying to help his brother see the streets, so whatever she had to say, he needed to pay close attention and listen.

"Oh what's good, Ms. Cox? what you got for me?"

He passed the blunt back to Trap and told him to hold on.

"Well, we just got back some information from the police department about the vehicle that rammed into your car."

This was music to his ears. He had wanted so badly to get payback on the person who got his brother in this predicament. The person responsible for the hit and run was going to have to try and run much farther now, since their identity was about to be revealed. At first, he didn't know how he was ever going to make it up to Cash for not telling him about the gun, but now he suddenly came up with a plan.

"So, you know who it is?" he asked.

"Yes, the vehicle belongs to Shantell Mosely, but we are still not sure if she was the driver or not."

"Hold on for a second, Ms. Cox." He couldn't believe the name she just said. "You said Shantell Mosely?" He asked her again, to be sure he heard her right the first time.

He knew Shantell's last name began with a M, but he wasn't sure if it was Mosely or not.

"Yes, Shantell Mosely. Why? Do you know her?"

She was asking too many questions while he tried remembering her last name. He knew what else to ask in order to find out.

"Nah, I don't know her, but ummmm…what kind of car did they say it was?"

"Um, let me see…" He heard her shuffle some papers around before she spoke. "Yes, here it is: a 2016 green Lincoln Towncar. Are you familiar with that vehicle?"

BINGO!

He knew exactly who was responsible for his brother's incarceration. Shantell was beginning to cause him more problems than he could stand. She just couldn't let go of him for nothing in the world. Now, he understood why, all of a sudden, he hadn't heard from her. It was all starting to make sense.

"Nah, I can't say I am, but thanks for the update. What are they talking about on my brother's case?" he asked, trying to change the subject.

"Well, I've talked to the Prosecutor and they want him to plead to a 922(e), possession of an illegal firearm by a convicted felon. In return for not going to trial, they promised not to pursue the enhancement for the obliterated serial number. He's looking at about 46 to 62 months if he pleads."

Damn! For a gun charge, Money thought to himself. That was a lot of time for just carrying a gun. Hearing that devastating blow intensified the hatred he had in his heart for Shantell. If his brother had to serve that much time in jail, Money was definitely going to make her pay.

"Got damn, Ms. Cox, it was only a pistol charge. You can't get it any lower than that?" He was pleading with her to do something. He wanted to help his brother as much as possible, but with numbers like that, he seemed helpless.

"I understand your concern, Mr. Lewis, but this is a serious charge on the federal level. Now, I suggest he take this deal because his fingerprints are all over the weapon and they are talking about running the probation concurrent."

There was a pause between them as Money contemplated the offer.

"Okay then, I'll holla at him and let him know what I think about it, but you can explain it better to him than I can," he said, giving it some serious thought. "When is the next time you're going to see him?"

"Well, that's the other reason I called. The $2,500 you gave me to represent him has diminished and I am going to need $5,000 more at his bond hearing in order to complete this deal."

Was he hearing her correctly? First, she tells him that his brother is looking at almost five years in prison, and then she has the nerve to ask him for some more money. He didn't want to give her any more money since his brother wasn't getting out, but he knew better than to let him go in the courtroom with a public defender.

"Alright, I got you," he agreed. "I'll be down there to drop off the money tomorrow morning. Is that okay?"

"Yes, that's fine, and if I am not here, you can leave it with my secretary, okay?"

"Alright then, just make sure you get down there and let him know about the deal and I'll take care of that bitch."

"Ummmm, excuse me?" she replied, wondering who he was referring to.

Money had forgotten he was still on the phone with an officer of the court. He had Shantell on his mind the whole conversation and couldn't wait to see her. The weed had him trippin', so he went ahead and ended the call.

"Oh my bad, Ms. Cox, I was talkin' to you and my homeboy at the same time. I'm sorry for that," he said, hoping she bought it.

"Oh, okay, well, have a nice day and I'll hear from you tomorrow." They both hung up.

Good, she bought it, he thought. When their call ended, he went back to telling Trap about the fight between Peaches and Jasmin, but in the back of his mind, he was trying to figure out how he was going to repay Shantell for all the trouble she caused. He knew revenge was best served cold, so he planned on serving her the coldest dish ever.

***

Cash was blowed after his visit with Ms. Cox. He couldn't believe he was actually about to take a plea for something that wasn't his. It was a lot for him to take in for the moment, so he told her to stall the deal until he could officially make up his mind. When it came to his freedom, he wasn't so willing to give in to a plea deal that would take five years from his life on the streets.

During their conversation, he felt like she gave him some good advice, but the fact that she kept bringing up him assisting the government was beyond his reasoning. She kept proposing stuff like getting him a 5k 1 or a rule 35(b), and Cash wasn't trying to take that route. That route, to him, was for cowards and he planned on being a man about his. He wasn't the type to drop a dime on someone else because he slipped. It was his problem, so he was going to deal with it, and she was going to have to start respecting that.

On his way back to his cell, he glanced into every block he passed to see if Miss Black was working today. At the moment, there was a black dude, whose pants were too tight for him to be comfortable, escorting him back. Cash could tell the government had completely brainwashed him because his demeanor was all jacked up. The worst part about it: he had the nerve to rock a Boosie Fade, but without the fade.

"Man, I like that haircut, dawg, who hooked you up?" he asked, trying not to laugh. He stepped into the sally port on his cell block and waited on his response.

"Oh, you like it, bro?" he replied, falling right into his joke. "My girl hit me up. You think she did a good job or what?" He turned around giving Cash a 360-degree view of his soup—bowl haircut.

Cash broke out laughing as he continued walking into the block. He'd seen enough for one day.

The block he was housed in contained bars, so he was able to communicate with the inmates on other ranges in his block. Being somewhat of a hood celebrity, Cash understood the respect his street cred got him, so whenever someone shouted out to him, he made it his business to speak. When he entered the range, he went straight for the phone. That was his exit outside of the jail's walls, so he tried his best to stay on it. He needed to speak with his brother about this deal. He knew they were coming up there to see him Saturday as usual, but he figured this couldn't wait.

After speaking with Money for 15 minutes, it was confirmed. His best bet was to plead out to the gun charge. In his mind, five years wasn't really that long, but when you're doing time for someone else's trouble, it seemed a lot longer. If his support system remained strong, he could do it with ease.

He could count on Jasmin to play her part, but Peaches on the other hand was another story. It was funny to him how she had the audacity to play the victim after their little brawl in visitation. When she finally got around to writing him, all she did was complain about Jasmin's behavior when, in all actuality, she initiated the whole thing. It was just crazy to him how she couldn't figure out why Jasmin stole off on her. To him, she got exactly what she deserved, and although Jasmin sucker punched her, she still put her ass in check.

After he ended the call with Money, he looked up at the clock on the wall and seen that it was 7:30, which meant Peaches would be out of class.

He dialed her number.

After the phone rang twice, she picked up. "You have a pre—paid call from…Cash…an inmate at a correctional facility. Press three to accept the call…"

He waited as the recording played, wondering why it was taking her so long to accept.

"Hello," he said, after hearing her accept.

"Hey," she replied dryly.

He knew she wouldn't be too thrilled to hear from him and he felt the tension.

"Hay is for horses," he replied, using him and Money's favorite line, "but what's good?"

"Nothin', everything is okay," she stated dully. "So you good?" He knew she was still upset about what had happened in visitation, so he started the conversation off first.

"Baby, listen, that shit that happened between you and Jasmin shouldn't have occurred. I wasn't takin' her side either when

I called you to the window. It's just that, you are supposed to be more mature than that ma."

"Mature!" she objected, as if it left a bad taste in her mouth. "What's so got damn mature about that bitch stealin' off on me, Cash? I'm tellin' you boy, when I catch that little girl, I'll be sure to give her a mature ass whoopin', how about that?"

He knew she meant every word too. Peaches could fight, but from what he witnessed the other day, she was going to have to come correct if she thought about confronting Jasmin again. He didn't like the thought of the two women he cared about fighting and going at each other. He was about to go down the road and needed for them both to stay by his side for support.

"I feel you ma, but shawty ain't even tryin' to see you head up," he lied, trying to stroke her ego. "That's why she stole off on you."

"Oh, I already know that bitch don't want to see me," she stated with confidence.

"Check this out though, boo. I ain't call to talk about her; I called to talk about us."

"What about us?" she snapped.

Damn, he thought. That came off real cold and he didn't know how to respond. She was really trippin' on him.

"Why you gotta come at me like that?" he replied, hurt by her response.

"Because you're the one who had that bitch all up in the window in the first place, Cash! What the fuck is really going on between you two, because I don't have time for these stupid ass games you playin', nigga!"

"Look," he snapped. "I already told you that she's a friend of my brother, so stop asking me these dumb ass questions." He was starting to lose his cool because she had him down bad. He didn't want to tell her the truth because she probably would leave him and he wasn't ready for that.

"Ummmm hmmmm, well," she said, calming herself down so she could deliver the final blow, "why was she in the car with you when you got into that accident?"

What the fuck! He thought to himself. He didn't expect her to know that much. He wondered how she found out but knew better than to ask. That would've been a dead giveaway that he was doing something he had no business doing. Whatever excuse he planned on using, he needed to come up with it pretty fast.

After taking too long to respond, she continued.

"What… you can't talk now or something?"

He knew he was busted, so he broke it down to her the best way he knew how.

"Look ma," he began, tired of them arguing back and forth. "I'm going through a lot right now dealing with these people, and I really don't know how to explain myself because I don't want to lie to you." He didn't know how to explain him and Jasmin's relationship, but he wanted to keep it as real with her as possible.

"I need you to believe me when I say this…I'm not fucking shorty and that's the honest to God truth."

He waited for her to respond but could only hear her sobbing through the phone. He didn't like hurting her, but he also wasn't trying to be alone. He needed more time to work things out with her and was hoping she could be a little understanding and patient with him.

"Hello," he called out, trying to get her attention. "Hello," he repeated.

"I love you Cash, with all my heart, but you make it so hard for me to trust you," she cried.

It was tearing him up on the inside to hear her cry. He never intended for the call to take a wrong turn. He felt responsible for breaking her down, and knew deep down this was the last thing they needed right now.

"Listen babe, I'm sorry about everything I'm putting your through, but I need you to be strong for me right now. I just spoke to my lawyer today and it's not looking too good for me."

"What do you mean?" she asked concerned.

"Well, I'm looking at five years, give or take a few months, but hopefully I won't have to do the whole five."

The phone beeped twice, letting him know their time was almost up.

He needed to get a clear understanding with her about where their relationship was going before the phone cut off. This was his last call before they locked down for the night and he wanted to end it with her still being there for him.

"Listen, the phone is about to hang up and we about to lock down, so I won't be able to call back, but I love you Peaches. You know that, right?" There was complete silence on the other end of the line.

He hung up the phone and headed off towards his cell. Tonight, he wouldn't get a good night's rest because in the morning, he wasn't sure if things would ever be the same.

***

Shantell didn't feel like herself. The person she'd become was disgusting and she desperately needed some help. After the police linked her car to the accident, Macon's finest came to pick her up for questioning. The detectives who interrogated her didn't buy her story. Her statement about how it all went down was inconsistent, plus there were plenty of eyewitnesses at the scene, so they locked her up and charged her with felony hit and run.

Luckily, she got off with a slap on the wrist when the judge gave her a $25,000 bond. So, she called her husband, who was at work at the time, to come and bond her out. Roger didn't have to go work out of town that week, so she knew he would be available.

Previously, he had noticed the damage done to her car and asked about it, but she tried covering it up by lying and telling him that somebody backed into her. Now, since her lie was exposed, Roger was really upset. Because of her lies, he had to withdraw a large amount of money from their savings account in order to get her out.

Shantell just couldn't control herself. After the intentional car crash, she began feeling bad about what she'd done and her emotions were causing her to make bad decisions. She had even started snorting cocaine on the regular. She was going through a stage of depression that made her unstable. She needed relief from the world, and her new best friend, a white girl by the name of cocaine, was her only outlet.

A couple of her friends were already using cocaine, so she knew who she needed to talk to in order to get some. She'd been offered it plenty of times before but always refused to indulge, but now since life was becoming such a burden, she looked forward to enjoying her stress reliever. Her first time experimenting with the drug changed her whole perception about it.

On her lunch break at the hospital, she stopped by the ladies room to take a few hits. At first, she didn't even think she was high but later on found out it made her more attentive and active. She then dismissed the notion that cocaine was such a bad thing. For a while, she was too embarrassed to let anyone find out that she was using, but after snorting for weeks, she started feeling more and more relaxed around her friends.

During their usual lunch break hour, she and some co—workers would all chip in and buy a quarter ounce to snort. That eventually made matters worse because whenever she wasn't at work she would crave the rich man's high. This ultimately led to her wanting to search for some on her own. She started asking around and eventually found a reliable supplier.

Over time, she lost focus on the things most important to her and her marriage began to skate on thin ice. She and Roger argued in the car the whole way home after he bonded her out of jail. They cursed and fussed at each other non—stop. She was upset with him because deep down inside, she felt like everything was his fault. He stayed on the road so much that she felt neglected. She cooked, cleaned, and ran his bathwater every night while he was home. She figured that after constantly maintaining their home, she could expect to receive a little attention from him every now and then. She wanted to enjoy having sex with her husband on a regular basis, but when he got off from work all he wanted to do was sleep. He always complained about being tired and she was beginning to get tired of his ass. It seemed like the only time he made love to her was when he was drunk, and that only lasted for a few minutes. She was sexually repressed and that's what she believed led her to sleeping with a teenage boy.

The point of the matter was that Money knew how to take care of business when it came to satisfying her. He spent countless hours learning how to eat her pussy just right before stroking her down. Now that he was brushing her off she couldn't take it. He had her hooked on the dick like a fiend, and she needed to find a rehab to wean herself off of it.

When they made it home, Roger told her they would finish their conversation once he got off work. She got out of the car and headed towards the front door. Roger drove off, not caring to see if she made it in the house or not. As Shantell stepped into the house, she thought about how tired she was and quickly ran upstairs. She needed a boost, so she headed to her secret stash spot to retrieve her quicker—picker—upper. She was so focused on getting high that she never even paid attention to the fact that the front door was open.

***

This was the moment he'd been waiting for. Money watched as Shantell came bursting through the front door. He stood in the corner of her living room, ducked off, and dressed in all black. In his hand, he carried a snub-nosed .38 revolver, which he clenched tighter and tighter at the thought of finally getting revenge.

Shantell ran into the bedroom and quickly tried remembering where her secret stash was. She walked over to the closet and opened it. That's when she remembered she hid the cocaine in one of her shoe boxes, but which one? Her closet was full of shoe boxes, so she began searching through them one by one until she came across her pair of red bottom heels.

She knew Roger would never go through her shoes; that's why she chose it as her hiding spot. After retrieving her bag, she took out her key chain from her purse and dug in. The substance ran down the back of her throat, making it numb, causing an instant high. Afterwards, she headed back downstairs to get a glass of water from the kitchen. On her way to the kitchen, she stopped in the living room, sensing that something was wrong. As she turned around to confirm her intuition, Money jumped from out of the corner and smacked her across the face with pistol.

She fell down, hitting the hard wood floor, clutching her face from the painful impact. The bag of coke she was carrying was now laying in front of Money. When he noticed it fall, he reached down and picked it up. While she was still laid out on the floor, he looked over the contents. He knew it was cocaine from having dealt with the drug on the regular. At that point, he didn't care to waste any more time. He snatched her up by her hair and put their faces close to each other so he could look her in the eyes.

"Bitch, what the fuck is wrong with you?" he growled.

Looking into her eyes, she could tell that this was not the same little boy she nursed back to health in the hospital. This person in front of her was mad, very mad, so she began to fear for her life.

"Money, please don't hurt me," she begged, sobbing from all the pain she was enduring. "I didn't know that was your brother in the car. I'm sorry, and I promise I'll leave you alone."

She was trying to loosen his grip on her hair because it felt like he was about to pull her scalp off. The pain in her jaw was beginning to intensify as well but the pain of him pulling her hair was much worse.

Money then placed the pistol up to her chin as he spoke.

"Bitch, shut the fuck up," he whispered in her ear. "Do you know what the fuck your stupid ass did?"

She was afraid to answer his question, because she didn't want to answer it wrong and make him madder than he already was. She looked into his eyes seeking for some kind of forgiveness, but she didn't see any. All she saw was a man possessed by a demon.

He could see the fear in her eyes and that's when he knew he had her just where he wanted. To see her jaw begin to swell made him want to continue. He had pure hatred in his heart for her and looked forward to making her feel his wrath, especially after learning that she was using cocaine.

With a fist full of hair, he yanked her over towards the closest chair and made her sit down.

"Bitch, you better not move either," he dared, pointing the gun's nose at her chest. "Where did your husband go?" he asked, glancing over his shoulder to look out the window.

She began looking around erratically when he asked about Roger. He wouldn't be getting off of work for a few more hours and she didn't want him to get caught up in the middle of her mess. She thought about telling Money a lie but he had a look on his face that said a million words. She began panicking when he pulled the hammer back on the pistol, blurting out the first thing that came to mind.

"Work," she uttered, deciding to tell the truth.

"What time does he get off?" Money looked at his watch to see what time it was.

"5:30," she barely spoke, trying to avoid the pain of her broken jaw. It was 3:15.

Money needed for Roger to be there for his plan to be complete. He didn't mind waiting, because she was definitely going to get what she deserved once Roger got there. He walked into the kitchen and grabbed a chair. He placed it in front of her so he could watch her while they waited on Roger to get home. He wanted complete silence. Every time she tried whimpering something to him, he would shush her letting her know to remain quiet. He was not trying to hear her excuses or apologies. He had only one mission and that was to get payback for what she did to his brother.

***

At 5:45, Money heard keys jingling outside the front door. He got up from the chair and indicated with his index finger for her to remain quiet. What he didn't know was that she didn't have the energy or courage to say a word.

When Roger walked in, he stopped by the living room and turned on the lights. He looked and saw that Shantell was sitting in there with her hands over her jaw. As he approached her, the cold steel of Money's pistol touched the back of his neck, bringing him to an abrupt halt. Then, out of his natural reflex, he threw his hands up to surrender.

"Whoa, what is going on here?" he asked looking scared to death.

"Aye dawg, don't make no quick movements alright, because I will send your ass on a permanent dream, ya feel me!" Money was calm and demanding as he patted Roger down for any weapons.

"Okay, so what is this about, money or some..." He was interrupted by the force of Money's pistol digging into his neck.

"Man, shut the fuck up, first of all." Money wasn't trying to hear his irritating voice. "And no fool, this ain't no 211," he replied, taking a quick glance around the room, then laughing. "Nigga, what is you talking about? Y'all ain't got shit worth taking in this bitch anyways."

He walked Roger over to the chair adjacent from his wife and made him sit down. He looked at his wife and saw that her jaw had swelled to the size of a baseball. He immediately began to get angry but stayed seated. He tried looking into her eyes to reassure her that everything was going to be okay. In return, all she could do was look away because she knew that all this was her fault.

Once Money had him situated, he stood off to the side and began to talk.

"Check this out bruh, this bitch right here," he pointed his pistol at her, "is scandalous, and she's been fucking around on you for the past few months with me." He paused to see his reaction.

At first, he was looking at Money, but after hearing him reveal that he was fucking his wife, he directed his attention toward her.

"Is this true, honey?" he asked, looking at her tear-streaked face.

She had no response for him. All she could do was cry from the physical and emotional pain she was enduring. She realized that Money's plan for revenge was not to kill her but to destroy her marriage and possibly her life.

"Yeah, it's true, nigga!" Money interjected, looking at Roger like he was stupid. "You think I'd come over here for nothing and make this shit up? Huh?" He knew Roger was a square but he didn't expect him to be this naïve.

"No, I believe you, because it's written all over her face." Roger was hurt. He couldn't believe she would do this to him. After all the hard work he'd put into their marriage, it disappointed him to find out she was sleeping with another man.

"Let me ask you a question though, homie," spoke Roger, bringing his attention back to Money.

"Nigga, I'm not your homie, so let's get that straight," he corrected him, raising his pistol to Roger's chest. "And you get only one question, so ask!"

"Why did you come over here and do this?"

Money could tell he was hurt. He had the nerve to ask about his intentions when his wife was the one cheating. He figured, only love could make someone that foolish.

"Well," he began, "this stupid ass bitch ruined my family's life, so I thought I would come over here and personally return the favor." A smirk broke across his face as he lowered the gun. He knew she'd be on the verge of suicide after this, so he finished what he had left to say so he could go. "Enough of these questions, though," he pointed the gun back in her direction. "Keep this bitch in check, or next time I promise I won't be so nice." On that note, he turned around and headed for the door.

"Hold on for a second," said Roger, getting up from the chair to face Money. "I got some secrets of my own I want to share, since we are sharing secrets."

Shantell's eyes flew open wide. She couldn't say much so she just looked at her husband surprised, wondering what kind of secret he was keeping from her.

Money, on the other hand, didn't care.

"Well, check this out," he said, getting both of their attention. "I don't want to hear your 'Trapped in the Closet' confessions, so save that for when I'm gone. This ain't no R. Kelly remix, nigga. Fuck is wrong with you?"

Roger understood him clearly because he was the man with the gun. He was just glad to make it out of that situation alive.

As Money exited their home, he shouted over his shoulder, "And if anybody calls the police when I leave, they might as well call the coroner too and make a reservation, if you know what I mean."

CHAPTER 19

VICTORVILLE

After going to court and being sentenced to 65 months, Cash was on his way to prison. He received a plea deal for his guideline range of 57— 71 months, where he hoped to receive the low end of the deal. However, the judge, considering Cash's probation, sentenced him to 65 months instead. It wasn't the best deal but it sure wasn't the worst, so he accepted it and moved on.

The U.S. Marshals came to pick him up from the county jail and transport him to Jones County. This jail housed federal inmates until the Bureau of Prisons came and picked them up. Their transportation route was very different from the state. When they arrived to pick him up, even though he knew where he was going, he wouldn't know how he got there. This tactic, which was developed for the high-profile criminals they transported, was used on the regular.

Cash stayed in Jones County for a week before being transferred to Atlanta United States Penitentiary, which was also used as a transfer facility. Once he arrived there he began to inquire about where he was designated. He'd spoken with the counselor to find out if he was going to remain close to home, but it turned out he was going to be shipped farther away. All he kept hearing in his head was the agent's voice telling him over and over again how he was going to a USP. Now, he knew for sure, because the counselor told him, he was going to USP Victorville.

Victorville, California, also known as Victimville, was gang-land. Its gruesome acts of violence, mostly by homemade weapons, made it one of the most dangerous federal prisons in the United States. It was established that a United States Penitentiary was far from being a Hilton or a Four Seasons and in order for you to walk within the general population, you needed your paperwork.

Paperwork was court documents explaining a prisoner's reason for being incarcerated. These documents would tell if they ever assisted the government in any prosecution of another person. Snitches were prohibited from living in general population, along with rapists and child molesters. So, if a prisoner couldn't produce their paperwork, they'd be forced to ask to be placed in protective custody.

Usually, they were given a 30-day time frame to get these documents. Failure to get them resulted in you asking for protective custody or getting stabbed, then forced into protective custody. Either way, you were going to get up out of there, with or without violence.

USPs had always been known for their brutal acts of violence towards staff and inmates. This was because most inmates in a maximum-security prison had very lengthy sentences, all the way up to life. These individuals are sometimes depressed or even miserable because their family, friends, or loved ones have deserted them, or they are left with no hope of ever getting out.

To make matters even worse, 90 percent of the prison population carried some form of homemade weapon for protection on them daily. This fostered an environment that should never be taken too lightly because at any moment, or anywhere, something could pop off.

Ultimately, Victimville is where Cash was headed and he made up his mind that he was going to stay clear out of trouble if he could avoid it. His plan was to mind his own business, and with any luck he could make it back home on time with all of his teeth and ligaments intact. He stayed in Atlanta's holdover for two weeks before they finally shipped him to California. For Cash, flying was a new experience. He enjoyed every minute of it, except for the part where his ears popped from being at such a high altitude.

When he finally made it to the prison, he was exhausted, plus the receiving process was time-consuming. Having to strip down to his bare ass, squat, and cough had him feeling violated. Compared to county living, Cash was willing to endure such humiliation in order to live a better life while serving his time.

After the intake process, each inmate received a bed roll and was led to their designated unit. When Cash made it to his unit, he and some of the dudes he came with just stood in the middle. Cash observed how all the inmates stared at them with hard looks. As they waited for the unit officer to inform them of which cell they were going into, a couple of men approached them and began asking questions about where they were from.

As he continued looking around, he couldn't believe how diverse the unit was. There was a good bit of whites and hispanics who seemed to have their own sections in the unit. There were even some Asians and islanders too. Cash thought to himself, I wonder if any of them chinks know Kung Fu?

"Lewis, you're in cell 224," the Hispanic unit officer informed him.

He didn't know where the hell that was, so he walked off in search of it. He was amazed by the amount of Mexicans housed in the unit. It was probably the most he'd ever seen in his life.

As he was walking up the steps to go to on the second floor, two inmates approached him: a dark—skinned dude with dreads that resembled palm trees, and a high—yellow dude with a bald head.

"What's good dawg? Where you from?" asked Palm Trees.

"Georgia," replied Cash, watching them both to see why they approached him.

"Okay then, we from the Souf too," stated the yellow dude. "I'm Joe Joe from Baton Rouge," he greeted Cash, giving him some dap.

"I'm Smoke form Palm Beach," said Palm Trees, giving him some dap as well. "What they call you, bruh?"

"Cash."

"Okay then, Cash," replied Joe Joe, putting too much emphasis on his name. "What cell they got you in?"

"I think he said 224," he answered, trying to read the both of them.

He could already tell Joe Joe was the clown type by the way he responded when he told them his name. Smoke, on the other hand, was serious. He watched Cash as much as Cash watched him, letting him know he was not the only one trying to read.

"Oh, that's empty, so you straight. You got a cell by yourself," stated Joe Joe.

Walking to his cell, Cash felt relieved about not having a cell mate. He wasn't too enthused about sleeping in a cell with a complete stranger, so now he felt a little bit more comfortable. While he made his bed, Smoke and Joe Joe gave him the rundown of how the spot was being run. They told him he had 30 days to get his paperwork, which he already knew from other dudes in transit. They gave him a care package that included hygiene products, food, and some used shoes so he wouldn't have to continue walking around in his bus shoes.

He already had $1,000 in his account, so anything they gave him he planned on giving back. His brother had put the money in his account while he was in Atlanta, so all he had to do was make it to commissary.

He asked them if anybody there was from Georgia, and they told him yeah, just not in their unit. He was going to have to wait until tomorrow to see who was there representing the red clay.

"Lockdown in five minutes!" yelled the guard from the officer's station.

Joe Joe and Smoke both gave him some dap and told him to be up when the doors popped.

"We'll introduce you to the homies tomorrow," Smoke told him, walking out of his cell.

When the guard locked his door, he sat on his bunk and took in his new domain. There was a grey-colored desk with a chair attached to it, two lockers, a porcelain sink and toilet, and a set of bunk beds. The walls were painted white and grey and looked kind of clean.

For a minute, he couldn't actually believe he was in the feds. He knew tomorrow would be a day to remember, so he laid down to get some rest. After a long trip across the United States, he needed to relax a little bit and build his energy level back up. Whatever was coming his way the next day, he needed to be ready for it.

***

Cash awoke when he heard the C.O. unlock his door. It was 6:00 and he was still tired, so he remained in the bed for a few more minutes. He planned on getting some more sleep in before he had to face his first day in prison, but somebody came knocking on his door.

"Aye dawg, you gotta get up when them doors pop and have your shoes on," stated Joe Joe, sticking his head in the door.

Cash looked at him like he was crazy for coming to his door so early in the morning. He wanted to tell him to close his door so he could go back to sleep, but decided it was probably in his best interest to get up. Remembering that he was in a penitentiary helped him realize every decision from now on could place him in a life-or-death situation.

"Alright, I'm up," he replied, getting out of bed.

"They about to call chow too, so if you tryin' to go, you better come on." Joe Joe closed the door and took off.

Cash got up, washed his face and brushed his teeth. After getting himself together, he waited for them to call chow, and then they took off out the unit.

On his way to the chow hall, Joe Joe introduced him to some of the dudes from the south. They were all supposed to be part of one group, or in prison lingo, one car. The southern states all ran together in order for them to remain strong in numbers. The Crips and Bloods had an alliance for the same reason. Basically, whatever geographical area you came from, that's who you ran with.

After breakfast, he came back to the unit and got on the phone. He needed to call his brother to let him know that he'd made it to Cali.

***

Money was in the process of running from a chick with a meat clever when he heard the house phone ring. All throughout his dream, he went on dates with different women and at the end of each one, some girl would chase him around with a knife. As he sat up, realizing it was only a dream, he said to himself, "Why is bitches always causing me problems?"

"Boy, get your ass up out of that bed!" shouted his mother, storming through his bedroom door. "You need to get up and find something to do, cause you ain't gone be layin' around here all day. Here!" She thrust the phone in his face.

"Who is it?" he asked, grabbing it from her.

"It's your brother," she answered before walking out.

Hearing it was Cash on the line made him wake all the way up.

"What's up, bruh?" spoke Money, getting out of bed.

"What up, my nigga? Man, get your ass up, still sleepin' and shit." Cash was glad one of his siblings was home for him to speak to. He tried talking to his mother for a brief moment, but that didn't go so well. She was too busy running around the house looking for a drink, so he asked to speak to his brother instead.

"Man I'm up, so what's good?"

"Shit really, I'm just coming back from chow and thought I'd call to see what was going on."

"Man, just the same ole shit, you already know how mama is, coming through here making all that fucking noise early in the morning." He sat up to put on a pair of his Polo jeans. "But ummmm, you done made it there."

"Yeah, and this shit crazy bruh. These niggas on some military-type shit around here, talkin' bout be out of bed when they pop the doors."

"Who? The inmates or the C.O.'s?" Money asked.

"The inmates," he answered.

"Damn, what they got going on over there?"

"Hell if I know," said Cash, "I'm not really feeling the environment, something about if you stay ready, you won't have to get ready."

"Ready for what?" Money was confused.

"War I guess."

Money burst out laughing over the phone. "Man, get the fuck out of here."

"Funny, huh!" Cash began to laugh himself.

They talked for the rest of the 15 minutes and then hung up.

Money finished getting dressed in a white t—shirt and a pair of brand-new Air Force Ones. He stepped into the bathroom to check himself out and noticed he was in need of a crisp line up. He had to maintain his pretty boy image, and along with the dreads he was now growing, that would require him spending more time on his look.

For the past year, he had been wanting to try something new for a change, so he began growing his hair out. His dreads were beginning to lock and he needed to keep them presentable. He made a mental note to go get them re—twisted when he had some extra time on his hands.

Right now, though, he had bigger things to worry about. It had been almost a year since they closed down their trap and Money needed some work bad. He figured that since the feds were watching the connect there was no need for him to holler at Cash anymore about Big Pete. So, he thought long and hard about what his next move should be.

He remembered meeting a dude a while ago at the gas station. The guy had pulled up to the pump next to him in a green Charger sitting on 24—inch chrome rims. When the man stepped out of the car, Money could see he was sporting a thick gold chain that held a big ass medallion around his neck. Then on top of that, he had a mouth full of gold teeth. His intuition told him this dude had to be a dopeboy, and after having a brief conversation with him, he turned out to be right.

They began engaging in a conversation about cars, but then the discussion veered off into numbers, dopeboy numbers. These were numbers that Money could relate to as they proceeded to speak in dopeboy language. When he realized he possibly found himself a connect, he logged the dude's number into his phone. He wanted to make sure when the time presented itself, he would surely put it to use.

***

"Yo Cash!"

He was leaning up against the wall in the dayroom looking at TV and listening to his mp3 player when Nut called him.

Nut was sitting down playing cards when he signaled for him to come over by the table. He wasn't in the mood to talk, so he hesitated at first, but after thinking that it might be something important, he made his way over to see what Nut wanted.

As he walked up, he eyed the card players to see if anything was wrong.

"What up?" he asked, removing one of the ear buds from his ear.

"You just got that Jeezy 101, right?" Nut asked without looking up from his hand.

"Damn nigga, how you knew that?" He had just bought the album off the computer this morning, so he wanted to know how Nut knew.

"I heard when you were sampling the tracks earlier. I was sitting in the booth right next to you," he replied, turning to face Cash.

Honestly, Nut was one ugly dude. He had bumps all over his face that made him look like he should've been the spokesman for Star Crunch. On top of that, he had enough butter on his teeth to cook ten bags of popcorn. He was an alright dude, but Cash didn't really mess with him like that. For starters, Nut messed with homosexuals and Cash considered that a big no no. Not only did he mess with boys, Nut didn't hustle, work, or try to even get an education. So, in his book, he was a nobody Cash preferred not to socialize with, especially since dummies walked a very thin line in the penitentiary. The only thing Nut had going for himself was that he was an avid knife pusher. He had only been locked up for three years but had stabbed four people. That gave Cash more of a reason to stay clear away from his ass.

"Damn dawg, you need to miss something sometimes," Cash told him, stating his disapproval of Nut's nosiness.

"Nah, it ain't nothin' like that, bruh, I just wanted to see if I could catch a few songs later on my nigga."

Cash looked at him like he was stupid. He didn't do for people who didn't do for themselves, and that was one of the things he kept in mind when dudes asked him for stuff.

"Nah dawg, you need to try and catch a book or something, because this shit ain't gone help you, pimp." He backed away from the table, letting him know their conversation was over.

Posting back up against the wall, Cash laughed to himself as he thought, "that nigga better worry about catchin' AIDS instead of catchin' some songs."

Cash had been at the prison now for a couple of weeks, and the personalities surrounding him never ceased to amaze him. He mostly just sat back against the wall in the unit and observed how dudes continuously tried to run game. The ones approaching him tried to run game, coming with the same see—through tactics he saw on a day—to—day basis. They all apparently liked using the same tired ass line: 'What's up bruh, this must be your first spot?' He assumed they were just hoping he was green, but to the contrary, he was two steps ahead of the game.

As he went back to watching *Love and Hip-Hop*, he noticed the dark— skinned Mexican who always stayed in his cell sitting at the computer. He heard some of the dudes in the unit call him Migo. Rumor had it, Migo was half-black and half-Mexican, but due to his lack of socializing, it was never confirmed. Cash peeped how Migo never watched TV unless it was the news, and he barely went outside.

When he was done on the computer, he got up and headed to his cell. Cash admired how he carried himself. He wasn't like everybody else and conducted himself like a leader, making Cash wonder what he was locked up for in the first place.

Cash continued watching Migo. Before he walked into his cell though, Migo turned around and looked dead at him, letting him know he knew he was being watched. Cash wanted to look away when they locked eyes, but he didn't want to give off the impression he was scared. Instead, he held his stare a little while longer before finally looking away.

When he glanced back over to see if Migo was still looking, he noticed Migo waving his hand for him to come over, then proceeded to walk in his cell. At first, Cash thought he was trippin' and looked around to see if he was waving at someone else, but there was nobody near him, so he knew Migo's request was directed towards him. He wanted to see what was up, so he headed over to his cell. When he walked up, Migo had his back to the door, so he knocked to get his attention. Without turning around to see who it was, Migo waved for him to come in.

He opened the door and stepped in, instantly noticing he had way too many books in his cell. There were books all over the place. From the top of the lockers, to under the beds, there were books everywhere.

Before Cash got a chance to speak, Migo spoke first. "Que pasa, Cash?, por que me estás mirando tanto, amigo?"

Cash only understand one word, his name.

"What?"

Migo laughed.

"I said, why are you watching me so hard, homie?" Migo repeated himself.

He couldn't read Migo like the rest of the guys he encountered. He kept a pleasant smile on his face, giving Cash an awkward feeling.

"I'm not watchin' you dawg, you just too busy watchin' me."

"Is that right?" Migo crossed his arms, pondering his statement.

"Yeah, that's right."

There was a moment of silence as they both just stood there staring each other down.

Cash, for the first time, realized Migo was a little bigger than he was. He was athletically built and appeared to be in good shape, but Cash had other options on the table besides fighting.

Tucked in his waist, right in front of his dick, he carried a 7 1/2-inch piece of steel. It was a gift from the homies once his paperwork cleared. They wanted all the homies to be strapped just in case anything popped off. He kept his piece on him at all times because not only was it sharp as hell, it floated, meaning it could pass through any metal detector.

He wasn't quite ready to use it this early in his bid though, but he made up his mind that if this Mexican started to act crazy he was going to blast him out of his socks. Truth be told, at the end of the day, he'd rather catch a body than be a body.

Migo noticed Cash move his hands towards the front of his trousers, so he spoke to break the tension.

"Man, be cool dawg, I'm not trippin'. I just called you in here to introduce myself." He was shaking his head from how aggressive Cash was acting. "My name is Migo," he stated, stepping forward with his hand extended for Cash to shake.

Cash calmed his nerves and shook his hand.

"That's what's up, I'm Cash."

"I know your name already. Have a seat." Migo gestured for him to sit in the plastic chair by the door while he sat down on his bunk.

They started off talking about why they were in prison, which eventually led to them discussing plans for when they made it home. Cash began to speak to him on the regular. They started to build a real friendship as they shared personal stories about their life on the streets. Migo turned out to be real cool, and the cooler he got, the more information Cash was able to get from him.

Turns out, Migo was connected to the Zeta Cartel. This interested Cash and made him want to know more about him. Not only could he have possibly found a connect to shop with when he got out, but he could have also met a real black Mexican.

CHAPTER 20

MIGO

"Say bruh, how much are you tryin' to spend?"

"Man, to be honest my nigga, I want to make sure the shit some good first before we even start talkin' numbers, ya feel me?"

Money was in the middle of conducting business with Q, the dude he had met previously at the gas station. It seemed to him Q was more concerned about how much cash he had than how much dope he was trying to cop.

"Look dawg," said Q, "here's what we can do, because I don't travel with work on me my nigga. Meet me at Taps tonight and I'll put something in motion for you, alright?"

"That's what's up, but what time?" he asked.

"12:30 good with you?"

"Yeah, 12:30 it is."

"Alright then, I'm gone, playboy."

"Be easy bruh."

They both pulled off in opposite directions.

Money knew that after their brief talk this was the deal he needed to start back making money. Things were moving slow around the city and he needed a way to speed things up.

With Cash in Cali serving a bid, Money saw hard times up ahead, so he decided to do something about it. He knew Shay liked having nice things, and if nice things was what she wanted, then nice things was what he planned on giving her.

***

"Migo, you crazy as hell!" laughed Cash while he and Migo were in the cell talking.

Over the past couple of months, he and Migo had spent a lot of time together. After their initial confrontation, they got pretty close. Migo recognized Cash as someone he could build with and learn to trust, so he allowed him into his circle.

"No, my friend," said Migo, shaking his head. "Why are you laughing?"

"Cause, you tryin' to say I can't speak Spanish, but shit, neither can you," he continued laughing.

"No, there's a difference, hermano. I speak in the same manner as you, just in a different language."

"Man, I know that, I'm just laughing at how you sound sayin' it… key yon da waaaaay."

Migo couldn't do nothing but laugh at how his silly friend was pronouncing the phrase he commonly used to greet people. Migo was trying to teach Cash how to speak Spanish, but he kept laughing when Migo pronounced words for him. He was having a hard time understanding the difference between formal and informal speech. Migo knew if Cash learned to speak Spanish fluently, he would have a chance at doing business with his uncles when he got out. That would give Migo exactly what he needed, a middle—Georgia distributor.

"Lockdown in 15 minutes," yelled the C.O.

"Alright, that's enough key yon da way for today my friend. I'll get at you tomorrow," said Cash, bumping Migo's fist.

"Okay amigo, buenas noches, Dinero," he replied, saying Cash's Spanish nickname.

"Whatever," he replied walking out.

Walking up the stairs to go to his cell, a dude from D.C. approached him and asked if he had any snacks in his cell to munch on. Cash looked at him like he was crazy and walked past him. They had barely spoken before, so what made him think Cash would feed him anything other than steel?

"Say slim, I know you just heard me."

Cash stopped and turned around. "Nah nigga, I'm part deaf," he replied, irritated by how the dude was calling him outside his name, "and my name is Cash."

D.C. smirked.

"Nigga I know your name, but that ain't what I asked you, slim."

Cash couldn't understand these dudes. It was known throughout the feds that dudes from Washington, DC were cut from a different cloth, but the fact that this dude was going out of his way to get into Cash's was beyond him. He tried his best to keep his circle small to limit any unnecessary trouble coming his way, but clearly that strategy was not working for him today.

"Say, my nigga," Cash said seriously, "what part of me tellin' you my name is Cash you don't understand?" He walked towards D.C. with his hands in front of his trousers, preparing to draw. He didn't have time to play, so if trouble is what the dude wanted, trouble is what he was going to get.

D.C. smiled, knowing he'd gotten under Cash's skin.

"Damn shawty, I was just messing with you fam. Don't do me nothin', holmes." He backed away from Cash with his hands up and walked off.

Cash shook his head, turned around, and went to his cell. He couldn't stand most of the cats that were housed with him. Most of them thought they were slick and that's what irked his nerve. He knew they were mainly trying to cut into him to get to know him, but he wasn't trying to make any new friends.

When the C.O. locked his door, he felt a slight bit of relief. He knew while the door was locked he was safe and could get a good night's rest.

That is, at least until the morning.

***

The vibe in Taps was off the chain. It was pure paradise to a hustler who knew how to break it off. Ass over here, titties over there. It was a sugar daddy's playground and a dopeboy's handout spot. At that very moment, a tall, light—skinned, pretty chick with thick thighs and plenty of ass was bouncing her as to Rae Sremmurd's "Throw Sum Mo," while her current customer, Money, threw some more.

Taps was not only a strip club but also a place to conduct business. A lot of drug transactions took place in Taps' parking lot and a lot of local dopeboys met there to handle their illegal business. Why? Well, the loud music gave them the opportunity of not being caught on a wire, and plus, the comfortability of seeing beautiful, half-naked women walk around kept the tension down in the club.

He had been in Taps for over an hour when he saw Q walk through the door. He was by himself as usual, which Money thought was a very good thing. There was no need in having an entourage when you were trying to conduct low-key business. He secretly admired Q's style and how he carried himself, but he wondered if it was just an act.

"What up Money! What's good?" yelled Q, as he approached Money, who was currently seated at a table enjoying a lap dance.

Money placed two $20 bills in the dancer's garter belt and lightly gave her a dismissive smack on the ass.

"I'm straight, fam, how about we head on over by the bar and grab us a drink?"

"Yeah, let's do that."

When they strolled through Taps, damn near every stripper in the club walked up to Q and gave him a hug, each whispering something in his ear before walking off. Money thought to himself, this nigga must live in this bitch the way these hoes jockin' him! For Money, this was only his third time, which was hardly enough times to remember.

"Hey Q!" shouted the sexy bartender when they approached the bar, "What can I get for you and your cute friend here?" she asked, leaning over the counter to check Money out.

"Hey Ebony. Just bring us a bottle of Ciroc, alright!" "I gotcha," she replied before walking off.

"Alright, let's get down to business," said Q, sitting at one of the bar stools. "Here!" He tossed a hard, glittery white ball in Money's lap and told him to check it out.

He picked it up, looking at it with a puzzled look on his face.

"What's this?" he asked.

"That's what you been asking for, ain't it?" he replied, looking at him suspiciously.

"This crack?" Q laughed.

"Nah fool, that's fish scale."

"Okay then, that's what's up!" he stated, still checking out the little ball.

He remembered when his brother copped some fish scale from his connect, so he already knew the quality of the dope was good.

"So, what do you want for a quarter piece of this shit?" he asked, anxious to get down to business.

"Well, I gotta get 10 for a quarter," he said, meaning $10,000.

"Damn my nigga, at least make a nigga want to come back and fuck with you!" He knew the dope was definitely worth it, but he clearly wasn't trying to pay that much. He was trying to come up, so if Q wanted his money, they were going to have to negotiate a better deal than that.

"Say homie, you ain't even spent a dime with me yet and you already complaining." Q didn't like how Money was trying to talk him down on the price. He knew the quality of his dope was good, so the thought of him even willing to do business with Money should've been taken into consideration.

"Here you go Q!" shouted Ebony, placing the bottle of Ciroc down in front of them, along with two cups.

"Here you go, ma," he said, handing her two $100 bills. "And thanks," he winked, letting her know to keep the change.

He poured himself a cup and took a sip while Money pondered on the price. He wasn't going to change it, so the next few words that came from Money's mouth better make sense or else he was gone.

"Check it out," Money leaned over towards Q so he could hear him clearly. "How about I snatch that from you for the 10 and come back in three days looking for a half at a better price? How does that sound?"

Q couldn't believe Money's nerve coming at him like that. Three days was considered excellent hustlin', especially if Money could come back with enough for a half-a-brick. Something didn't seem right, though. He knew from experience in order to move that much work and make double your money required having a top-paying clientele. Either that or Money was working for the feds. So, to be sure, he threw something out there to see if he would bite.

"Nigga, I don't care if you came back in ten minutes and got a whole block, I'm still gone charge your ass like everybody else," he stated sternly, paying close attention to his reaction.

Money looked shocked and felt disrespected. He knew right then it was time to go. For Q to come out of his mouth sideways at him had him heated, and for a split-second, he contemplated hitting him over the head with the Ciroc bottle, but instead, he kept his composure and stood up from the bar. He reached into his pocket and pulled out a wad of cash, peeling off four crisp $100 dollar bills and tossing them on the counter.

"Don't even trip big dawg, but thanks for your time, boss," he stated before walking off towards the exit.

Q remained seated at the bar replaying their conversation over in his head. He knew from his response Money was legit, because if he was working for the feds, he would have either tried to continue negotiating or paid the price he offered.

On the real, Q liked how Money was so adamant about returning for a half-a-brick. If he could flip a quarter in a day or two and make almost double, he was a hell of a hustler. So, after making sure he wasn't being set up, he grabbed the four hundred dollars off the counter and headed towards the door. He planned on catching Money in the parking lot to give him back his money so they could continue doing business.

****

Cash was already up and dressed when the C.O. unlocked his door. He had programmed himself to wake up 20 minutes before the doors popped, so when they did, he could be up and out of the way while his celly got ready.

About a month ago, he decided to take in a new celly. He knew not having one wouldn't last long, considering how they were always bringing in new people off the bus. Based on what he'd seen lately, he wasn't trying to get a weirdo as a cellmate, so after peeping out the scene in the unit and picking out the best prospect, he asked Jay from South Carolina to move in with him.

Jay and his celly weren't getting along, so Cash pulled him to the side one day and told that if he wanted to, he could move in with him. Jay was thankful and the very next day, after getting it approved by the counselor, he moved in. Jay was a laid-back type of dude who always stayed to himself. He worked in the kitchen on the p.m. shift, so Cash gave him the morning time in the cell all to himself. He knew once 12 o'clock came around, he would have his alone time in the cell, so he didn't mind giving Jay his in the morning.

Now, after a month of living with Jay, he realized it was the best move he could've ever made. Not only was Jay laid back, he was pretty cool too. All he wanted to do was work, read, and do his time, and Cash didn't see anything wrong with that.

Walking down the tier, he noticed that no one was at the computer and figured he'd hit up Jasmin. A week had passed since he had spoken to her, so after checking his email for messages, he went to the phone and called her.

The phone rang twice before she picked up. "Hello?"

"You have a call from a federal…"

"Hey boo," she sang, greeting him.

"Damn girl, you accepted that motherfucka quick," he replied.

"Boy whateva," she said, giggling because he was right.

"Ummmm hmmmmm, sounds like somebody's been waiting on daddy to call."

"And you know it," she replied in her goofiest voice.

They both laughed.

He spoke to her for 15 minutes and after telling her how much he loved her, he hung up. He finally came around to using those three words of affection, because for one, he truly meant it; and two, he knew deep down inside, she loved him too. Jasmin had been playing her part in his life since day one, and he wanted her to know she had a special place in his heart.

People were starting to come out of their cells when he noticed his celly sitting at the computer. He had forgot his ID, so he headed back up to his cell to get it before they called chow. Walking along the tier though, he felt something was wrong. The D.C. dude he got into it with last month was leaning on the rail in front of his cell, which was strange since he stayed downstairs.

Walking to his cell, Cash noticed when he raised from the rail and started walking his way. When he looked at him, he could see it written all over his face, he was up to something. Just as Cash was about to approach him, he felt two sets of hands grab him from behind. He tussled with the two dudes trying to pull him into a nearby cell. As he reached for his knife, the two dudes, who he could now see were also from D.C., kept grabbing his arms, making it impossible for him to get ahold of his weapon.

When they got him in the cell, the D.C. dude that was posted on the tier before, ran into the room and closed the door. He pulled out a knife of his own and Cash knew right then he was in a world of trouble. He was trying to break free from their grasp but was unsuccessful. Everything was looking bad and no matter how this situation turned out, Cash knew it wouldn't end well.

CHAPTER 21

SHU

"Say what?"

"He's in the SHU sir, but I cannot give you any more details…"

Money hung up the phone because he wasn't trying to hear anymore; he'd heard enough. "What the fuck is bruh on?" he said to himself. He wondered why he hadn't heard from Cash, so when he called the prison to find out, he was not pleased to hear that he was in the hole. He knew being in prison wasn't a walk in the park, but he at least figured Cash could stay out of trouble for a couple of years.

Moreover, he had other things to worry about. He'd been riding around town all day trying to gather his thoughts and come up with a new plan on how to move the dope he had. After walking out of the club that night, Q ran outside and caught up with him before he could make it to his car to continue discussing business.

Evidently, he changed his mind about the price and gave Money the respect he deserved. That respect came with a $8,800 dollar price tag, which Money thought was a hell of better start than the original $10,000 he initially offered. He even told Money if he could come back in three days with $16,000, he wouldn't see a problem with giving him half a kilogram of cocaine. Money figured that was reasonable, since the whole kilo went for $34,000.

Either way, he was definitely satisfied, because after getting it rocked up, he knew he was looking at double his money in no time.

"Hello," said Money, answering his cell phone.

"Hey young man, how's it going?" Mr. Mac greeted him.

"Oh, what's up, Mr. Mac? How's business treating you?"

"Business is fine, Money. How's your brother doing?"

"He's doing fine; I just talked to him the other day." He didn't feel there was a need to tell Mr. Mac about his brother being in the SHU, so he lied.

"That's good, that's real good, son."

He knew Mr. Mac had love for his brother because he would always call to find out how he was doing and check up on him.

"Well look, I got a few dollars over here for his commissary whenever you get a chance to come by and pick it up."

"Alright Mr. Mac, I'll be through there before you close the shop today. Is that cool with you?"

"Sure son, come on by, and don't be a stranger just because your brother is gone. Come on by and get that car detailed every now and then."

"I'll be sure to do that, Mr. Mac."

"Alright then."

"Holla," said Money, ending their call.

It was time for him to swing by the block and see how Trap and Scrappy were coming along with the work he gave them. After breaking the quarter brick between the three of them down, they had all gone their separate ways. There was no longer a trap for them to hustle out of, so they sold it the best way they knew how.

***

"Man, shawty can suck a mean dick my nigga, straight up!"

"Yeah dawg, but shit, compared to her fuck game, she killing it."

186

Cash and Joe Joe were sharing stories about when they were free. They ended up being cellies in the SHU after the melee occurred in their unit.

Turns out, when Cash was pulled into the cell, Jay witnessed the whole set up. He rushed and alerted the rest of the guys from the south about what was going on, and they ran in the cell just in time to save Cash from getting demolished. One by one, they pulled the D.C. boys out of the cell and went to work. Knives, locks, and fists was the only means of communication between the two groups determined to win the battle.

Now since it was over, he and Joe Joe were stuck sharing a cell. Most of the people involved got caught, but some got away. Cash didn't mind being in the SHU, because he was thankful to be alive. He figured as long as his time continued to roll, he was good.

"Man, I heard them Georgia Peaches be off the chain down there in the A," said Joe Joe, getting excited about the women from Georgia.

"Yeah, they alright," Cash replied, as memories of him and Peaches floated across his mind.

All of a sudden, their cell door tray flap opened.

"Yeah, what's up?" yelled Joe Joe from the top bunk.

Chow wasn't for another two hours, so it was odd for the C.O. to be opening their flap.

The C.O. tossed a brown paper bag into their cell and shut the flap back closed. That's when Cash knew what it was.

"Alright G.A., that's good lookin'," he yelled to the C.O., getting off his bunk to retrieve the package.

There was a C.O. from Georgia working in the SHU when they got back there, so after Cash found out, he made it his business to let him know they were from the same geographical region. He received a little favoritism from him every now and then, but that was pretty much it.

Cash already knew how to get contraband from general population, he just needed for someone to bring it back there to him. So, after fraternizing with the C.O. for about two weeks, he convinced him into transporting a few items to the SHU. This time when he grabbed the bag from off the floor, he saw that Migo sent him three bags of coffee.

"Say bruh," Joe Joe called him, "Who sent that one?"

"Migo," he replied, placing the three bags of coffee on their desk, next to the five they already had.

"I see why you fuck with that Mexican so tough, he a real motherfucka."

"Yeah, you see them fake ass niggas ain't sent a nigga shit back here."

"I'm tellin ya," Joe Joe agreed, getting down from off the bunk to fix himself a cup.

"Straight up bruh, that's why I stay to myself. I can't wait to get home and fuck with nothin' but bitches."

There was a long moment of silence between them after Cash's last statement. He was waiting for Joe Joe's response, but once he thought about it, he realized he wouldn't.

"Damn, my bad, my nigga," he apologized, remembering he was around someone who would never see the streets again.

"Man, I'm not trippin' on that shit," replied Joe Joe, dismissing his apology.

Joe Joe was serving two life sentences and 40 years for robbing a bank that ultimately led to him killing a pregnant woman during a high-speed chase. They gave him life for the woman and life for the fetus, leaving him with no hope of ever going home. He ended up having to plead guilty in order to escape the death penalty. He was stuck with the consequences of his actions for the rest of his life, and Cash felt sorry for him.

When they got through fixing themselves a cup of coffee, they went back to sharing their past experiences living in the streets.

***

"Oooooooh baby, that feels so good," cooed Shay, as Money continued sucking on her clit.

His head was between her thick caramel thighs, sucking away at her juicebox while her eyes rolled around in her head.

"Damn Money, what are you doing to me baby?" She tried to control herself, but he was too much for her.

Slurp…mhmmmmmm

He was enjoying every minute of eating her pussy. He had a lot of tricks up his sleeve to satisfy his woman, and the more he used them, the more she fell in love. He was stepping his game up in the lovemaking department. There was never a time when Shay was not satisfied with his tongue action, and although he didn't like to admit it, he owed it all to Shantell.

He was getting ready to turn it up a notch as he reached over and grabbed an ice cube out of the bowl on the side of the bed. He even had fruit diced up from earlier to add some sweetness to their lovemaking.

He let the ice sit in his mouth for a minute while he continued to rub her clit. When he knew it was time, he plunged back in instantly making her back arch from the cold sensation of his tongue licking the outer walls of her precious kitty.

"Sssssss—," she sighed from the unusual feeling.

"Hold on baby," he told her, getting up to change his position. "Turn around for daddy."

She turned around and positioned herself in the doggystyle position. He was turned on by the sweat glistening on her beautiful brown skin. The ice cube he was still holding in his mouth was pretty much gone, so he bent down behind her ass.

"Come on Money and stick it in," she begged, realizing he was teasing her.

"Hold on girl, be patient." He blew the cool breeze in his mouth down the crack of her ass. He smacked her on the ass, then went back to rubbing on her clit. He knew she didn't like when he teased her, but he wanted build the momentum up high enough so when she nutted it would drive her crazy.

Shay couldn't take it anymore. She reached behind her while still in doggystyle position and grabbed ahold of his wood. Stroking it a couple times to make him think she was trying to please him, she got into position and backed all the way onto it, wrapping her tight, wet walls around every inch of him.

"Mhmmmmmmm," they moaned together.

She slowly rocked back and forth, creating a nice, slow rhythm. He grabbed her hips to keep the motion going and watched as his lil man slid in and out of her pretty pink pussy. She started throwing it back, allowing him to go deeper and deeper inside her, hitting her spot.

"Whose pussy is this?" he asked, demanding an answer.

Smack!

"Yours!" she cried out in pleasure.

Smack!

"Sound off!"

"Ssssshh baby, it's yours!"!"

"Is it?" he asked, pumping harder and harder.

"Oooooh baby, I feel it," she whined, grabbing a handful of sheets for support.

"You what?"

Smack!

"I said I feel it," she said, digging her fingernails into the comforter.

"Cum then."

Smack!

"Cum for daddy.

"I feel it, baby." She grabbed ahold of his thighs. "I'm about to cum. Aaahhhhh," she screamed, rocking harder and harder, releasing her cream all over his genitals.

When she nutted, so did he, making them both gasp for air as they collapsed onto the bed. He wrapped his arms around her as they laid there, his semi-hard dick still inside her. As they laid there trying to catch their breath, they slowly closed their eyes and fell asleep.

***

A few hours later, when she awoke, she reached behind her to pull Money closer, but realized he was gone. She rolled over to the side of the bed to see if his clothes were still on the floor, but they were gone.

"God, I hate when he does that," she said to herself, disappointed he wasn't there for another round.

She knew he was probably out hustlin' and didn't really mind, but she was going to make it her business to let him know not to leave next time without letting her know.

Laying there in bed, she reminisced about their long night of pleasure. She loved Money, and after thinking about all the wonderful memories they'd acquired, she knew he was the right one for her. He treated her like a queen, and that's what she loved most about him.

She suddenly heard the phone ring.

"Ugh," she groaned, looking over at the clock, "it's too early for this shit." She reached over to the nightstand and picked up the phone.

"Hello," she answered hoarsely.

"Good morning to you too, bitch!"

She rolled her eyes at the sound of Peaches' voice. She needed some more beauty sleep before she began gossiping over the phone.

"Hey girl," she replied dryly.

"Hey hell, girl get up, 'cause I'm about to come scoop you up."

"For what?" Shay cried.

"Because we having a girls day out, that's why!"

She was too tired to get up and didn't understand why her friend was calling to go out so early. She wanted to get as much sleep as possible before her day started.

"Shay?" Peaches called her. "This bitch better not have hung up on me."

Shay had done closed her eyes and dozed back off.

"Girl, I hear you," she said, waking back up.

"You better," she replied with an attitude.

"I just feel a little sick girl, that's all. Must have been something I ate," she said, getting up to go in the bathroom.

"Yeah, Money's dick!" Peaches laughed.

"Whateva, hoe," she shot back, dismissing her comment. "When are you coming?"

"I'll be there in an hour."

"Alright, let me get ready then."

"Bye bitch."

"Bye."

She turned on the shower and looked at herself in the mirror. Her hair was all disheveled and wild-looking, but she also looked sexy. She took a few seconds to pose and admire her naked, curvaceous body. She was truly pleased with her shape, blowing herself a kiss before getting in the water.

CHAPTER 22

SWEET LICK

Months had passed since the night in the strip club, and since then, Money and Q had been doing business. Money supplied Trap and Lil Scrappy with all the cocaine they needed while making moves on his own. Because of him everybody ate, but that's because everybody knew they had a position to play. So, Money made sure he did his part and kept the drugs on deck.

When Cash got out the SHU and got his privileges back, he called Money and told him to send Jasmin out to Cali to see him. Money didn't see any problem in making that happen, and plus, he figured he could make it worth his time.

A couple of days later, he called her at work and told her to stop by Tha City to discuss something important. After being told that it involved Cash, after work she immediately headed over to the projects to meet up with him.

When she pulled onto the street where his mom lived and noticed the dudes standing on the corner by the house, she decided to drive by and see if any one of them was Money before she called him. As she was pulling up, he stepped away from the crowd, signaling for her to stop. When she did, he walked around to the passenger side and got in.

"What up J?" he greeted her, closing the door as he got in.

"What's up, *brother-in-law?" she replied smiling. "Now tell me what's going on with my baby."

"First off, pull off, 'cause we can ride and talk at the same time."

She looked behind her and noticed the line of cars beginning to form behind her, so she pulled off.

"Listen," he said, making sure he had her undivided attention. "Bruh wants me to send you on a first-class trip to California."

"What?" she replied, shocked. She couldn't believe it. She did want to see Cash but going all the way to California by herself was another thing. She had never traveled out of the state of Georgia, so to leave and go over three thousand miles away from her home was something she wasn't sure she could do.

"Don't worry about nothin'," he said, seeing her reaction, "I'm gone pay for everything first class."

"But I don't know how to get…"

He put his hand up to silence her.

"Look, whenever you can get some time off, I'm going to book you a round-trip flight and have Enterprise set you up in a car with a GPS system, so you will know where you are at all times."

"Well, why can't you go with me?" she asked, thinking how uncomfortable it would be to travel that far alone.

"J, I can't. I gotta watch the block, and plus he didn't ask for me, he asked for you." He knew that would make her feel special.

She pulled over to the side of the road so she could think. She already knew her answer, because she wanted to see Cash more than anything in the world, but she needed it to sink in a little before she spoke. It had been almost two years since they had seen each other, and that was when she attacked Peaches. They had banned both of them from coming back up there, so the opportunity to see him was overwhelming.

"Okay," she finally agreed, "but let me holla at my boss first to see when I can take off."

"Alright," he said, knowing she would go. "But check it out. I need you to take this with you." He pulled a clear plastic bag from his pocket containing 12 small balloons.

***

"Man, I feel you dawg, but damn, why all of a sudden you gotta change the spot?" asked Money.

"Because I'll feel more comfortable doing it this way," said Q.

Talking with Q over the phone, Money was trying to figure out why he was changing their meeting location. He was about to cop three bricks of cocaine and 15 pounds of weed, which was the most he had ever purchased. However, for some strange reason Q wanted to change the location of where they planned to meet.

Money wasn't feeling it, but he had to go along with it, because he and his crew needed to re—up. It was income tax time, and they weren't trying to miss out on collecting a few income tax checks. Finding another connect to supply him took time, and time wasn't something he had right now.

"Alright, my nigga," he replied, ultimately giving in, "but we can't keep doing this switch around shit, ya feel me?"

"Oh, don't worry, fam, I got everything under control. Just be there tonight at 10:30, okay?"

"Alright then, pimp. 10:30 it is."

***

Money pulled up at the meeting spot at 10:30. Q had set the time for them to be there, but from the look of it, he was going to be the one running late. Money scanned the area for any sign of an approaching vehicle, but didn't see one. He was going to give Q 15 minutes before he pulled off. He picked up the duffle bag containing the 80 thousand off the floorboard and opened it so he could quickly recount it.

He and his crew had come a long way. He knew they weren't kingpins or nothing like that, but he figured for being on their side of town at their age, and doing those kind of numbers, they were doing pretty good.

From up ahead he saw headlights coming towards him. A black Tahoe pulled up, cutting the lights off before coming to a stop. He could see Q through the front windshield, so he grabbed his pistol from under his seat and placed it on his waist as he got out. Q did good business, but Money knew you could never be too careful when dealing with dudes in the dope game.

Q exited the SUV when he saw Money get out with a duffle bag.

"Man, you got a nigga out here waiting on your ass and shit. What's up?" asked Money, giving him dap.

"Man, this stupid ass bitch wouldn't get off a nigga dick, dawg," he smiled. "You know how it is."

"Nah, not really," he replied, knowing business always came before pleasure. He thought Q knew that too. "But anyways," he continued, "where is the work, bruh?" He wasn't feeling Q's vibe and was ready to go.

"Come on over here," Q told him, walking towards the back of the truck.

As they made their way towards the back, Money was starting to get annoyed because Q kept rambling on about some chick he just met and how she could suck a dick for hours. Money had his mind on other things besides getting his dick wet and Q was making him feel uncomfortable from the way he was acting.

"Come on dawg, let's just handle this business and get the fuck outta here," Money urged, getting irritated.

"Hold your horses playboy, why you so high strung?" "Man, I got better shit to do, my nigga, that's all."

"Alright then, just be cool," he stated, bending down to open the trunk.

As soon as he did, somebody raised up from the backseat with a single-barrel sawed-off shotgun. Money never even got a chance to react as he stared down the barrel of the gun.

Boom!

A round of buck shots lifted him from the ground, jerking his body backwards as the duffle bag fell from his grasp. He flew a few yards back before hitting the pavement.

"Stupid ass young nigga," Q said to himself, walking over to pick up the duffle bag.

His partner in crime and best friend, DJ, hopped out of the back of the truck, smiling from how easy their plan was. It was a vicious set up, something they did on the regular as dopeboys slash jackboys. It was a part of their MO to trick local dopeboys into trusting them, then later on robbing them once they got their money up. Most of the time their plan worked perfectly, but this time things were a lot different.

Pop Pop Pop Pop Pop Pop

"Oh shit!" shouted Q, running to take cover behind the Tahoe as gun shots erupted around them. "Who the fuck is that?"

Pop Pop Pop Pop Pop Pop

What they failed to realize was that Money was smarter than the average dopeboy. After feeling awkward about Q switching the meeting location, he decided to bring someone along as insurance just in case things didn't turn out how they were supposed to.

Trap was laying down in the trunk of Money's car when he heard the shotgun blast. Instantly he knew it was time for him to put in some work. So, after releasing the string he held to keep the trunk door closed, he got out, clutching his AK—47 assault rifle and ran towards the front of the car, sending round after round towards the back of the SUV.

All along, Money had been prepared for the unexpected. He picked Trap up along the way to make sure the deal went smoothly.

Pop Pop Pop Pop Pop Pop

Glass shattered all over them as the truck's windows were shot out. They remained ducked off behind the truck until the opportunity came to fire back. They couldn't get a peep to see who was shooting at them, or even which direction the shots were coming from.

"Damn man, where the fuck this…"

Plow!

Q nearly jumped out of his skin when he heard the gunshot come from behind him. Frozen with fear, he witnessed DJ's brain matter ooze from his head. There was brain splatter all over him and the taillight.

While Trap kept them distracted with a hailstorm of AK rounds, Money recovered from the gunshot blast to the chest, and sneaked up behind them, placing a bullet in DJ's head. When Q looked up and saw him, he couldn't believe his eyes. Standing in front of him, wearing a bulletproof vest, Money was very much alive. Q knew at that moment he had made a mistake by not putting one in his head.

Before he could react, Money placed his Glock against his forehead and pulled the trigger, blowing Q's brains out the back of his head.

Pop Pop Pop Pop Pop Pop

"Trap!" Money yelled, trying to get his attention.

The gunfire suddenly stopped.

"Money, you alright?" he asked, creeping towards the back of the truck with his AK aimed in Money's direction.

"Yeah cuzz, I'm good." Money stood up from behind the truck and met him halfway.

Hoping the dope was there, they began searching the truck.

"Damn!" Money shouted after realizing nothing was there. "There ain't shit in this bitch!"

"I know my nigga, fuck it, let's go."

They both ran to the car and jumped in. They didn't want to be anywhere near the parking lot when the cops arrived. They could hear the police sirens approaching, so they pulled off leaving in the opposite direction, but not before splashing the Tahoe with gasoline and setting it on fire.

***

"Cashmere Lewis," the unit officer yelled, "report to visitation."

"Bout time," Cash said to himself, heading to his cell to get ready.

He was sitting in front of his cell reading a magazine as he waited on them to call him to visitation. It was Jasmin's third day coming to see him that weekend. During the first two days she snuck the weed filled balloons in through her pussy, passing them off to him when they kissed.

The guards were already aware how the inmates got drugs into the prison, but it was just the matter of catching them. Cash knew it was all about timing, skill, and technique, so he made sure Money prepared her in case anything went wrong during their visit. To make sure she was ready, he made her walk around for a couple of days with paper filled balloons in her mouth so she could get use to hiding them while she talked.

Now, since their drug smuggling was complete, it was time for them to fully enjoy each other. After being searched, he stepped into visitation and quickly scanned the room. He saw her sitting towards the back by the vending machines, so after turning in his I.D. to the officer at the front desk, he headed over to where she was seated.

"Hey babe," she greeted him with a hug and long passionate kiss.

"What's good baby, did you miss me?" he asked while they held hands.

"Boy shut up," she smiled, breaking away from their embrace. "I saw yo ass yesterday, didn't I?"

"Yeah, but shit, 24 hours is a long time to be away from someone you love," he replied sitting down across from her.

"Mhmmm hmmm," she mumbled, gazing into his eyes, "well, in that case, I did miss you. Probably more than you'll ever know."

He liked her response but was more interested in what she had on. She was rocking a pair of baby blue pumps with matching earrings, along with a skintight one-piece jean outfit that zipped up from the sides. She had gotten her hair done real nice before leaving Georgia because she knew that he wanted her to be all dolled up. She was rocking some braids but kept them tied together in the back of her head so he could see her pretty face.

"Look," she said, gesturing for him to lean in closer so she could whisper to him, "Money told me to tell you that the connect or something thought he was sweet, so he sent him down south to retire." She looked at him to see if what she had said made any sense.

He nodded his head letting her know he understood the message.

"Good lookin' out ma, but anyways," he said, changing the subject, "you looking real good today, you know that, right?"

She blushed.

"You think so baby?"

"I know so," he replied, correcting her.

As they sat there enjoying each other's company, he thought about the message his brother sent. He didn't like how Money was out there killing people, but he did understand how serious the dope game was. Knowing how it could get wicked at any time is what kept him worried. Being the oldest, he felt like he had to be the responsible one for his brother when it came down to taking care of business, but now that he was locked up, he had to take the back seat and let Money do whatever he needed to do to stay alive.

CHAPTER 23

BOUNCE BACK

Two years later, Cash was all set to go. His brother had mailed him a pair of Gucci Air Force Ones along with a Gucci outfit to wear on his release date. The time had finally come for him to leave prison and return to the streets.

Before leaving, though, he left his contact information with some of the guys he had befriended while incarcerated at Victorville. He urged them to keep in touch and stay out of trouble, but he knew the second request would fall on deaf ears.

"Say Cash, eat some pussy for me dawg!"

"Yeah, me too!"

"Me three!"

The entire unit said their goodbyes and wished him well. As he was being released from the prison the only thing running through his mind was how he was going to get to the money.

He was scheduled to take the bus back to Georgia, but after being informed it was a five-day trip, he made plans to catch a plane. He knew catching a flight back home would buy him some spare time before he reported to the halfway house.

"Alright Mr. Lewis," spoke the C.O. escorting him to the bus station, "You know the rules of your furlough. Your bus should arrive at 11:30, so make it your business to be on it." He looked at his watch before continuing. "You got about an hour before it arrives, so I suggest you sit inside until it comes."

After hearing the officer's advice, he got out of the transportation vehicle and headed over towards the entrance of the Greyhound Bus Station. He walked in and stood behind the tinted glass in the waiting area and watched as the fat, sloppy-looking officer pulled off. That was his cue to call a cab and get to the airport.

He walked to the front desk to get some change for the payphone, then walked over to the phone booth. After picking up the phonebook, he looked around and noticed how the bus station was damn near empty. There appeared to be a drunk guy sleeping on the floor, and a Hispanic woman sitting on a bench with her two children.

Looking through the phonebook, he found the number to a local taxicab company. He picked up the payphone and began dialing. After calling a cab, he tried calling Money's cell phone number.

"4...7...8...9...7..."

"Excuse me sir, are you lost or something?" He heard a female voice behind him.

When he turned around to see if she was talking to him, his face lit up with joy.

"Oh shit, girl!" he shouted in excitement, wrapping his arms around Jasmin. "You just couldn't wait for daddy could you, huh?"

They embraced for a juicy kiss.

He didn't expect to see her there waiting on him even though she had come out there several times to visit.

"Girl, you sure do know how to make a nigga day," he stated, smiling.

"Well, I try." She replied, smiling in return. "Come on." She grabbed his hand and led him outside.

As they stepped out of the bus station he saw that there was a Lincoln Navigator stretch limousine parked outside by the curb. Shocked, he looked at her and smiled.

"This for me?" he asked rhetorically.

"There's more," she said, right before the driver opened the back passenger side door.

"Surprise!" shouted his family as they all climbed out of the limo one by one.

Standing there, his world began to feel a whole lot bigger. Ms. Tina, Money, and Mercedes all ran up and gave him a hug. Reality had set in, and he was thankful to have his family there by his side.

This was his first day to a new beginning and he was ready for what came next.

***

After being home for two weeks, Cash couldn't get comfortable. He had to serve 90 days in the halfway house before he could go on home confinement and wasn't feeling that.

Although Macon's halfway house was better than most and the staff seemed nice, he wanted to be totally free to do whatever he wanted. However, he knew he had to be patient. When they allowed him and the other inmates to go look for a job, he took that as an opportunity to get away.

Every morning he received a pass to go look for work, Jasmin would be waiting around the corner for him in her car. They would spend those mornings together making love before it was her time to go to work. Then she would allow him to take her car to go look for a job but looking for employment was the last thing on his mind.

He rode through Tha City and observed the new breed of hustlas that was on the block. Taking notes, he devised a plan on how he and his crew were going to take over the neighborhood, and then the city. Money was pretty good at hustling, but to Cash, he was only making pennies compared with what he had in store for them. His focus was on meeting up with Migo, because he knew Migo was the missing piece to the puzzle. The new connect he was about to bring to the table was the answer to all of their problems and was going to make them millionaires. Cash just needed a little time to put everything together.

"Say bruh," said Cash speaking to his brother, "I got a connect in Texas that's tryin' to break us off."

"Oh yeah," replied Money, interested in what his brother had to say.

"Yeah, he gone hit us off with them thangs for 14 a piece. We just got to go and get'em ourselves, ya feel me?"

"Bruh, you know you talking about trafficking, right?" Money didn't like the idea of them transporting drugs across state lines. He knew how serious of a crime it was and wanted to make sure Cash knew too. "Dawg, you just bounced back and you mean to tell me you trying to jump out there like that?" Money paused to hit the blunt he was smoking. "Maybe you should think about this a lil' more before you make your mind up for sure," he stated, attempting to pass Cash the blunt.

"Bruh, you must be tryin' to send me back?" Cash asked him, dismissing his brother's ignorance.

"Damn, my fault, bruh," he apologized sincerely, realizing his brother still had to take piss tests.

They were parked in front of Money's house, sitting in his car. Cash had another two hours before he had to return to the halfway house, so he decided to spend it with his brother discussing their future.

As they sat there brainstorming, Cash began to grow impatient with Money. He didn't understand why his brother was so skeptical about the idea of them going to get their own cocaine. He knew at fifteen-thousand a kilogram they could see triple their money, and that's a risk he believed was worth taking. He didn't want to sell drugs for the rest of his life, so while sitting in prison, he came up with a plan to expedite the process of them becoming multi-millionaires.

He wanted to become a successful businessman his community could one day respect, love, and cherish, giving back to the community he grew up in. He wanted the next generation to have a better chance at living a good life. Everything had already been preplanned in his head, but in order for him to bring it into fruition, he had to convince Money that his vision was beneficial to all of them.

"Man, I don't know cuzz," he shook his head.

"Man, listen, I know what I am doing, fam. I just need you to follow my lead."

Money was still skeptical about the idea of them driving hundreds of miles with cocaine in a car. The farthest he'd ever traveled for some dope was to Atlanta, but now Cash wanted him to take a trip all the way to Texas.

"Why you trust this chico so much, bruh? He could be tryin' to set a nigga up. Did you ever think about that?" he added objectively.

Are you serious? Cash thought to himself.

"First off, bruh, that chico's name is Migo, and secondly, yeah I fuck with him." Cash was getting upset at how his brother was questioning him like he didn't have confidence in him or something. "Bruh, Migo held me down in there like a real nigga when I was on lock, so I trust him. Plus, the nigga even taught me Spanish dawg… comprende?" They both shared a slight laugh.

Money pondered the idea for another two minutes before responding, making sure that his answer wasn't being influenced by his high.

"Well look," he began, facing his brother, "I'm down with you on this, bruh, but when we get to Texas, I want some of them fine ass señoritas to go with them bricks, alright?"

Cash couldn't do nothing but smile. He knew his brother all too well, and if that's what it took to get him to go along with the plan, then so be it. In a couple more months they would be on their way to Texas, and then from there, to the top.

CHAPTER 24

BRICKS

"Hey girl!" shouted Peaches. "I'm glad you're here," she said, running around Mercedes' car to give her a hug.

Mercedes was accepted to Spelman after scoring a big four-teen—thirty on her SAT, putting her in the spotlight of most Ivy League schools. Her preference wasn't to attend an Ivy League school, though; she wanted to go to Spelman. So, after filling out some admission forms and receiving an academic scholarship, she was finally at the school of her dreams. She figured the best person to show her around campus and give her the rundown would be her brother's first love, so she called Peaches the moment she entered Atlanta.

"Peaches, I am so glad to be here, it's so amazing," she stated excitingly, grabbing her bags from out of the trunk.

"Well, hold your horses, because there are some rules you need to follow if you want to make it here, sweetie."

"Rules?" Mercedes exclaimed.

"Yes, rules."

Peaches was a respected member of the Alpha Phi Alpha sorority and she knew what it took to make it through college, especially when it came to dealing with the men. She knew it was her responsibility to make sure Mercedes became aware of everything that went on in college, hoping she'd catch on quick and conduct herself appropriately. Spelman was an all-girl school, but the men were not too far away from campus for her to still get involved in their foolishness.

Once they made it to Mercedes' dorm room and unpacked her belongings, Peaches sat her down for a little one-on-one girl talk.

"So, how do you like the campus so far?" asked Peaches, wanting to know if actually being on campus made the same impression on Mercedes as it did with her a few years back.

"It's nice and all, but I'm ready to party," she replied cheerfully. Peaches smiled.

"Girl, you got the wrong idea already."

"How? Don't act like you don't get your groove on up here, miss thang, cause I know. Plus, it ain't like my brother still got that thing on lock," she laughed, pointing at Peaches' pussy.

"Please don't go there," she replied, dismissing her silly statement as she got up from the bed to go look out the window.

She thought about Cash often and wondered how he was doing. She really did miss him, but there had been too much bad blood between them for her to reach out to him now. She figured he wouldn't want to talk to her anyways, since he believed she deserted him. Deep down inside though, she felt like she did, but in order for her to keep her grades up she had to put school first. She cut him off because he was putting her through an emotional rollercoaster. Her grades began to fall from losing focus, so she did what she had to do to pull them back up.

"Damn girl, you miss my brother, huh?" Mercedes asked, getting up to stand next to her.

"Yeah, but I know he probably hates me," she replied on the brink of tears.

Mercedes rubbed her back to try and comfort her. "Awww, don't worry about it girl. If it's meant to be, it will be."

Peaches nodded her head knowing there was some truth to her statement.

"Plus he's been real busy lately running around." Mercedes walked back over to the bed and sat down. "Last time I called him I think he said he was in Texas or something like that."

"He's out?" she asked surprised.

"Well, yeah," she answered, unaware that Peaches didn't know. "He's been out for almost a year.

***

"Qué tú pienses de ésto, Manny?"

(What do you think about this, Manny?)

"Yo no sé, todavía pero, parece pero que Migo confía en este Negro." (I don't know yet, but Migo seems to trust this nigger.)

"Sí, él me dijo que hicieron tiempo juntos en California, pero tú sabes como yo siento sobre esa gente."

(Yeah, he said they did time together in California, but you know how I feel about their kind.)

Cash, Money, Migo, and his uncles, Manny and Negro, were all sitting at a table discussing business. Migo's racist uncles assumed Cash didn't speak Spanish, so after talking in English for a while, Migo's uncles began speaking to each other in Spanish.

Migo knew Cash understood every word his uncles were saying, because he'd taught him how to speak and interpret Spanish. He wasn't too concerned about their disrespectful dialogue though, because he had already advised Cash how his uncles were. He knew once they approved the deal for him to do business with Cash, they would totally be out of the picture.

Cash, however, was becoming uncomfortable, and decided this would be the perfect time to reveal to Migo's uncles that he could understand every word they spoke.

"Oye Migo, por favor dirle a tus tíos que la raza y color no es tan importante," stated Cash, knowing they would understand him clearly.

(Say Migo, please inform your uncles that race and color is irrelevant when it comes to doing business.)

Migo looked at his uncles shocked faces and said, "I believe you just did, my friend."

Money was sitting their completely lost. He had no clue as to what was being said. All he knew was that there were some beautiful women at the mansion they were meeting at, and he couldn't wait to get one of them back to his hotel room.

"Motherfucker, you understood us the whole time and you didn't say a word, why?" asked Manny, upset about being caught off guard.

Cash sensed the tension in the air and said, "With all do respect Mr. Manny, I am not concerned about how you may feel about people of my color. My only concern is if we can do straight-up business, that's all."

After calming Manny down, he continued.

"I came here on account of Migo and the love and respect I have for him. He knows me personally and I think by him trusting me to do good business, I think you should have faith in his judgment that I am a good businessman."

When Manny looked at Negro for his response, he nodded his head for them to continue.

Although Cash would be directly going through Migo for the cocaine, Migo thought it would best if Cash built his own relationship with his uncles first before they proceeded to negotiate numbers. He knew after his uncles accepted Cash, his request for more cocaine would be granted with ease.

"Uncle Manny," a gorgeous Hispanic girl with hair hanging down to her voluptuous behind spoke, interrupting their conversation. "Can I drive your Maserati to the mall, because my car is still in the shop?" She looked around the table and smiled after realizing she was now the center of attention.

"Sure, Latina," he okayed, waving her off so they could resume their discussion.

Before leaving, she glanced around the table once more and locked eyes with Money. The lust she saw in his eyes turned her on. Liking what she saw, in return she decided as she turned around to walk away that she would advertise her curvaceous rear end for him, attempting to entice him into wanting her even more.

Money was mesmerized by her beauty. The way she sashayed away from the table was more than enough to convince him that he had to stick his dick in her. As he began to imagine how good it would feel to slide his manhood between her ass cheeks, Cash elbowed him, steering his attention back to their meeting.

"Okay, look," Migo finally spoke, "Cash can be our middle Georgia distributor since we already have one in Atlanta. I know he has what it takes to make us some real money, so I think we should give him a chance."

"We understand Migo that you trust this fellow, but what kind of assurance can you give us on our cocaine?" Negro asked while rubbing his chin. Cash didn't understand why they would need assurance for something he was paying for.

"Señor Negro, I'm not coming down here to get any cocaine on consignment," Cash corrected him. "I came to get ten kilos at fifteen—thousand apiece."

The uncles looked at each other and began laughing.

"Cash, we don't move anything less than a hundred units at a time," replied Manny.

Cash looked at Migo for some kind of explanation but realized after seeing the look on his face he wouldn't get one. A hundred kilos. here was no way in hell they could move that much dope in a month. He wasn't even sure if Macon consumed that much dope. He thought real hard about what his next few words would be.

"I'll tell you what," he said, quickly devising a plan, "Give me a hundred at ten-thousand apiece, and I'll have your money in a month's time."

"Hold on for a second," Money interjected, leaning over to whisper into Cash's ear. "Bruh, what the fuck are you doing?"

"Man, let me handle this, my nigga, because I know what I'm doing, alright," he replied, assuring him that everything would be okay.

Money looked at him like he was crazy. A hundred bricks was way too much dope for them to move in a month, but he decided to let Cash finish what he started. However, after their meeting, he planned on giving him his input on the deal.

"So, what do you say?" asked Cash, looking at both uncles. "Do we have a deal?"

Cash winked at Migo to let him know he had everything under control.

Manny and Negro whispered back and forth to each other for a couple of minutes before responding.

"You have a deal, Cash," Manny finally answered, reaching over the table to shake his hand.

"A deal it is," he stated, grabbing ahold of Manny's hand to seal the deal.

After a few more seconds of exchanging handshakes, they were all in agreement. Cash would report to Migo, and Migo would report to his uncles, who in return would supply them with the cocaine. Just that quickly, Cash had negotiated the deal of a lifetime. He knew instantly from this day forward their life would never be the same.

***

"Bruh," said Money, leaning his seat back in the rental Migo had got for them. "Please explain to me how we're going to move that much dope in a month?"

"Listen my nigga, at ten-thousand apiece, when bricks are going for 34, how can we go wrong?" He constantly checked the rearview mirror to see if they were being followed, because he wasn't so sure Migo's uncles wanted them to leave alive. "Plus, I already did the math. When we get back to the Mac we gone make a couple of quick flips to get our paper straight, and then in no time we'll be able to cop a 100 bricks ourselves."

Besides them having to find a way to sell all that dope, Money didn't like the fact they would be transporting so many kilos of cocaine across the United States. This was an endeavor he wasn't trying to participate in, but knew his brother was right. At ten-thousand a kilo they could become millionaires in less than six months, so why not take a chance for a short period of time to retire at a young age?

"Well, I guess since that's over we can chill now," stated Money, closing his eyes to get some rest.

"Chill!" Cash shot back, trying to understand what his brother was talking about. "Man look, we gotta start looking for buyers, my nigga, and get these fools their bread. I ain't tryin' to be fucked up with them cartel niggas over some money."

"Shit, we can't get no customers while we out here," he contested.

Cash looked at his brother and smiled.

"Yeah, I guess for once bruh you're right," he agreed.

They were on their way to the Ramada Inn to enjoy the two jacuzzi suites Migo had arranged for them. He wanted their stay in Texas to be as comfortable as possible and looked forward to showing them a good time later on that night when they attended one of the hottest strip clubs in Houston. They were going out to celebrate their new partnership.

Before leaving the mansion, Migo told Cash he would call him later that evening to discuss the details of their agreement. He apologized to Cash about being blindsided by the 100-kilo deal. Migo knew his uncles were only testing Cash, but either way, it was done. Now since they were officially working for the Cartel, it was time to go celebrate.

Cash pulled into the hotel parking lot. As they got out and headed towards the elevator that would take them to their floor, Money said, "What do you think about Latina?"

"I think," Cash said, putting emphasis on his words, "you need to stay away from her and leave her alone." Cash stopped walking, putting his hand up on Money's shoulder to stop him as well. "Bruh, stop thinking with your dick and be smart about this, okay? We don't need no bitch fucking this up for us, and I don't have time to babysit you either, so I'm gone need you to move with some sense." He then continued walking to the elevator and pressed the button.

"Nigga, I'm not thinkin' with my dick," he stated in defense as the elevator doors opened and they got on. "You didn't see how she was checking me out?"

Cash burst out laughing.

"Fool, she was only looking at your ass because you was drooling on the table like a fucking baby. She probably wanted to run in the house and get your stupid ass a baby bib," he said, still chuckling.

"Man whateva," Money replied angrily, shooting out of the elevator when it stopped on their floor. He wasn't trying to hear any more of what Cash had to say.

Cash's room was at the other end of the hallway, so when he stepped off the elevator he headed in the opposite direction, but not before shouting to his brother to be ready in a half—an—hour. Migo was going to pick them up at six—thirty, and he wasn't trying to have him waiting.

Money didn't like how his brother kept trying to boss him around. He knew what Cash was saying was right, but he just didn't like how he had to be right all the time. Messing with Latina may not be the best idea, but how would they know unless he gave it a try? He knew from the way she looked at him, she wanted him, so he wasn't imagining things.

For now, he listened to his brother, but as soon as he got a chance, he was going to find out if what she had between her legs was as good as she looked.

When Money made it to his room, he slid the room key card in the door and opened it. When he walked in and turned on the lights, he saw two completely naked Hispanic women lying in his bed. Realizing Migo had blessed him with some welcome gifts, he smiled and closed the door.

"And this nigga talkin' about not thinkin' with my dick," he said to himself, getting undressed to join the party.

CHAPTER 25

FRENEMIES

"Baby, how much longer are you gonna be gone?"

"We should be on our way back tomorrow, why?"

"Because I miss you and I want some dick, that's why."

That brought a smile to Money's face.

While Cash and Migo were enjoying themselves in the strip club, Money was in the car explaining to Shay why he hadn't returned from their business trip. He knew she missed him, because he missed her too, but for now she was going to have to be patient.

"Alright Shay, I'm gone make it my business to be back in the Mac by tomorrow, okay?"

"You promise?" she whined, thinking about how good it would feel to have him inside her.

"I promise."

"Alright then, I love you and stay safe."

"I will, and I'll see you and AJ soon," he assured her, not wanting to spend any more days away from her or their son, Armani Junior.

As soon as she hung up he got out the car and went back inside the club. Rubbing his hands together, the idea of seeing some ass clapping began to excite him.

***

"You see them over there, Cash?" asked Migo, tilting his head in the direction he wanted Cash to look.

Cash looked over to where the group of black dudes were partying and said, "Yeah, why?"

"Well, those little bitches are my frenemies, and I owe them big time." Cash nodded his head as if he understood what Migo was talking about.

From what he gathered, Migo didn't like these guys, but for what reason he didn't quite know yet. What he did now was that he was sure he was about to find out.

"You see," Migo continued, pausing to take a sip of his liquor, "before my incarceration, the one over there in the green shirt getting a lap dance was one of my local distributors."

Cash saw the dude he was referring to.

"So, what happened?" he asked, realizing Migo was going somewhere with this.

"Well, I guess when I got sent to prison, he thought his debt was clear with me or something, because he didn't pay one of my associates when I sent him to collect from that motherfucker."

Cash knew right then why their friendship had gone bad. He could tell by the look in Migo's eyes that this beef was far from over, which gave him a pretty bad feeling about how this night would turn out. So far, it was all good as they sat back, ducked off in a private booth towards the back of the club.

Earlier when Migo picked them up from the hotel, Cash was impressed. He pulled up in a stretch black Cadillac Escalade limousine sitting on some 26-inch rims. The limousine was being escorted by two regular Cadillac trucks that held armed bodyguards. Cash didn't understand the need for all the extra security, because he didn't come to Houston for trouble, but what he would soon find out is that the city had trouble of its own already brewing.

"Man, what's up?" asked Money, sitting down in the booth. He glanced around at all the half-naked women walking the floor. "Why y'all over here looking all serious and shit? Let's get some of these bitches over here," he said, unaware of the tension in the air.

When Migo looked at Cash, Cash shook his head. It never ceased to amaze him how his brother could just come into an environment without observing the scene first. He and Migo was obviously engaged in a serious conversation when he walked up, but he seemed to overlook the seriousness in their demeanor. Cash didn't like it and was about to pull him up when Migo spoke first.

"He's right," Migo agreed, ordering one of the bodyguards to go fetch them some entertainment.

The bodyguard wasn't gone 45 seconds before returning with some of the sexiest women the club had to offer. Two slid in the booth between the three of them while two others began dancing.

Cash had to admit, he was starting to enjoy himself and he saw that Migo was too, but their conversation before Money's interruption had him thinking about what Migo was saying about his so-called frenemies.

What did he have in store for them? Was he trying to tell Cash something?

He decided on letting it go for now and have fun since Migo and his brother was obviously enjoying the big titties and large asses that were shaking in their face.

***

After enjoying themselves in the club, Migo, Cash, and Money all jumped into their limousine and called it a night. They were drunk and high, and for once, Cash had a really good time.

Cash sat up in his seat and said, "Migo, I appreciate the love, homie, straight up."

Migo was too busy looking out the window to pay Cash any mind. Revenge dripped from the tip of his tongue as he waited for the action to begin. "Cash, come over here," he said, gesturing with his hand for him to come take a look.

Cash moved over next to Migo so he could look through the tinted window. "You too, Money," said Migo.

As they sat there looking, Migo started talking as if he was narrating a story.

"Sometimes my friend, when you think you're getting away, you really are just digging your grave even deeper." He pointed towards the group of dudes standing beside a candy-painted, older model car.

Looking closer, Cash noticed that the group of dudes Migo was pointing at were the same guys from inside the club, the ones he called his frenemies. He glanced over at Migo and noticed the cold stare he held.

Migo smiled as he continued talking. "You see, not everyone is loyal. Loyalty is something that should never be taken for granted because it can cost you dearly."

They were watching the group from behind the glass when one of the Cadillac trucks escorting them pulled up in front of the group. The crowd of people didn't even notice when the truck came to an abrupt halt and the doors flew open.

Pop Pop Pop Pop!

A hailstorm of gunfire erupted, causing everyone in the crowd to scatter, running for cover.

Pop Pop Pop Pop!

Cash and Money watched in shock as two of their bodyguards exited the truck with fully automatic sub—machine guns and began shooting.

The group of dudes that were once standing in front of the older model car were all laid out on the ground. They never even had a chance to run from the bullets that riddled their bodies.

Before getting back into the truck and speeding off, the bodyguards walked around to the bodies and gave each a head shot.

Cash and Money both looked over at Migo, who was now turning back around in his seat with a sinister smile on his face. Not a word was said between the three as the limousine proceeded to pull out of the club's parking lot.

CHAPTER 26

TRAFFICKING

"So, how was your trip?" asked Jasmin, walking out of the bathroom with only a towel wrapped around her.

Cash was laying down on the bed watching *Scarface* while she took a bath. When he got out of prison he moved in with her, just like they had planned when he was in California. She had moved out of her mother's house 15 months earlier and had gotten an apartment for them. She wanted Cash to come home to her every night, so she made it a priority to have him a home already established when he got out.

"I guess it was okay," he said, still thinking about the display Migo had them witness a few days ago.

"Well," she began, crawling onto the bed to cuddle up next to him, "I'm glad that you're back. Did you miss me?"

"What do you think?" he replied looking into her beautiful eyes and kissing her on the lips.

They had been up all night making love, which prevented Cash from getting any much-needed sleep. He was tired, but every time he tried to close his eyes he would think about how Migo had those dudes executed outside the club that night. He saw something in his eyes that night he'd never seen before, and it made him wonder if he had made a deal with the devil.

Was Migo really that dangerous? Or was his uncles the real driving force behind his madness?

These were questions he asked himself repeatedly. He knew from the meeting at Manny's house he could not be careless in how he conducted business with them, so as soon as they got back to Macon, he and the crew met up to discuss their next move.

In Scrappy's grandma's basement, they devised a plan to get their own places, but designated her house as their official meeting location. During the meeting they discussed how much dope they needed to move in order to pay the plug their money. They all agreed to sell each kilo for a set price, and instead of keeping all the cocaine at Scrappy's grandma's house this time, Cash came up with a better idea.

They all agreed to keep the dope at a 24-hour storage place. That way, when they needed to re—up, everyone could have easy access to it at any given time. They all liked the idea, so that's what they did.

Now, since everything was in order for him and his crew to move forward with their empire, he needed to spend time with Jasmin, because he knew when it came time to hustle, she would hardly get a chance to see him.

"Baby listen, I'm gonna be traveling back and forth to Texas once a month for now on until my business get under way. How do you feel about me not coming home some nights?"

"Baby, I'm cool with it as long as you're careful." Jasmin knew what was going on, but she trusted him enough to make decisions for the both of them. "Just promise me one thing," she said, curling up under his arms.

"Anything."

"When your business gets up and running, I want you to stop going to Texas and we start a family."

He didn't see anything wrong with that. He loved her and planned on someday marrying her, so making that small commitment to her would be nothing.

"You got it lil mama," he assured her, kissing her on the forehead before covering them both up with the blanket so they could get some sleep.

*****

2 weeks later

"Here goes your ID's and your uniforms, fellas." Migo handed Cash and his brother two fake military ID's that identified them both as privates in the U.S. Marine Corps.

They were going to be driving a Chevy Suburban loaded down with cocaine dressed as Marines. Migo thought the idea was brilliant.

At first, Cash didn't have a clue as to how they were going to traffic the 100 kilos, but after Migo called him and told him he had it under control, he relaxed. Plus, he had to admit it was a good idea. It's just, the thought of carrying a life sentence around was easier said than done.

"Where's the dope?" he asked Migo, looking through the truck's back window. From what he could see, there were only two duffle bags in the back seat, and from his years of experience with handling dope he knew 100 kilos couldn't fit in those two bags.

Migo walked to his H2 and opened the back door, pulling out a device that appeared to be a handheld video game system. He walked back over to where Cash and Money were standing and turned it on. He held the device up towards the truck as if to take a picture and that's when they saw it.

Hidden within the inner walls of the truck there were 100 kilos of cocaine neatly packed throughout the vehicle. Cash was impressed. Not only did Migo set them up with the best disguise ever, he gave them a vehicle that looked too damn good to be true.

Migo turned off the x—ray device and looked at his friend. "So, what do you think?"

Cash smiled and gave him a pat on the back, letting him know that he was pleased.

"Aye Migo," said Money walking towards the house, "I need to use the bathroom before we go. Where is it?"

"Upstairs on the right, Money, you can't miss it."

***

Entering the house through the back door, Money was surprised at how big the house was on the inside. From the outside it appeared that Migo stayed in a regular-sized, middle-class home, but as he looked around, he became even more interested in how Migo was living.

He tried remembering the instructions Migo gave him on how to find the bathroom, but realized he forgot. So, he decided to stroll around until he found one.

He walked around the kitchen and into the living room where there was marble flooring everywhere. There was black leather furniture sitting in front of a custom made fireplace and hanging from the chimney was an oval-shaped TV.

"Oh shit, this nigga got a round TV in this bitch," he said amazed as he continued walking through the house.

When he saw a staircase leading to the upstairs floor he remembered Migo saying something about going upstairs. As he walked to the top of the stairs he realized there were two hallways with plenty of doors. He didn't know which one to take, so he hurriedly picked one to walk down in search of the restroom.

Walking down the hallway, he stopped and looked at some pictures that caught his attention. There was one picture of Migo and his uncles standing side by side next to what appeared to be a black man. He wondered who the guy standing so close to them was, because the vibe he got from Migo's uncles was that they really didn't associate with black people like that. Making a mental note to run it by Cash, Money proceeded down the hallway.

The first room he passed, the door was wide-open and the room appeared empty, so he kept going. The second one he came across had the light on, but the door was closed, so he knocked on it to see if anybody would answer. He figured if it wasn't the bathroom then whoever it was that answered the door could probably point him in the right direction.

He heard some one's bare feet walking across the floor, so he stepped back and waited for them to open it. When the door swung open, a smile broke across his face. He stood there looking at the woman dressed in some pink, skintight booty shorts and a white tank top.

It was Migo's cousin, Latina.

"Yes?" she said, eyeing him suspiciously.

Money hesitated for a minute before finally speaking.

"Ummmmm, my bad, ma," he apologized, looking down at her cute, manicured feet, "I was looking for the bathroom," he said, gesturing with his hands for her to point him in the right direction.

She smiled after realizing he was the same guy from her uncle's house. She thought he was cute and was hoping she would one day get a chance to see him again.

"Yeah, it's this way," she said, stepping out of the room to show him where it was.

As she led the way, she made sure to give him a good look of her ass as she sauntered down the hall, her right and left cheek bouncing one after the other. She knew he would be looking, because there weren't too many guys from around her way that could resist staring at her perfectly round behind.

He watched her every move, and despite what Cash had told him, he had to have her. Even after advising him to stay away from her, he figured he couldn't miss out on this opportunity. He knew if he could get her on their team, then maybe she could persuade her uncles into giving them a better deal on the cocaine. It was a move he was willing to make for the team, he just hoped

Cash would eventually realize it was a good idea too. After all, if anybody could pull it off, it would definitely be him.

"There it is right there," she said, pointing at the first room at the top of the stairs. "You got it from here or do you need some help?" she asked flirtatiously.

She eyed him seductively as he walked pass her.

"Well, since you asked…" he began.

"Yo Money, hurry the fuck up man, because we about to go!"

He shook his head when he heard Cash yell from downstairs. "Alright, here I come!" he shouted back, pulling out his cell and handing it to her so she could log her number in.

He walked in the bathroom without closing the door so she could peek in.

After entering her number into his phone, she walked in the bathroom behind him. He was relieving himself as she walked in and placed the phone on the counter.

"Make sure you call me, papi," she told him, taking a quick peek at his manhood before walking out.

Once he finished, he washed his hands, grabbed his phone, and headed downstairs. He knew Cash was ready to go, so he wasn't going to hold him up any longer.

***

After ten hours of driving from Texas, they finally arrived in the Peach State. Exiting I—85, Cash stopped in a city called La-Grange, just over the Georgia state line, to get some gas. He thought it would be best if he did all the driving on the way back, because between the both of them, he knew he was the more responsible driver. Money liked to talk on the phone too much and look for women while he drove, so Cash made sure to do all the driving himself.

During half the ride back, Money was asleep, so Cash enjoyed most of the trip in peace. When he wasn't asleep, though, he played video games on his phone or texted. They only went over the plan on how to get rid of the dope once, because Cash didn't think it was necessary to try and beat it into his head how important this was. Plus, Money knew exactly what he was doing when it came to selling dope.

Money never brought up how he ran into Latina in the house earlier and got her number. He thought it would be best to leave Cash in the blind for a while, at least until he figured out how he was going to get her to become a part of their team. He was hoping once he put some dick in her life, she would be so sprung on him, she would be chasing after his dirty drawers just to get a whiff of him.

"Say bruh," said Cash, looking over at his brother, "go in and pay for the gas and bring me Crunk Juice back."

"Alright," he replied getting out of the truck.

Cash got out and pumped the gas. He looked around to see if anything looked suspicious or out of the ordinary, but everything seemed fine. He felt better knowing they were back in Georgia. From where they were it was only a two-hour drive before they reached Macon, so he relaxed a little.

His nerves had him on the edge going through the two checkpoints they had to pass in order to get out of Texas. Border Patrol dogs circled their vehicle at the checkpoints to see if they were transporting drugs or illegal immigrants across the U.S., but lucky for them, Migo was a professional when it came to wrapping cocaine.

He wrapped each kilo with five layers of his secret mustard sauce. The sauce temporarily disguised the scent of the cocaine for 72 hours, but then the rest was on them. Cash knew within three days they would have the dope broken down and ready for distribution back in Macon.

Money came out of the gas station and got back in the truck. When Cash looked at the bag in his hands he asked, "Where's my Crunk Juice?"

Money dug in the bag and pulled out a Red Bull, handing it over to him. "Bruh, they said they've never heard of a Crunk Juice."

"Man, that's crazy," Cash replied, cranking the truck up, "Let's hurry up and get the hell out of this country-ass town."

Ten minutes into the drive, he saw a sign that read, "Macon 82 miles ahead," so he leaned back and put the truck on cruise control.

***

"Got damn cuzz, this shit a lot of work," complained Lil Scrappy.

"Man listen," Cash began, getting irritated, "We're almost done, so stop bitching and take that side off so we can count these bricks." He pointed towards the side of the truck that was still intact.

For the past four hours they had been stripping off the exterior part of the truck, using screwdrivers, wrenches, and pliers to break the truck down, removing one piece at a time. They removed brick after brick of cocaine, stacking them neatly to the side of the garage so they could keep count. They were almost finished and couldn't wait to see what it felt like to be in the presence of Mexico's finest cocaine. Cash and Trap had already finished their side of the truck, so they began counting the bricks until their numbers matched.

Money and Scrappy were in the process of removing the fender wall of the truck when Cash informed them they were still eight bricks short.

"My nigga, we about to be kingpins in this bitch, you know that, right?" Trap said excited.

Cash nodded his head as he gave him some dap. "I don't know about kingpins, but millionaires for sho."

After finally stripping the truck down and removing the 100 kilos, they quickly began putting the truck back together. They needed transportation not registered to either one of them to re-locate the drugs. Instead of moving the whole 100 at one time to the storage, Cash decided it would be wise to only move a third of it just in case something went wrong.

So, once the truck was loaded down with the first 30, Cash hopped in and drove to the storage place to make the first drop. He brought Scrappy along to help him carry the dope inside so it wouldn't take that long. Trap and Money on the other hand, stayed behind to unwrap the ten they were going to keep over there to break down. Half of that was going to be cooked into crack, while the other half was going to be distributed as cocaine.

***

Over the next three weeks, Cash and his crew sold every sin-gle one of those bricks, accumulating $2.2 million in cash. They kept six—hundred thousand of it in the safe at Scrappy's grandma's, which left them with about four—hundred thousand apiece.

Times were good, and their names were beginning to ring in the streets. Their acceleration in the drug trade eventually forced them to expand their empire, so each member of the crew relocated to his own side of town. Cash and Jasmin moved to the north side, which was considered the white folks side of town. He chose that side because the crime rate was low, and since he promised her a family one day, he didn't want to raise their chil-dren in the hood.

Money remained where he was at on the west side. During his brother's incarceration, he had made a name for himself that was loved and respected on the West. Plus, he had some young soldiers under his command that worshipped the ground he walked on, so he thought it would be best to stay close to them.

Scrappy relocated to the East, while Trap moved to the South. They all had a position to play in order for them to execute their plan the way they wanted, to completely take over the city.

Since the dope was gone, Cash had to hurry up and get back to Texas so they could snatch another 100 bricks. This time though, he would be bringing 1.6 million dollars with him. A million was for Migo and his uncles, while the rest was towards another 100 bricks. Each member invested a hundred and fifty thousand apiece towards their next purchase, so when the dope made it back, they would only owe the connect $100,000 apiece. With 25 bricks, each one of them was looking at a pretty hefty profit.

"Migo," Cash said after hearing someone answer the phone.

"Hola mi amigo, qué pasa?" asked Migo.

(Hello my friend, what's good?)

"Necessito ir a recoger a las regalos para mi familia."

(I need to come down there and pick up the gifts for my family)

"Le gustaron los otros que le mande," he replied, catching onto Cash's lingo.

(Ah, so they liked the other ones I sent down there.)

"Sí, le gustaron, pero los niños lo han usado todavia. Necesito de me mandes los otros lo más pronto posible."

(Yeah, but the kids done ran through them already, so I need some more asap.)

"Cuando tengas tiempo pasa por aca que yo tengo mas disponible?"

(Well, when you get a chance, come on back down here and I'll have you some more ready, alright?")

"Ok ya voy de camino."

(Alright then homie, I'm on my way.)

"Tú dices hoy?" Migo asked, wanting to be sure.

(You mean today?)

"Sí hoy, mi hermano," Cash answered before hanging up.
(Yeah, today bruh.)

There was nothing else to be said. The city was starving and their clients were begging for some more dope, so Cash called Money and told him to get ready, because they were on their way back to Texas.

CHAPTER 27

MILITARY

"Mhummmmm Papi, where have you been all my life?" Latina moaned, rolling over in bed to cuddle up under Money.

He smiled and kissed her.

They were shacked up at the hotel, having countless hours of sex, and he couldn't get enough of the tricks Latina had under her sleeve. She sucked his dick for hours, and he didn't know if could take it anymore.

As it turned out, Migo couldn't move as fast as Cash had anticipated, so he and Money checked into the Holiday Inn Express until he could get the bricks together for them. When Cash dropped the money off, Migo assured him that within 72 hours he would have the cocaine. So, in the meantime, instead of driving back and forth from Georgia to Texas, he decided they would stay in a hotel until Migo produced the dope. That was music to Money's ears, because ever since the day he had run into Latina at Migo's house, he wanted to get back to Houston to knock her socks off. They talked over the phone on the regular, where they agreed once they had the opportunity to hook up, they would.

So, after him and his brother made it to the hotel, he checked into a room and told Cash he needed to use the car. Cash didn't mind, because he had already planned to get some much-needed sleep.

"Bruh, don't do nothing stupid," was the only thing he remembered Cash saying before giving him the car keys and going to his room.

After unpacking his stuff, he called Latina to find out if she was ready to meet up. He didn't want Cash to know they were fooling around just yet, so he instructed her to go get them a room at another hotel down the street from their hotel.

When they got there, they immediately began tearing off each other's clothes like two lovers who had been separated for years. With Latina bent over in the doggystyle position, Money drilled her from behind.

"Ahhhhhh!" she screamed from the pleasure of his dick expanding her pussy's inner wall. Digging deeper and deeper as he thrust his hips forward into her, her ass cheeks repeatedly slapped up against his thighs.

For hours they sucked and fucked each other, trying to make the other tap out. In the midst of their sexcapade, Money's phone started ringing, so he pulled his dick out of her and answered it.

"Yeah, what's up?" he answered, thinking it was Cash calling to complain about him not being back yet.

"Hey baby, are y'all on y'all way back?"

He sat upright when he heard Shay's voice on the line. He wasn't expecting her to call so soon, since he told her they were going to be gone for two days.

"Nah babe," he said, looking back at Latina as she laid there naked.

"We gotta wait a couple more days and then I'll be on my way, why? You need something?"

"No, not really, I'm just bored and miss you, that's all."

He felt bad for cheating on Shay after hearing her say that. He knew she deserved better, but right now he couldn't see passing up on such a good-looking piece of pussy.

Latina didn't appreciate the hold up. She had waited all month to get him inside her, so she didn't like how some other chick was getting in the way.

She rolled off the bed and walked around it until she was standing in front of him, giving him a clear view of her naked body.

He held his index finger up, signaling for her to give him a minute, but she wasn't trying to hear it. She kneeled down between his legs and told ahold of his semi—soft dick. Placing it into her mouth, she slowly sucked on it until it became hard. He groaned as he leaned back on the bed.

"Yeah baby, I can do that," he said, answering Shay's request to bring her back some souvenirs, "but let me get back to you boo, cause I gotta take a shower."

"Well, alright then, I love you," she sang.

"Ummmmm, I love you to," he replied.

After ten minutes of orally pleasing him, she decided to make her move. She stood up and climbed on top of him, positioning herself so she could slide down his pole. Before he could contest her jumping onto him without a condom, the warm walls of her pussy enclosed around his dick sending him straight into a state of euphoria.

Her pussy felt so good he couldn't even build up enough strength to toss her off. She continued riding him while his face made all kinds of expressions. She knew she had him right where she wanted him when she saw his eyes roll to the back of his head. Her goal was to get pregnant so they made the prettiest little baby.

As her tight pussy stroked him repeatedly, Shay's number one rule played in the back of his head, "If you fuck around on me, you better strap up." He couldn't believe he was breaking that rule. He knew fucking Latina raw was wrong, but he couldn't bring himself to end what they had going on right now.

***

When Cash awoke, he was surprised to see his brother had already made it back to the hotel. He assumed Money was going to meet up with a chick he met on social media, so he didn't have a problem with him using the car. For him though, this trip was strictly for business.

After being incarcerated for almost five years, Cash thought differently about life. He wanted to be a one-woman man, because Jasmin had proved to him that she was all the woman he could ever need. She had been down with him so long he couldn't picture himself making that kind of commitment to any other woman.

He loved her deeply, but sometimes memories of Peaches would resurface in his mind. She once played a significant role in his life and he wasn't sure if he could ever stop loving her, but one thing he knew for sure, Jasmin deserved his heart more than Peaches did.

"Hello," he answered without checking the caller I.D.

"Es la hora mi amigo," stated Migo before hanging up.

(It is time my friend)

Cash jumped up to get ready. He called Money's phone to inform him that the bird had landed, and to be ready to leave in 30 minutes.

Money wasn't ready to go, because he at least expected to spend one more day with Latina's freaky ass before they left. However, it was time to go and make some more money, and nothing was supposed to get in the way of that.

After packing everything up, they headed downstairs. As they strolled through the parking lot, Cash tossed Money the car keys.

"What you giving me these for?" he asked confused.

"What you mean? It's your turn to drive," replied Cash, getting in on the front passenger side.

Money walked around to the driver side and got in. "So, you want me to drive to Migo's house, or you want me to drive all the way back."

"Listen fam, I trust you, but if I can't trust you to drive us back safely, then there's no reason for me to fuck with you at all then, right?"

He nodded his head, agreeing with Cash 100 percent. He was just glad his big brother had finally begun to see things his way.

***

"Yeah, we should be back in Macon in 6 hours, sweetheart."

Cash talked to Jasmin over the phone while Money drove them back to Macon. He was impressed with his driving, because not one time did he turn the music up loud or check his phone. For the first couple of , they were having a good conversation about their future, but then it was temporarily put on hold when Jasmin called.

"I know, I know babe, be safe," he said, letting her know he knew to be careful.

"I love you too, later." He ended the call.

"Ahhhh, I love you too, Cash," sang Money, making fun of him.

"Shut up fool," Cash smiled.

"Man, listen, when we get back and flip these bricks, I'm gone call Migo and tell him to have another 100 on deck in two weeks."

"Yeah, cause I know once we hit the city I'm probably gone be sold out in a week."

"Damn, the west pumpin' like that?" he asked, not really convinced the west side could consume that much dope in a week.

"Shit, I got niggas coming from outside of the Mac to cop too, so…"

Whoop Whoop!

The sound of a police siren silenced them both.

Cash sat back and looked at his rear side mirror. "Is that the police?" he said more to himself than his brother. Leaning forward and checking the mirror closer, he saw that it was definitely a cop car coming up behind them, and fast. However, he couldn't tell for sure whether the cop was pursuing them or someone else.

Money clicked the turn signal to switch lanes attempting to get out of the car's path, but there was no hope. As soon as he switched lanes, so did the State Trooper, pulling up right behind them.

"Oh my God bruh, they on us," Money panicked.

Cash glanced over at him and noticed he was shaking. Sweat beads were forming on his forehead, and Cash could tell he was about to lose it.

"Bruh, be easy and don't panic," Cash told him.

"Man, Shay gone leave me my nigga if I go to jail," he complained.

Cash looked at him like he was crazy.

"Driver of the Charger, pull your vehicle over now!" The State Trooper bellowed over his bull horn.

"Man, I'm fixin' to let him feel this Hemi bruh," Money sat up straight and took off his seat belt.

"No!" shouted Cash, hoping his brother would calm down. "My nigga, pull this bitch over and chill the fuck out, cause we good, alright."

Money thought about it for a second, then decided to listen to his brother. He clicked the right-hand signal and pulled over to the side of the road with the State Trooper pulling up right behind them.

"Bruh, just remember the script and chill out, cause you acting too fucking nervous right now."

Cash saw how scared he was and started second guessing his decision allowing him to drive them back. On top of that, he had the nerve to be thinking about his bitch when there was a possibility they could be spending the rest of their lives in federal prison.

"Listen," he said, opening the glove compartment box to grab the insurance card and registration. "We good homie, just give him these and show him your military ID."

"Alright bruh," he replied, taking the documents, "but I didn't even do nothing."

"You probably was just speeding. How fast were you going?"
"I think like 88.

The speed limit was only 75, so Cash assumed that was it. He began regretting not paying attention to his brother as he talked on the phone.

The Trooper waited a good 15 minutes before exiting his vehicle. When Money realized the Trooper was a black man, he started feeling a little better, because he figured he had a better chance with a brother than with a white guy.

When the Trooper approached his door, he rolled down the window and held out his ID, insurance, and registration cards.

***

"So, what is there to do up here?" asked Mercedes.

"Listen, Mercedes," said Peaches, raising her hand to stop her from walking any further. "Girl, you gotta hold yourself down up here, otherwise Atlanta will chew you up and and spit you out if you let it."

They were walking across the school's campus, having a conversation about how Mercedes needed to conduct herself once Peaches graduated. This was her last year at Spellman, so she was going to be leaving her to fend for herself shortly. However, she vowed before leaving to give her all the tools and advice she needed in order to succeed when she was gone.

"Well," Mercedes began walking again, "I know what I want to do, so as long as you point me in the right direction, I will be good."

"Oh, I got you girl, so you ain't even got to worry about that."

They continued on up the hill until they reached their dormitory, then they parted ways. Seniors stayed on the second floor, while freshmen stayed on the sixth, so Peaches left her on the elevator when it stopped on her floor.

"Bye girl, I'll catch you later," she said, heading to her room.

"Alright then, see you later," replied Mercedes.

Peaches was in a rush, because she was having hot flashes. During their walk back from Wal—Mart, they talked about Cash, which brought back memories of when they spent time together. Throughout the walk, she reminisced on how good it felt to have his head between her thighs as he ate her pussy. The whole time Mercedes was talking, Peaches was fantasizing about her and Cash making love. As moisture began building in her panties, she felt her pussy juice dripping down her leg. On top of that, the skin-tight Spandex she wore made matters worse, because now everyone could see that she was wet.

When she made it to her room she quickly pulled out her keys and unlocked the door. Walking in, she was glad to see that her roommate was gone, so she hurried up and ran into the bathroom, closing the door behind her. She opened the cabinet under the sink and grabbed some pictures and her box of sex toys. For a minute she pondered on which toy to use, then after making up her mind, she grabbed her six-inch vibrating dildo. She had to relieve some of her hormonal stress, so she placed the pictures and the dildo on the sink and took off her pants. Then with two fingers she started probing around in her pussy. She wanted to build the momentum up, so when it came time to really go to work half of her job would already be done.

She looked at his picture and closed her eyes, imagining him touching her and playing with her pussy. She pictured him holding her from behind while he explored her most precious jewel. She deeply missed him and loved the way he use to handle her body when they made love. When she realized she was moaning, she knew then she was ready.

She grabbed the dildo with one hand, and with the other she grabbed his picture. She then proceeded to lay down on the floor so she could focus. After turning on the vibrator, she held the picture of him with no shirt on up to her face. Lusting over Cash's picture, she slowly began to insert the dildo in and out of her throbbing hot pussy.

Lying there, she used her imagination to facilitate the process of reaching an orgasm. She knew with time, she would get over losing the love of her life for her career, but for now, she was doing what it took to satisfy her desire.

***

"Son, please step out of the car for a minute," ordered the State Trooper.

Money looked at Cash for help, but the look in his eyes told him everything he needed to know; he was on his own. As Money got out of the car, Cash began to say a silent prayer for the both of them. He knew if things went bad, they were going to be in big trouble. Getting busted with 100 kilograms of cocaine was not the type of story he wanted to be on the news for. He preferred being on the news for giving back to the community, not for being recognized as a kingpin. While he sat there waiting for their fate to be determined, he too began to think about his woman.

Money and the Trooper stood face to face behind the Charger. Money looked into his eyes for a sign, but didn't see any. It was as if he was reading a blank page in a book. He had no clue what was about to happen, but if things started to go left, he was going to find out if the Trooper was trained for hand-to-hand combat.

"Now, son," the Trooper began by placing Money's military ID on the back of the trunk next to the insurance and registration cards, "you and that other boy in the car are in the military, is that correct?"

"Yes sir," he answered with no hesitation.

"So, tell me why are y'all leaving Texas again?" he asked, as if he heard him wrong the first time.

"Because we have family down in Houston, sir, and we went to visit them before reporting back to base."

"Which base?" asked the Trooper eyeing him suspiciously.

"The Marine Corp Logistics Base in Albany, Georgia, sir."

The Trooper picked up his ID and looked at it again. There was something really wrong with this picture and the trooper wasn't buying his story. The State Trooper had been in the military before and he knew what a real service member looked like, so when Money presented him with an identification that contradicted protocol for the service, he knew something wasn't right.

"Look," said the trooper, placing his hand on his firearm, "I know you are not in the military, and I'm pretty sure you boys are involved in something you shouldn't be."

Money's heart stopped. It was all over. They were going to prison forever and he would never get the chance to feel Shay the way he'd felt her so many times before. He was going to have to live without her and their child. This was turning out to be the worse day of his life.

"But I'll tell you what," he continued with a slight smirk, "we might be able to work something out."

After holding his breath for the past 30 seconds, Money exhaled.

"What… what… what do you mean?" he stuttered nervously.

"Well," he said, taking off his hat, "I have two twin boys who are about to graduate from high school, and they are both considering enlisting in the military as well. The REAL military," he stated with heavy sarcasm.

Money nodded his head for him to continue so he could get to the point.

"You see, I don't want them to, because I know how it is in the military, but they want to be able to take care of their college tuition on their own, you know, to lighten the burden on me and my wife."

Money was trying to figure him out, and the reason behind him telling him this story. Obviously, he was considering giving them a way out of the situation, but the story he was telling him seemed to be going on and on.

"What exactly can I do to make your life a little easier, sir?" he asked, getting straight to the point.

The trooper smiled, "I thought you'd never ask. I want you to go back to your friend in there and y'all put together, how you young folks say, ten bands, and bring it to me. Then, I'll send y'all on your way."

Money couldn't believe it. The trooper was as crooked as his smile, but he was glad to know that today he would not be going to jail. He held up one finger as if to say 'give me a minute,' then walked back to the car and got in.

"Bruh, listen," said Money, getting in with a smile plastered across his face. "This motherfucka said he wants ten bands and we're good."

"Say what?" replied Cash, surprised at what he was hearing.

"He said, give him ten thousand dollars and he will let us go, so give me half to put with the five I got."

They both pulled out their knots and began counting. While Cash counted out his five grand, an idea came across his mind that could possibly prevent this from ever happening again. He knew once this cop took their money, he was going to be in a position to stop them again, so before Cash gave him his money, he gave him some instructions to go along with it.

Money got out and headed back towards the trooper who held a wide grin on his face. He handed over the ten thousand in a McDonalds bag and asked the trooper a question.

"Say trooper…" he peeked at his name tag to know exactly who he was dealing with, "Stevens. How about we set up a little contract with you that will ensure future passage through this way. How does that sound?"

"Well, I see you're getting smarter by the minute, son."

For the next ten minutes they negotiated a deal for clear passage in the future. It was agreed that whenever they planned on trafficking through his state, Trooper Stevens would give them information on the best time to traffic their dope. He also agreed to provide them with secure transport through the state of Mississippi and train them on how to evade other law enforcement personnel along the way.

All he asked for in return was that he received twenty—thousand a month for his service. Money thought it was pretty fair considering the valuable information he was going to provide them with. So, they exchanged numbers and ended their conversation.

As he turned to walk away, Trooper Stevens called after him. "Mr. Lewis."

Money turned around at the call of his name, "For God's sake man, cut your hair and change those ID's. No one in the military wears dreads, and it's how I knew you were lying all along."

Money thought about it and knew instantly what he was talking about. His dreads were a dead giveaway.

CHAPTER 28

A GHOST

6 months later

"It's that time ladies and gentlemen, now coming to the stage representing that ten—a—key state, we got your boy Yooooooo Gotti!"

The DJ was making the announcement everyone was waiting for. The hip-hop artist, Yo Gotti, hit the stage to perform one of his hottest singles, "Errrbody." The atmosphere in Stacks was live. Fans from all over packed the club waiting on their chance to party with one of the rap game's realist.

Cash, Jasmin, and Shay all watched his performance from their private section in VIP while Money stood behind Gotti on stage as part of his entourage. He was up there supporting the 75-thousand-dollar investment he put into bringing the rapper to the city. Lately, promoting shows had become one of his most lucrative hobbies, and it was something he really enjoyed. He was beginning to develop a reputation throughout the music industry as the go to guy for artists who wanted exposure. His entertainment company TBD, To Be Determined, was taking off, and if everything continued to go right, he planned to bring home some of the biggest stars to bless the music industry. Nodding his head back and forth to the music, he took in the scene and realized he was in his mode.

"This is where it's at, y'all. Mac—Town, let's keep this thang crunk!"

the DJ shouted over the club's massive speakers, playing another one of Gotti's tracks.

Cash was on cloud nine and didn't want to come down. He had been smoking some chronic he got from Migo the last time they traveled to Texas. Over time, the trip back and forth got easier and easier, so Cash didn't see how they could be stopped.

Trooper Stevens held up his end of the agreement and supplied them with all the help he could. He even persuaded a few more troopers from other states to participate. Although it cost him and his crew more money, it felt good to know that their dope was secured by the best insurance company in the U.S.; the State Patrol Office.

While partying with his girl and his brother's fiancée, Cash finally realized they were on top of the world. They had acquired a level of success beyond their wildest dreams. They were millionaires, and Cash and his crew were the people to see when it came to getting dope in the state of Georgia. Their empire had gotten so large it expanded across Georgia into counties as far as Bryan County, right outside of Savannah. They had come a long way, but in the back of his mind Cash was feeling like they were doing too much. He knew the history of the dope game, and he knew their time would be limited at the top if they didn't diversify, so he started thinking about an exit strategy that would secure their future without it being in a grave or a jail cell.

"Cash!"

"What's up?" he replied after hearing Shay call him.

"Can we go backstage after this and meet him?"

"Yeah babe, I want to meet him too," Jasmin chimed in.

Cash smiled.

"Man, y'all can do whatever y'all want to do with them around y'all necks," he said, pointing to the Gotti staff passes they were wearing.

He knew they enjoyed being around celebrities just as much as he did. With these new social media sites blossoming, he expected to see them posting selfies with Gotti tomorrow. He had a few of his own on there, but he was beginning to get tired of flaunting his affluent lifestyle for the world to see, especially since his perspective on success had changed. He was ready to move on and leave the dope game alone, but first he had to decide who he was going to trust with the connect.

Scrappy and Trap were both doing their own thing. Scrappy opened up a chain of soul food restaurants that was inspired by his grandmother's cooking. When Ms. Scott found out that her son was becoming wealthy selling drugs, she immediately made him invest his money into something legit to cover up his illegal activity. Trap, on the other hand, was more into putting his money back into the streets. He opened a few barbershops and detail shops to employ his family and friends. He wanted everyone a part of the struggle to eat, so he provided small businesses to the community allowing everyone he knew a chance at receiving a slice of the American Pie.

Cash knew he had to do something, but instead of dwelling on it at this moment, he decided to let it go and have fun.

"Y'all want to go downstairs and dance or do y'all just want to continue standing here looking beautiful?"

They both chuckled at his compliment.

"Come on baby," said Jasmin, grabbing his hand and leading the way.

He admired how good she looked in the La'Quan Smith dress that hugged her curvaceous body from all angles. Her blue Tom Ford boots matched her earrings and lipstick, making her look like the Queen of the Nile. He watched her backside as she led the way down to the dance floor. Her dress kept trying to reveal her round ass, so she constantly pulled it down to avoid exposing her assets.

When they made it downstairs, some of the guys from Gotti's entourage immediately left the stage area and began following them. Money had it arranged that nobody was to get too close to Gotti while he performed and nobody was to mess with his family. He hired additional help to ensure that if anything popped off, the odds would definitely be in their favor.

Jasmin grabbed ahold of Cash's hands and wrapped them around her as she swayed her hips from side to side. She grinded and whined her body to the rhythm of the beat. She enjoyed dancing with him because of their emotional attachment. She got turned on after noticing how everyone's attention was on them and not Gotti.

Cash was high and in the zone. As Jasmin nearly made love to him on the dance floor, he looked around the club, observing his surroundings. He knew he stuck out like a sore thumb in the crowd, especially since he was wearing a fifty—thousand-dollar chain. The fifteen—thousand-dollar white gold Cuban Link necklace he wore around his neck held a thirty—five-thousand-dollar charm that was the outline of Georgia. Eighty baguettes sat in the outline of the custom-made piece. Plus, on top of that, he was sporting a Gucci outfit costing more than a couple of the cars in the parking lot. With all that glitter and bling, he was considered someone of a higher class, but that didn't mean he was immune from getting jacked.

While they continued dancing, he glanced around to see if there were any familiar faces watching them. In the midst looking he stopped and locked eyes with a pretty face standing off to the side of the wall near the bathroom. His vision was a little blurred from being intoxicated, but as he focused, he slowly began to recognize the face that was obviously staring back at him.

"Peaches," he whispered to himself, not really sure if his eyes were deceiving him. He rubbed them in an attempt to clear his vision, but by the time he looked back over towards the wall, she was gone. It was like he had seen a ghost, but there was no mistake in what he saw. Peaches was definitely in the building.

"What's wrong babe?" asked Jasmin, looking concerned. She knew something had caught his attention because his hands had stopped caressing her body.

"It's nothin, ma," he replied, kissing her on the lips. "Why don't you and Shay go on backstage until the show is over."

He quickly glanced at his watch and saw it was two—thirty.

"The show should be over in about ten more minutes, because bruh said he was supposed to perform for a lil over half—an—hour."

Reluctant at first, because she felt something was wrong, but already knowing he could handle himself, she decided to comply with his request.

"Alright, but make sure you grab us a bottle from the bar before you come back there, because I want us to continue this dance when we get home," she stated seductively, reaching behind him to grab his ass.

He jumped from the awkward feeling and smiled.

"Girl, you better stop playing."

She grabbed ahold of Shay's hand and headed off towards the backstage entrance.

Cash ordered the guys with them to watch over the girls. He personally didn't feel the need for any security in a club where at least a hundred members from their crew roamed around. If somebody ultimately decided that tonight would be their night to die, he didn't see a problem with granting them that wish.

When he saw the girls walk through the backstage door, he knew they were safe and out of sight. So, he headed over to the bar to grab a bottle of Ace of Spades for later. He knew when Jasmin got drunk she got freaky, so he was going to make sure he got her exactly what she wanted before the night was over.

While standing at the bar waiting on the bartender to serve him, he felt someone tap his shoulder. When he turned around to see who it was, there she stood looking as good as ever. It was the ghost he had seen earlier.

Peaches.

***

"Man, what the fuck is bruh doing?" Money said to himself as he watched his brother walk towards the bar. He had given specific orders for two members of his entourage to watch over him, but from what he could see they were nowhere in sight.

Even though their crew were scattered throughout the whole club, with the capacity of people stretching over two—thousand it wouldn't be too hard for someone to go for Cash's chain, then duck back off into the crowd. He walked over and instructed two more of the bodyguards on stage to go over by the bar to watch his brother's back. Never taking his eyes off Cash, he stayed posted on stage behind Gotti until the show was over.

***

"Hey handsome," Peaches greeted him.

"Hay is for horses, remember?" he stated with sarcasm before turning around to face her.

She sensed the tension between them and assumed he wasn't too pleased to see her. He was definitely not the man she knew many years ago. This new person looked at her differently than the man she once loved. As she looked into his eyes, she felt like she was looking into an empty freezer in the projects. The sparks and flames that were once there when he used to look at her were gone and she could do nothing but blame herself. She had caused him to be so cold, and for the hundredth time in her life she regretted leaving him like that. She traded the love of her life for a career that she wasn't sure would make her happy, and now she had to sit back and watch as he loved someone else.

"Ummmmm, I saw you over there earlier dancing with your girl and I didn't want to interrupt," she said, attempting to start a conversation.

"Well, I'm glad you didn't," he replied, cutting her off.

She glanced down at her shoes to avoid eye contact with him, because she didn't know what else to say. He was brushing her off, which made her feel stupid for even approaching him. She desperately wanted to hear him say he missed her and still loved her, but she knew that would never happen. He had a new woman in his life, and from the look of it, she had complete control over his heart. So, she decided instead of further humiliating herself, she would just turn around and walk away.

Before she could get away, though, he reached out and grabbed ahold of her wrist.

"Where are you going, ma?" he asked, not wanting her to leave just yet.

"I don't know what to say to you anymore, because I know you hate me," she admitted on the brink of tears.

Cash had to admit, no matter how hard he tried to disconnect himself from her, he couldn't. He still didn't like to see her cry. He had once loved her with all of his heart, and now that she was back in his presence, those same feelings began to resurface.

"Check it out," he said, removing his hand from her wrist to place under her chin, so she could look him in the eyes. "How about we sit over here and have a drink, you know, to catch up on the good times." He ushered her over to the barstool next to his.

She smiled, accepting his invitation.

He waved for the beautiful bartender to come back over and take their order.

"Excuse me, could you give the lady here whatever she wants, and bring me a Goose and cranberry, hold the rocks."

"Sure," the bartender replied, taking Peaches' order before rushing off to get them their drinks.

He placed the bottle of Ace down in front of him and sat down beside her. They stared at each other for a minute before he complimented her on how stunning she looked. She had her hair done in a bob with two bangs and was dressed in a sexy two-piece leather skirt suit. She had really blossomed since the last time he saw her. He noticed how she had picked up a few pounds in all the right places too.

"So," he started off, "what are you doing here?"

She didn't want to begin lying to him since she knew it wouldn't do any good, so she told him the truth.

"Shay told me you would be here, and I wanted to see you," she answered truthfully.

Ain't this a bitch, he thought to himself. It had slipped his mind how close Shay and Peaches were, now realizing where Shay's loyalty remained.

The bartender interrupted their conversation for a moment to serve them their drinks.

"That'll be $16.80, sir."

Cash pulled out a wad of money and handed her a hundred-dollar bill. "Keep the change," he told her, grabbing his drink and taking a gulp.

"Why do you want to see me after all this time?" he asked, suspicious of her intentions.

"Why not?" she replied, gazing into his eyes, "I really do love you Cash and I can't stop thinking about you, no matter what I try to do. I'm sorry for leaving you like that, I just didn't—"

He stood up, cutting her off.

"Listen, I ain't mad at you, shawty, but for you to sit up here and say you love me don't mean squat shit to me anymore."

She looked away to conceal her hurt. She knew he had a good reason for feeling the way that he did, and she couldn't blame him. She left him in prison with no kind of support and there was no excuse for her actions. She chose to pursue her career over her heart, and now she had to pay the consequences.

"Cash, I'm sorry," she apologized, begging for forgiveness.

"I am too," he said before kissing her on the cheek and walking off. He couldn't stay any longer. Hearing her confess her love for him made him feel awkward, and he wasn't about to allow his emotions to reveal how he felt in the club. The truth was he still had feelings for her, but to jeopardize what he had going on with Jasmin was just not worth it.

Yo Gotti's performance was over, and he and his entourage were leaving the stage. When Cash began heading over towards the backstage door he saw Jasmin standing there with Shay outside the door. From reading the look on Jasmin's face he could tell that she had seen it all.

CHAPTER 29

A SILENT PRAYER

The next morning, after going home and fighting with Jasmin about why he was at the bar with Peaches, Cash went out for a ride to clear his head. He felt bad about the whole thing but tried convincing her that the whole encounter between them was innocent. Deep down inside though, he knew he still had feelings for Peaches, but he wasn't trying to rekindle anything between them. At one point in time, he had thought they were the perfect couple, but that was over and he wasn't going to lose Jasmin over something that no longer existed.

Jasmin meant the world to him and he wouldn't trade her for all the riches in it. When they made love, it was as if the heavens opened up for him, allowing him to have his very own angel. She was there for him when he was locked up in YDC, she was there for him when the feds shipped him way out to California, so he'd be damned if she wasn't going to be there when it was time for him to ask for her hand in marriage.

So, after riding around town for two hours, he stopped by Kay Jewelers to check out a few engagement rings. If he wanted to keep Jasmin on his team and let her know how much he loved her, he was going to have to make a real statement. The six—and—a—half carat ruby diamond he was staring at convinced him that it was time. It was time for him to make up for all of his mistakes and set things right for a change. He wanted to change Jasmin's last name from Myers to Lewis and give her the life she rightly deserved. He promised her they would settle down and start a family, and now he was finally ready to fulfill that promise.

As the saleswoman handed him his receipt, she said, "I see there's going to be one lucky lady tonight."

"More like a lucky man," he replied, taking the bag that contained the two—hundred-thousand-dollar engagement ring out of her hands.

"Huh, ain't that a shame," she replied, disgusted.

Noticing the unpleasant look on her face, he realized she had misunderstood him.

"Say ma, you got me twisted," he began, making sure she understood him clearly this time. "I'm the lucky man, not her," he corrected.

She smiled, thankful that a man as fine as him didn't sword fight.

Cash walked out of the jewelry store and headed towards his car. He planned on making Jasmin the happiest woman alive after he purchased this last shipment from Migo.

***

"Excuse me nurse," said Money, trying to get the physician's attention.

He was at the doctor's office trying to get his test results back, so he could show Shay he was in perfectly good shape. She had instructed him to go take a physical at the local clinic before they got married, because she wanted them to get a family life insurance plan.

At first, he was suspicious of her intentions because he thought a life insurance plan wasn't needed. His family had no history of having any kind of genetic diseases, so he didn't think they needed one, but after speaking with her about it and realizing how beneficial it would be to their family, he agreed. He knew the position he played in the dope game, and figured if anything were to happen to him, he would want his family to have financial support when he was gone.

"Say, excuse me, nurse," he raised his tone. This time one of the receptionists came from behind one of the partitions to address him.

"Yes sir, how can I help you?" she asked with a bright smile.

"Ummmm look, I came down here to find out the results of my bloodwork."

"And your name is?" she replied, logging onto the computer.

"Armani Lewis."

As she typed his name into the computer, he took in her appearance. She was a cute sister with full, pouted lips and a nice set of titties. She had a decent-looking face, and from what he could see, her scrubs fit her well. He thought about asking for her number, but quickly dismissed the idea. He was marrying the love of his life in one month and still had problems being faithful. He told himself that once he said, "I do," everything else was out the door. The girl he had in Alabama, the one in Mississippi, and the twins he adored from Baton Rouge would all have to go. He planned on being a one-woman man. However, when it came to Latina, he wasn't so sure if she was willing to let him go.

His only interest in Latina was sex. It appeared lately though that her feelings were beginning to make her a little clingy. She even had the nerve to ask him if he would take her back to Georgia with him, which was definitely not going to happen. After telling her it wouldn't be a good idea, all hell broke loose. That's when he realized it was time to cut her off.

He was just waiting on their next trip to Texas to tell her face to face.

"Mr. Lewis." The receptionist called his name.

He looked up from staring at her cleavage. "Yeah?"

"Could I please see your ID?"

He pulled out his wallet and retrieved his ID, handing it to her. After verifying his identity, she told him to please wait for his name to be called.

Money went over to one of the couches in the mid—size office and sat down. As he waited for his name to be called to see the doctor, he grabbed an up—to—date *Vibe* magazine from off the table in front of him and began scanning through it. There was an article inside about successful marriages that caught his attention, so he sat back and began reading.

***

"So, you tryin' to tell us you're out of the game for good?" Trap asked, not wanting to believe what he was hearing.

"Yeah, that's basically it, bruh," Cash replied.

"Man, this some bullshit, Cash," Lil Scrappy complained, clearly upset.

They were having a meeting in the Waffle House's parking lot to discuss their empire's future. Cash had just dropped the bombshell that he was leaving the drug game for good, and from the look of it, it wasn't sitting too well with the guys who had been with him from the beginning.

They didn't understand why he wanted to quit. They were family, and in their eyes family never quit on family. They had been through so much together as a team; for Cash to just up and quit on them made it seem like he wasn't part of their team. However, they knew deep down inside he loved them, and even though he wanted out, he would always be there for them if they needed him.

After a brief silence between them, Trap approached Cash and gave him a hug.

"We always gone be family, my nigga, no matter what," he stated before breaking their embrace.

"That's what's up, my nigga," replied Cash, looking over at Scrappy, who had his back turned towards him.

Lil Scrappy was still trying to get it to register in his mind why this was happening? Was Cash scared? Or was he just pussy whipped? He couldn't figure it out. To have so much love and respect in the city you grew up in, it seemed crazy to just all of sudden give it all up. They had been through a lot to get where they were. Murder. Robbery. Extortion. Trafficking. Those were just some of the crimes they had committed in order to reach their level of success. So, for Cash to say he was giving it all up to live a square lifestyle was beyond Lil Scrappy's comprehension, but he ultimately knew he could never turn his back on Cash.

He turned around to face his friend.

"I don't know why you gone leave all this behind," he said, gesturing with his hands for him to look around at their exotic cars, "but I got your back homie. Even if you want to suit and tie this thang on out, alright."

They embraced for a moment showing each other there was no love lost between them, and then walked into the Waffle House to have lunch.

***

Stepping through the door, the doctor called his name. "Armani Lewis!"

Money had fallen asleep waiting for them to call him. The streets were weighing in on him so much, whenever he got a chance to sit down and relax, he would fall asleep. The clinic's quiet, serene atmosphere wouldn't allow his body to resist the urge to shut down. Once he heard his name being called though, he got up and walked over towards the doctor.

The doctor held the side door open for Money as he ushered him in.

"What's up doc?" he greeted him.

"The usual, Mr. Lewis, and yourself?" he asked in return, leading the way towards his office.

"Man, you know how it is. Just ready to make my fiancée proud."

"If only you knew, the doctor thought to himself."

They entered the examination room, where numerous pictures on the wall displayed the human anatomy. In the corner of the room a laptop sat on top of a desk. Money saw there were chairs on both side of the desk, so he sat down in the one reserved for the patient. Looking around, observing the room he noticed how clean and neat his office was. Last time he came, he sat on the examination bed while the doctor gave him a fullbody physical. This time he didn't even go near the long bed covered in wax paper, because he was only there for his results.

As they sat there, he waited on the doctor to finish reviewing his file. After flipping through a few pages, he laid the file down on the desk and looked into Money's eyes. The news he had for him was not going to be easy for him to convey. It was the part of his job he really didn't enjoy, but it was what he was trained to do.

"Mr. Lewis," he took his glasses off to message the bridge of his nose, "I have some disturbing news about your results."

Money looked at him, confused. "What are you talking about?"

"Your white T—cells are very low and some of them look abnormal." He paused for a minute to see if he could see if anything he was saying was registering, but from the lost look on his face, he could tell that Money didn't have a clue. "Now, I plan on doing some further testing to be sure, but—"

"Man, just spit it out," Money replied, beginning to feel nervous.

"Armani, your results indicate that you have HIV."

Money just sat there with a blank expression on his face. Looking into the doctor's eyes hoping that this was just one of the sick jokes he played on people about to get married. The letters he just used to describe Money's health had to be wrong.

There was no way in hell he could have HIV. He was in complete denial, and to him, the doctor was lying.

"D...D...D...Doc, I...I...th-th-think I heard you wrong or something. Please say that again," he stuttered, trying to make sure that he heard him accurately.

"Mr. Lewis," the doctor began, but was cut short.

"I said, say it again!" Money demanded forcefully, shaking from paranoia.

"You have HIV."

He definitely heard him right the first time. As he leaned back in his chair, he slowly closed his eyes. The room was starting to feel small, and he felt alone. His whole life flashed before his eyes. He had done so much in his life to be so young but felt like everything was now coming to an end too early. There would be no extravagant wedding to the woman of his dreams, because he was a walking dead man.

The doctor remained silent, giving him a chance to digest the information. He knew it was a lot to handle, so he gave him time to regain his composure. So far, he thought Money was taking it well compared to some of his other patients, who would cry and get hysterical. Money just sat there with his eyes shut tight, as if he were trying to figure out his next move.

He was right. Money was trying to figure out his next move, but first he needed to figure out who gave him such a dreaded disease. He knew for a fact it wasn't Shay, because she had gotten her results back two weeks ago and she was in perfectly good health. So, he replayed through his mind the many nights he engaged in unprotected sex, and there was only one name that came to his mind. Latina. Besides Shay, she was the only other person he had sex with without a rubber, and in his book that made her guilty.

"Mr. Lewis," the doctor's voice snapped him back to reality. When he opened his eyes, the doctor immediately felt uncomfortable. He didn't know what else to say, because he was afraid of what Money might do. His eyes were red like fire and the look on his face said murder. The doctor looked down at his keyboard to avoid Money's penetrating stare. After a few seconds, he noticed him get up and walk out of his office without saying a word. Usually, he would recommend for the patient to see a psychologist, but in this case, he assumed it wouldn't be necessary. Money's eyes told him everything he needed to know. Someone would die soon, and while he sat there glad that it wasn't him, he bowed his head and said a silent prayer for whoever it was about to feel Money's wrath.

CHAPTER 30

LATINA

"Bruh, is you alright?" Cash asked Money, noticing how quiet he was.

They were on their way to Texas to pick up some more cocaine and Cash couldn't figure out what was wrong with him. For the past few weeks, he had noticed a change in Money's behavior, but he assumed it had something to do with his upcoming wedding.

Cash was really proud of him for stepping up to the plate and making Shay his wife. He had known him to be a player most of his life, but who was he to judge someone else. If his brother could settle down and wife him one, then so could he.

"Do you hear me my nigga, or are you going deaf?"

Money turned his head to look him in the eyes. He had no words for Cash, because his heart wouldn't allow him to speak. It was as if his mute button had been turned on or something.

As Cash continued driving, Money just stared out of the window, watching the trees pass them by. It felt like everything in the world was passing him by, leaving him stuck in his own misery. Why would Latina do him like this? Was she so messed up in the head that she had to infect him with the worst virus known to mankind? Did she even know she had it?

At this point, it didn't even matter, because she could never take back what she had done to him. He was a dead man, because if the disease didn't kill him, Shay would.

Cash arranged with Migo's uncles for Money to take over the business, but he didn't care about that anymore. There was no hope for him and the future of their empire. It had all gone up in smoke when he disobeyed Shay's number one rule not to have sex without protection. He was going to pay the price for his mistake, but not before Latina paid hers.

Cash peered over at his brother and wondered what had him in such a messed-up mood. He decided to leave him alone for now though, because obviously he had something else going on. He knew how the street life could weigh-in on a person at times, so he hoped Money wouldn't allow it to affect the business they had going on. He needed him to be on his game when they made it to Texas, because to be officially over with the drug business was frowned upon by the cartel, especially at the level they were involved.

Cash knew a lot and to know that much about a major drug supplier without actually participating raised red flags. If Cash's intuition served him right, Migo's uncles would definitely have a problem with him leaving the drug game alone. He figured with a little bit of Migo's help, he could convince them that things would stay the same, allowing him to walk away a free man, free from trafficking charges, and free from ever going back to prison. That's what he wanted because he promised Jasmin he would live a criminal—free lifestyle. Cash just hoped that Migo's uncles would decide to let him live to fulfill that promise.

***

"What do you mean you want out?" asked Manny, with a blank expression on his face.

Cash knew Manny understood exactly what he was saying; he just wanted him to repeat himself. They were all sitting along the side of Manny's pool discussing how Cash wanted to hand all authority over to his brother. He had already mentioned it to Migo weeks prior to this meeting, but Migo told him, before it could be finalized, he would have to get his uncles' permission as well. Migo knew how his uncles were, and for someone to just up and leave without being in a pine box or barrel was something they were definitely not used to. However, since Cash had brought them so much money in the past year, he believed he had a good chance of walking away alive.

"Manny," said Cash, taking his time to choose his words wisely, "I want to raise a family and I promised my fiancée—"

"Fiancée!" Negro interrupted, now realizing that Cash was about to get married.

"When were you planning on telling us this?" asked Manny, with a slight smirk.

"I was going to surprise y'all with invitations, but obviously I spilled the beans a little early, huh," he stated with a chuckle.

"Well, I'll be damned," Manny replied, waving his arm for one of the girls standing by the pool to come to their table.

A sexy young Hispanic girl wearing a bikini strolled over to where they were seated. She had a pretty face that reminded Cash of the famous, deceased singer, Sabrina.

"Sí, Papi!"

Manny spoke to her in Spanish, requesting that she go in the house and grab them a bottle of champagne. Cash hoped the bottle was for them to celebrate his upcoming marriage and not his death. It was hard for him to read Manny sometimes because he never showed any emotion. Negro, on the other hand, was always emotional, wearing his true feelings on his shoulder.

As they sat there waiting on her to return, Migo decided to join the conversation to help Cash out.

"Uncle Manny, you trust me, right?" Migo asked his uncle.

Manny took his eyes off Cash and looked over at his nephew.

"Migo, the matter is not trust here, it's the way we do things. To allow him to walk away after knowing so much about us and our organization is unacceptable."

"But he's not completely walking away. His brother will be our man for Central Georgia, and plus we cannot pass this up. Have you reviewed the books lately?"

Manny raised his hand to silence Migo. The Hispanic girl was coming back over to their table with their bottle of champagne and five empty glasses. After she poured the champagne in each one of their glasses, Manny ordered for her to leave.

"Gracias, Madellina, you can go."

She glanced around the table and smiled, glad that she could play a part in their meeting. Once she walked away, Migo resumed the conversation.

"Like I was saying, we will still have a connection down there, and if anything were to go wrong, we could still go to Cash if we needed to."

Cash didn't want to be held accountable for anything dealing with drugs, so for Migo to say that caught him off guard. He didn't fully agree to what he was saying, but he knew Migo knew what he was doing.

The table was quiet for a moment.

Manny sat in his chair with his excellent poker face as usual. He knew Migo was right. Because of Cash they had a networking system that spanned across four states: Louisiana, Mississippi, Alabama, and Georgia. All of the state patrol officers Cash had in his pocket would surely go along with the deal. It was too much to lose and Manny was not in favor of losses.

He leaned over towards Negro and whispered something in his ear. After whispering back and forth to each other for a few seconds, their eyes circled the table and landed on Money.

During the whole meeting, he had sat there without saying a word. It was usual for him to remain silent while they discussed business but considering the fact that he played a significant role in this whole deal, it was time for them to ask for his input.

"So, how do you feel about this?" Manny asked Money.

Everyone looked at him, awaiting his response. He already knew it really didn't matter what he thought, because he was only there to agree with Cash. Whatever Cash wanted, that's what he wanted, because right now his opinion or life didn't even matter.

"Man, whatever you're expecting from Cash, you can expect that from me," he replied, supporting his brother 100 percent.

Cash smiled at his brother's arrogance. He knew Money was completely capable of handling the connect. He had the city behind him and all of his soldiers loved him.

As Money sat there taking in the stares from Migo's uncles, his phone beeped. He removed it from his belt clip and read the message he had from Latina. His blood began boiling at the sight of her name.

Before coming to Texas, he had texted her to meet up, so they could have some private time before he left. Now, as he sat at the table with her kin, he thought about how he was going to teach her a lesson.

When he read the text, it said for him to meet her at the Marriot in an hour. He was definitely going to be there, but first he had to make sure that everyone was cool with his brother falling back.

After hearing Money say that he could run the business just as Cash did, Manny stood up and handed each one of them a glass of champagne. He was willing to give Money a chance to continue doing business with them as long as Cash wasn't too far away. He knew that if anything went wrong in the course of them doing business with Money, they would kill them both.

"Let's make a toast, gentlemen," announced Manny, raising his glass.

Everyone stood up to join him in a toast.

"To Cash and his marriage, and our new number one distributor for the central Georgia area." They all tapped glasses and took a sip.

Money was in no mood to celebrate. He had other things to take care of. His mind wasn't on moving up in the criminal world because he was no longer concerned about power. His only concern right now was to seek revenge.

***

After the meeting at Manny's mansion, Money asked Migo if he could borrow his Maserati to go out and handle some business.

"Sure, just make sure you bring it back in one piece," he joked, winking his eye and passing him the keys.

"Don't even sweat it, playboy. I gotcha."

Money hopped into the car and sped off. He knew for the next couple of hours they would be busy loading the car, getting it ready for transportation. He knew that what he was about to do could get them all killed, but he didn't care. His heart was filled with rage, and he needed something to give him some relief.

***

After 25 minutes of weaving through traffic, he pulled into the Marriot's parking lot in search of Latina's car. When he saw her plum-colored Benz parked in the back of the hotel, he drove around to the front and parked just in case he needed to make a quick getaway. As he got out, he checked the text message again to make sure he had the right room number. The text said that she was in room 222, so he walked to the elevator and pressed the call button to go upstairs to the second floor. When the elevator door finally opened, there she stood with the hotel's ice bucket in her hands.

Money wasn't expecting to see her outside the room, but before he could utter a word, she lunged out the elevator and wrapped her arms around him. She placed her lips on his attempting to kiss him, but he just stood there paralyzed by anger. He wanted to wrap his hands around her neck and choke the life out of her right there on the ground floor, but he knew that wouldn't be wise. He wanted her to pay the ultimate price for destroying his life, but he knew he had to play things out smart, especially since he still wanted to see Shay and his child again.

She tried sticking her tongue in his mouth, but he wouldn't allow it.

He knew his hatred for her would probably make him bite her tongue off.

Sensing that something was wrong, she pulled back and looked at him. The hairs on the back of her neck stood up as she looked into his soulless eyes.

"Papi, what's wrong?" she asked, feeling something wasn't right.

He held an expression on his face that she had never seen before. Money was not the same person she remembered from the last time they were together. She knew he loved him some Latina, so for him to not be drilling his tongue down her throat while groping her butt made her feel like something was wrong.

Realizing he was beginning to scare her, Money quickly recovered his sanity.

"Nothing's wrong, ma," he assured her, grabbing her hand and stepping onto the elevator. "Let's just head upstairs to our room."

She hesitated at first, but then she succumbed to her desire to feel him inside her and stepped back onto the elevator.

"I was going to get us some ice, Papi, because the ice machine on our floor is broke."

Money pressed the button for the second floor.

"We ain't gone need no ice, boo," he replied mischievously, looking over her body.

He couldn't deny the fact that even with such a terrible disease, she still looked damn good. When the elevator stopped,

Latina led the way to their suite with him trailing behind her. He watched her backside as it jiggled and bounced from side to side. He knew right then in the back of his mind that before he killed her he would fuck her one last time.

***

"Okay Migo, and good looking out too, homie," Cash thanked his friend as he gave him some dap.

"Don't trip. I told you before, as long as you stay loyal I got your back."

Cash nodded his head in appreciation.

Migo had gotten him out of the situation earlier with his uncles during their meeting. When they left Manny's mansion, he told Cash why he interjected the offer for him to oversee Money's operation into their conversation. He knew that if his uncles didn't accept Cash's resignation, they would have executed him and his brother right there on the spot. Dealing with a cartel was no joke, and it's an implied understanding amongst those who do business with them that any agreement is considered a lifetime contract.

So, after realizing how close he was to death, Cash became grateful, vowing to someday pay Migo back. He really appreciated him for everything he did. He owed his success to Migo, and that was something he would never forget.

Feeling his phone vibrate, he said, "Hold on for a sec, Migo." After removing his phone from his hip and checking the caller ID, he saw that Money was calling.

"Man, where you at?" he answered the phone, growing impatient.

"Listen bruh, you gotta come and get me," Money whispered into the phone.

"Come and get you?" Cash asked, confused. Last he remembered, Money was supposed to be bringing Migo's car back.

"I think I killed her, dawg."

"Bruh, what the fuck is you talkin' about?" Cash walked farther away from Migo, so he couldn't hear their conversation.

"Latina," he said erratically, "I think I killed her, bruh. Shit, there's blood all over me!"

Cash closed his eyes and took a deep breath. Whatever Money was trying to tell him didn't quite register, so he took a few more seconds to make sure he understood clearly what he was saying.

"Bruh, are you still there?" He heard Money shout through the phone.

"Where you at?" asked Cash, trying to think quick on his feet.

"I'm at the Marriott."

"Stay there and don't move, I'll be there in a minute." Cash hung up without saying another word. He knew they were pressed for time, because whatever happened to Latina would not be a secret for much longer.

"Migo, my brother just called and said that he was on the way. I'm gonna go get our things from the hotel and meet him back here, alright?"

Migo was talking to one of his workers when Cash came back over there.

"Okay, I'll be here when he gets back," he replied, before continuing his conversation.

Cash quickly hopped in the car with the dope and sped off, praying to God that Money hadn't signed their death certificates.

***

Cash pulled into the Marriott's parking lot 15 minutes after receiving Money's call. The whole drive there he prayed for God to send them a miracle, because that was what it was going to take to keep the cartel off their ass if anything happened to Latina.

What the fuck was Money thinking? Cash thought to himself. He warned him about messing with her in the first place, but Money didn't listen. As he replayed their phone conversation over again in his head, he recalled Money saying something about he thinks he killed her, and that he had blood all over him. Those were descriptions of what he hoped hadn't transpired. He needed to know the facts so he could make the right decision on what to do next.

Circling the parking lot, he dialed Money's number to find out what room they were in. Before he could even hit the call button, he saw Money come rushing out of the side door of the building. He was moving quick and looking around as if the cartel already knew what he had done.

Cash stopped and unlocked the door so he could get in. When he got in, Cash noticed he had his clothes turned inside out. He had the look of a wild beast written all over his face.

"Man, what the fuck is going on, bruh?" asked Cash, demanding an answer.

"Pull off first, my nigga, and then I'll tell you what's going on," replied Money, looking around the parking lot as if the feds were about to jump out and arrest them.

"Where's Migo's..." he started to ask where Migo's car was, but as he was pulling out of the hotel parking lot, he noticed it sitting in one of the parking spaces towards the front.

"Nigga, I don't know what the fuck you done did to that girl, but you better start telling me something," ordered Cash, his tone revealing his anger.

As he drove, he glanced over at Money to let him know he was waiting for an explanation. Money's hands covered his face while he rambled. Cash couldn't understand a word he was saying because he was talking too low and wasn't making any sense.

"Nigga, speak the fuck up!" Cash shouted, getting his attention.

"She gave me HIV, bruh," he mumbled a little louder, in between sobs.

"What?" Cash asked in shock.

"The bitch gave me the package, bruh, that's why I've been acting like this. I'm dying fam and I didn't know how to tell you."

Cash looked at him like he'd lost his mind. He couldn't believe what he was hearing. Latina giving him HIV was a hell of a blow, especially since Cash didn't think his brother was stupid enough to have unprotected sex with her.

"Where is she?" he asked Money, checking the time on his Movado watch.

"In the room," he answered, still crying. "I think I beat her to death, bruh. First we started fucking and then when I nutted I lost it and went crazy."

Cash was at a loss for words. He knew from what he just heard they were dead men. Money had clearly crossed the line. He had caused them and possibly the rest of their family to see an early grave. He wanted to call Migo and explain the situation to him in hopes of resolving it diplomatically but thought better than to make that mistake. He knew from this moment on, they were going to have to stay low and off the radar, because once Migo's uncles found out what had happened to their niece, they were going to be at war.

Cash thought about putting a bullet in his brother's head and then delivering him to them personally. He knew his brother could be weak at times, but never in a million years did he expect him to do something so foolish. Part of him wanted to go back and see if she was alive, but his intuition led him to believe that it was already too late. Plus, the Marriott had cameras all over their hotel and he wasn't trying to be seen coming out of that room.

The car they were in was not registered to them, so he didn't care about the cameras in the parking lot. Once they made it back to Macon and the cocaine was removed from the car, he was going to get rid of it anyways.

In the meantime, since they were a half—a—day away from the city, he needed to call and put everyone on point.

"Trap," Cash said, once he heard him pick up, "listen, bruh. We Code Blue, homie. Close down everything immediately, because we gotta relocate, fam."

Trap began asking questions about what was going on, but when Cash reiterated his order, he knew he had to follow instructions. Code Blue was their signal for war, and since Trap knew they were on their way back from Texas, he assumed it had something to do with the cartel. Cash had prepared his team to shut everything down until the matter was resolved just in case something like this ever happened.

When he got off the phone with Trap, he felt a little better. He knew he could trust him to take care of everything and get their families to the safe house in Richmond Hill, Georgia. As he pulled onto the highway to head back to Georgia, his phone rang. He knew it was Migo before he looked at the caller ID. More than likely though, he was just calling to find out about his car, but Cash didn't have any explanation for him, so he didn't answer it. The truth of the matter was he was scared to answer the phone, because he didn't know for sure if Migo already knew about Latina. It wasn't like he wouldn't find out as soon as her body was discovered. His family ran many of the businesses in Houston, so it wouldn't take long for word to get back to him about his little cousin.

As he sped up, pushing the speedometer to 90 mph, he looked over at his brother who was slumped in his seat, staring out the window. He looked pathetic, and although Cash was angry at him, he felt sorry for him, too. Even though he was making deadly moves, Cash wasn't ready to drop him six feet just yet. Money was his brother, and he loved him 'til death; and from the look of it death would be coming pretty soon for them.

CHAPTER 31

BLACK

They were an hour away from Macon and his nerves were driving him crazy. Cash and Money rode the whole way back in silence. Cash didn't want to hear any more of his brother's excuses about why he did what he did, because he understood. What he couldn't understand though was why Money couldn't have followed his instructions and stayed away from Latina. Cash knew that only trouble could come from messing with a girl like her.

"Hello," Cash answered his phone after seeing it was Trap calling, "bruh, is everything taken care of?"

"Cash, what in the hell is going on?" Jasmin snapped through the phone.

"Listen, baby, I can't talk right now, and we are really pressed for time. Where is Trap?"

"He's outside loading our stuff into some SUVs. Baby, there's people walking around my house with guns telling me I have to leave my own fucking place, so you or somebody better tell me what is going on before I lose my mind."

He could tell by the crack in her voice she was scared and on the verge of breaking down. It was killing him on the inside to worry her like this. He wanted to reassure her like he always did that everything was going to be okay, but at this point he wasn't sure how things were going to turn out. Basically, everything was all bad, and if they didn't leave Macon ASAP, somebody was going to die.

"Listen, baby," he tried pleading with her. "Whatever Trap asks you to do, please do it. I cannot explain to you what's going on right now over this phone, so I'm going to need you to trust me. I'm on my way back."

He looked at his phone after hearing it beep and saw that he had an incoming call from Mercedes.

"Baby, hold on for a second, I got my sister on the other line." He clicked over.

"Cash!"

"Yeah Mercedes, what's good?"

"Lil ugly, why in the hell did you send these three fools up here to pull me out of class?"

"Listen, lil sis, they are going to take you somewhere safe because something has happened. I need for you to call me when you get there."

"But…" Before she could say another word he clicked back over to finish speaking with Jasmin.

"Jasmin, just stay calm and please do what they tell you until I get there, and I promise, baby, everything will be okay."

"No, my brother, everything will not be okay," stated Migo.

Cash looked at his phone to see if it was Trap's number, but the name clearly said Migo. Jasmin must have hung up while he was on the phone talking to his sister, allowing Migo's call to go through.

At first he thought about hanging up, but after quickly thinking it over, he didn't want to seem like a coward so he stayed on.

"Migo, I know it looks bad right now, homie, but I need you to work with me, family," he said, trying to buy them some time.

"Family!" scoffed Migo, not liking his choice of words. "Do you know what you've done?"

"Migo listen, I promise I can fix this if you give me some time."

"Cash, I'm sorry my friend, but your time has run out. My uncles have already green-lighted your whole family. There is nothing I can do."

Click!

Just like that, their friendship, his connect, and his peace of mind were gone. Money had cost him and possibly their loved ones their lives. He looked at his brother and shook his head as he put the phone down, letting him know that it was all bad. They were officially at war with the Zeta Cartel, but before he could strike his first blow, he needed to make sure that everyone he cared about was safe and out of harm's way.

*****

About two-and-a-half hours later, they were pulling into Bibb County. He knew better than to continue driving into Macon in the same car they departed Texas in, because they would surely be spotted by one of the cartel's loyal associates. So he stopped by the house of a girl in Warner Robbins he used to mess with and swapped cars.

When he got there, he told her he needed to use her car for the remainder of the day, offering to swap theirs out for hers. She didn't have a problem with it, since she rarely went anywhere, so he knew the car would pretty much stay parked while they were gone. He knew it was a risk leaving the dope with her, but right now that was a chance he was willing to take.

Shortly after the exchange, Cash and Money pulled into Macon in a black Honda Accord. It wasn't their usual type of transportation, but it was the perfect vehicle for them to stay off the cartel's radar.

Cash wondered how long they would have to stay low key. With the cartel being all over the city, he knew it would be hard for them to come up for air right now. Migo's uncles were well-connected throughout the south, so in order for them to stay alive, he needed to meet up with his most trusted friends so they could strategize on how to bring this nightmare to an end.

Ever since they had arrived in Macon, he had been calling Lil Scrappy's phone to try and get an update on the status of their traps. It was his job during emergencies to clean out all of their spots to make them look like abandoned houses. Unfortunately, though, he couldn't get ahold of him. So, he decided to call Trap back and find out if he had heard anything.

When he called Trap, he informed him that he hadn't heard from Scrappy since the Code Blue was issued. His only concern was to make sure their families were safe. Since Trap couldn't give him any information about Lil Scrappy's whereabouts, after ending their call he decided to head over to Scrappy's grandma's house to find out what was the status of their trap houses. They had millions of dollars stored in his grandma's basement, so Cash was hoping Scrappy had enough sense to retrieve their money before things got out of control.

After bending a few more corners he pulled onto the street that led to her house, but before he could drive any further he noticed that fire trucks and policemen were scattered everywhere up and down the street. People were gathered around staring at the house totally engulfed in flames.

As Cash pulled to the side of the rode, they both remained in the car as they watched from a distance the horrific scene and prayed that their money was not inside the burning house.

"Bruh, the Cartel is already here," stated Money, breaking the silence between them.

"I know, cuzz, and this shit just got real," he replied angrily, upset that they got to them first.

They slowly pulled away from the scene attempting to avoid any unwanted attention. Cash was at a loss for words, and he couldn't believe what was happening. Less than 24 hours ago, everything had been perfectly fine, but now everything was a complete mess.

As he turned down a side street to get back onto the main road; for the first time in a long time, he didn't know what to do.

***

"Señor Manny, hemos localizado a los principales objectivos," Manny's most loyal henchman, Black, informed him.

(Mr. Manny, we have located the main targets.)

He and three other Mexicans were parked in a van down the street from Scrappy's grandma's house. They were surveilling the home they just set on fire to see who would show up. Watching through binoculars, Black observed the black Honda Accord pull onto the street, and then after about three minutes, back up and pull off.

Black was trained to look for any suspicious activity once the bait was laid. While he and another henchmen sat in the front watching, two others sat in the back, clutching fully-loaded assault rifles. He had specific orders to call Manny as soon as the main targets were spotted.

"Están solos?" asked Manny.

(Are they alone?)

"Sí, jefe," he answered in return, waiting for further instructions.

(Yes, boss.)

This was music to Manny's ears. He was determined to get revenge for his niece. Although Latina had survived the brutal beating from Money, he assured her that they would not survive what he had in store for them.

"Mátalos, Negro, y como Latina está viva, deja que sus familias vivan tambien."

(Kill them, Black, and since Latina lived, let their families live as well.)

"Entendido, Señor. Se llamaré cuando éste sea terminado."

(Understood sir, I'll call you when it's done.)

After ending their call, Black looked at the driver and nodded his head, letting him know to proceed with their mission. The driver pulled off from the curb and began following the black Honda.

Within the next 20 minutes, Black planned on calling his boss back to deliver the good news that the hit was complete, so he could be on the next flight back to Mexico.

***

"Got damn, Money!" Cash shouted angrily, pounding the steering wheel out of anger. "What the fuck are we supposed to do now?"

They were sitting at the light waiting on it to change when Cash nearly lost it. He knew his brother didn't have the answer to their problems, but he needed to vent in order to release the frustration.

"I know I screwed up, bruh," cried Money.

He had been crying on and off the whole time they had been riding around the city. He felt terrible for the mess that he caused, but he felt even worse when he thought about the illness he had.

"Bruh, I'm already dead," he continued between sobs, "and I know I should have told you, but I didn't know how."

Cash looked at him and shook his head. He was pathetic, but he felt sorry for him. If only he would have listened, Cash thought to himself.

He reached over and hugged him because he knew Money needed his support. As they embraced, Cash noticed the van beside them door slide open. He watched as two masked gunmen in all black hop out, pointing guns towards their way.

As Cash realized what was going on, his feet pressed down on the accelerator, sending the Honda flying straight through the red light.

Gunfire erupted all around them.

Cash was trying to get away from the heavy gunfire as soon as possible. Looking in the rearview, he saw that the van was right on their tail. He swerved from lane to lane, trying to get away, and after about two minutes he was able to get a good little ways ahead of them. After feeling a sharp pain coming from his chest, he looked down and panicked.

"Money, I think I'm hit bruh!" he yelled hysterically. He was trying to keep his focus on the road, but the blood soaking his shirt made him go wild.

"Money!" he shouted, trying to get his brother's attention.

Cash looked over in his seat to see why he wasn't responding and nearly lost control of the car. The sight of seeing Money's body all eaten up from bullets almost made him throw up. Half of his head was blown off, with his brains splattered all over the headrest.

"Ah shit!" he screamed, looking at his brother's dismantled body as tears streamed down his face.

Losing his mind, he forgot to pay attention to the road ahead and ran another red light, colliding with another vehicle at the intersection.

Boom!

The car slammed into the side of the Honda, sending it tumbling down the street, flipping over six times before hitting a tree.

The van chasing them had slowed down as it passed the accident. Black didn't know if the driver was dead or not, but he knew the passenger was for sure. He wanted to pull up to the car, get out, and put a bullet in the driver's head, but he knew with all the spectators that wouldn't be a good idea.

So, they pulled off and parked around the corner. He was going to walk back around there on foot and make sure the job was done before he called Manny.

CHAPTER 32

TRAP

"What you mean he's dead?" Mercedes cried over the phone.

The Macon Police Department had just informed her that one of her brothers had been killed, and the other was in the hospital in critical condition.

Mercedes, Ms. Tina, Jasmin, and Shay were all housed at the safe house in Richmond Hill with Trap and over 30 of their men standing on guard. Everyone became hysterical after hearing from Mercedes what happened to Cash and Money. They all screamed and shouted for some kind of explanation as to why this happened, which made Trap and some of his crew rush into the house.

"What's wrong, y'all? What happened?" he asked, stepping into the living room where they were all gathered.

They were all in shock.

Trap walked over by Mercedes, who was still holding the phone and mouthed, "What happened?"

She reached out and hugged him for support because she wasn't sure her legs could hold her up any longer. The terrible blow of hearing her brother's fate nearly made her pass out; it was too much for her to bear. Trap held her for a minute until one of his soldiers rushed in to inform him that news had come back about Scrappy, and he needed to holler at him outside.

He guided Mercedes over to the couch and laid her down before walking out. He knew right now he wouldn't get any answers from the women, so he went back outside to get it from his men. As he walked out the front door he noticed all the sad looks on his men faces. It was a look he had seen so many times before. That was the moment he realized somebody had been killed.

He walked over to the soldier who had received the phone call and said, "Junior, what's going on?"

Junior was one of their most fearless lieutenants.

"Boss, they pulled two bodies from the fire. One was big homie and the other was his grandma."

Trap closed his eyes and shook his head. He began saying a silent prayer for his childhood friend when he was interrupted.

"There's more," another one of his men spoke up. "I just got off the phone with my baby mom and she said Cash and Money have been hit. Money didn't make it, but Cash is in ICU."

"Man, what the fuck is going on?" Trap shouted angrily, upset because someone was bringing the pain to their doorstep.

None of his men had a clue who was behind the hits. Most of them was on the phone trying to find out why the heads of their empire were being targeted, and by whom. They had no idea who was behind the attacks, but they knew whoever it was committing these acts had to be either crazy or dumb to pull a stunt like this.

Trap paced back and forth thinking about what to do next. As of that moment he was the only one capable of making decisions for their crew, and he knew he had to make the right ones. If Money and Scrappy were both dead, then that meant he and Cash were the only ones left. He figured whoever was causing this mayhem was trying to take them all out, and in order for him to find out who it was he needed to speak to Cash.

Without saying another word, he rushed back into the house.

"Y'all get everything together. We're leaving," he informed the women before walking back outside to instruct his men to do the same.

He got on the phone and told some of his men in Macon to go down to the hospital and guard Cash's room. If Cash was alive, he planned on keeping him that way, because he couldn't afford to lose another one of his friends.

He also didn't want to leave the girls out of his sight, so he decided to bring them along.

As they all got into the vehicles, he informed them that they were going back to Macon so they could be by Cash's bedside. Cash needed his family there with him for support, and although Trap knew Cash wouldn't have wanted the girls there for their own protection, he didn't trust leaving them in somebody else care. He made plans to arrive at Macon Memorial Center with 100 men, so if anybody tried anything, they were more than likely to receive the same fate as his deceased friends.

***

At the hospital, Trap and his men took post on the main floor and the third floor where Cash was being held in ICU. His condition so far was serious but stable. The doctor told them when they arrived that he was suffering from a gunshot wound to the chest and had severe brain injuries.

From what the doctor was telling them, Cash's head hit the front windshield when their car flipped over. When the paramedics arrived on the scene, he was unconscious and his vital signs weren't looking too good, so they rushed him into surgery to try and stop some of the swelling and internal bleeding of his brain. They placed him into a medically-induced coma until his vitals showed signs of him beginning to improve.

Trap urgently needed to speak with him to find out what was going on, because as long as Cash stayed in a coma, he would not know anything. His intuition told him the Cartel had something to do with this but he wasn't sure, and didn't feel comfortable starting a war without being 100% certain. He desperately needed his friend to recover so he could know who was behind all this drama. Only then could he seek revenge for his two deceased comrades.

"Trap!" someone called him.

He was busy instructing his men to keep their eyes open when he heard Jasmin call his name.

"What's going on, J?" he asked, walking over to where she and Shay was seated.

Shay was still trying to get over the fact that her fiancé and baby's father was dead. Trap could tell by the look in her eyes she was a mess. It broke his heart to see her like this.

"He's been out of surgery now for three hours, so ask the doctor if we can see him."

"Sure, baby girl, but I'm almost certain he's going to say no," he replied, knowing how serious his condition was. "Three hours is not nearly enough time for someone to recover from his type of injuries, J."

She lowered her head in disappointment. Cash was her everything, and although it hurt her to hear about Money's fate, she secretly thanked God that her man was the one still alive. It would've been a complete heartbreak for her if Cash had died, and she didn't know if she was ready for that.

Trap put his hand under her chin to lift her head back up.

"J, don't worry yourself more than you have to, alright," he said, encouraging her to stay strong. "Whoever did this is going to pay deeply, I promise."

She knew he meant every word, but she didn't want revenge to come out of this; she only wanted for Cash to be okay.

"Can I speak to the family of Cashmere Lewis?"

They all turned around to look at the doctor who had just stepped into the waiting area. Everybody stood up and approached him in hopes of hearing good news. Once they were all gathered around, he continued.

"I'm sorry to inform you all that after an unsuccessful surgery, Mr. Lewis has passed away."

"Oh my God noooooo!" screamed Jasmin, collapsing on the hospital floor.

Cries were heard throughout the whole room as everyone's world came tumbling down.

Trap punched the wall next to him. Hearing that his best friend was dead devastated him, and he didn't know how much more he could take before he spazzed out. He looked at the women he was instructed to protect as they cried their eyes out and felt sorry for them. He could feel their hurt and pain for their deceased loved one because he was in pain as well. After looking at their faces, he vowed to himself that whoever was responsible for this tragedy would surely pay the ultimate price.

***

Down the hall, getting onto the elevator, Black was on the phone calling his boss. He had gotten the news he'd been waiting for. Cash was dead.

He too was awaiting the update on Cash's condition. Instead of him and some of his men rolling up in there to finish the job, he decided to go alone. He noticed when Trap and the women arrived at the hospital they were being escorted by a large number of bodyguards. He wasn't about to lead his men into a suicide mission, so he told them to stay in the van while he went in to confirm whether he was dead or not.

When the elevator doors closed, he heard Manny pick up.

"Negro, qué pasa?" asked Manny.

(Black, what do you got for me?)

"Esta hecho, Jefe," he replied.

(Boss, it's done.)

He could almost feel his boss's devilish smile through the phone. Manny hung up without saying anything. That told Black that he was no longer needed.

As he stepped off the elevator and walked towards the exit, a light smile spread across his face.

***

Back in the waiting room everyone was still trying to get a grip on reality. Getting over Cash and Money's deaths would be hard.

Ms. Tina was stuck in a daze as she sat in a corner by herself. She had lost two children today, and as she looked at her third and final child, she began to weep.

Jasmin, Shay, and Mercedes were all holding each other, crying. They were there for each other and needed each other's support.

As he sat in his chair with his head down in the palms of his hands, Trap couldn't look at anyone. He had lost too many friends in the past 24 hours to console anyone and he needed some time to grieve.

As the doctor was making his way back over towards the waiting room to inform them they could come be with their dead, a nurse came running down the hall to catch him.

"Doctor, doctor!" she shouted, coming to an abrupt halt in front of him and the family.

"What is it, nurse?" he asked, patiently waiting for her to catch her breath.

Once she regained her composure, she said, "We have a pulse!"

To be continued...